Ironspark

IRONSPARK

C.M. McGuire

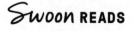

New York

A Swoon Reads Book

An Imprint of Feiwel and Friends and Macmillan Publishing Group LLC

120 Broadway, New York, NY 10271

Our books may be purchased in bulk for promotional, educational, or business use. Please contact your local bookseller or the Macmillan Corporate and Premium Sales Department at (800) 221-7945 ext. 5442 or by email at MacmillanSpecialMarkets@macmillan.com.

Library of Congress Cataloging-in-Publication Data

Names: McGuire, C. M., author.
Title: Ironspark / C. M. McGuire.
Description: First edition. | New York : Swoon Reads, 2020. | Audience: Ages 13–18. | Audience: Grades 10–12. | Summary: High school senior Bryn Johnson works with new friends to keep her family and town safe from murderous Fae while also dealing with panic attacks, family issues, and a lesbian love triangle.
Identifiers: LCCN 2019036131 | ISBN 9781250245267 (hardcover)
Subjects: CYAC: Supernatural—Fiction. | Fairies—Fiction. | Panic attacks—Fiction. | Family life—Fiction. | Lesbians—Fiction.
Classification: LCC PZ7.1.M443527 Iro 2020 | DDC [Fic]—dc23
LC record available at https://lccn.loc.gov/2019036131

Book design by Liz Dresner

First Edition—2020

10 9 8 7 6 5 4 3 2 1

swoonreads.com

To my little brother
No longer with us
Always here

One

In most fairy tales, the fairies are the good guys. They're godmothers or magical blue ladies who turn puppets into real boys. The problem with that is most fairy tales are sixty percent bullshit, thirty percent wishful thinking, and ten percent horrifying unknown. That's not to say there are no fairy godmothers; I just never saw one.

More often than not, I saw the other side of it: the blood-sucking, strangle-you-for-fun variety of fairy. For every benevolent shoemaker or wish granter, there was a killer. Which meant I needed to be ready. Steel-toed boots were always a good idea, and they went well with my dark clothes and roughly twenty thousand talismans, all silver and iron and anti-fairy. I could have pulled off the punk goth thing, except living with a single father meant no piercings or blue streaks until I was thirty or he was dead. And with a pair of twelve-year-old brothers, there'd be no slipping a stud out before I got home.

About the most I could do was cut my dark hair up to my chin and draw on some black eyeliner. My dad tolerated that much. But then, he didn't know exactly why I wore the steel-toed boots or why my jewelry included an iron nail on a chain. He probably suspected, though.

I checked the time. Eight-eighteen. The wind pierced through my dark jacket and into my skin like it had some kind of personal problem with me. I huddled into myself, drawing my knees to my chest. Somewhere out in the town, other high-school seniors were likely hanging out and drinking or smoking. Odds were they'd all die of lung cancer someday. Still, they were having fun and blissfully shortening their lives while I sat on a church stoop alone, waiting for some priest to get with the program and take me to kill some fairies.

The door to the church creaked open. I scrambled to my feet. Father Gooding stepped outside, a large, black duffel bag slung over one shoulder. He stooped just a bit, so it would be a little easier to make direct eye contact. Friggin' tall people. Hard to name the greater injustice: that he was six foot four or that I was five two.

"I apologize," he said, locking the door behind him. "The choirmaster called. I really couldn't hang up without arousing suspicion."

"So tell them," I said, and I hated the tight, wheezy tenor of my voice after too long in the cold.

Gooding arched a brow. "That's awfully rich coming from you, Miss Johnson. Does your family know about your extra-curricular activities?"

"The whole reason my dad moved here was because of the fairies," I reminded him. "And because he knows you protect people from them."

Gooding gave me that oh-so-disappointed Catholic look of his and sighed. "Bryn, we discussed this. What I'm teaching you is dangerous. Potentially life-threatening. Your family deserves to know in case I have to call them to the hospital." The same lecture he'd given me for the last three years, ever since he first agreed to take me as his apprentice.

"Well, you haven't yet," I pointed out. Gooding's little half frown would have made a marble statue confess its sins. I diverted my gaze. "You know my dad's got a lot on his plate, and Ash and Jake are just kids. Besides. You said it yourself: You need the help. There's too many of them popping up lately."

Gooding's lips thinned, but he stopped angling for direct eye contact. Once again, Gooding chose the high road. He just loved to do that. Sometimes that worked in my favor; sometimes it drove me crazy. But it was too cold for me to decide whether his prissiness was a blessing or a curse.

"Come along, then, Bryn."

Gooding took off across the long stretch of yellowed grass behind the church, and I had to half jog to keep up with his sweeping gait. Well, at least it warmed me up.

"You're right, though," he said. "This is the third call from Postoak Road this month. They're getting more active."

Another visit to Postoak Road, easily the crummiest place in Easterton, Pennsylvania, but not for the reasons most people thought. By day, Postoak Road was an overgrown stretch of dirt with a line of ancient houses held up by sheer willpower. At night, it turned into the hottest haunt for all of fairykind and the practical classroom for my anti-fairy education. Holy water for redcaps, gifts and thank-yous for brownies, seeds or salt for boggarts, dropping down and praying for a little good luck with garden gnomes.

And now an "exorcism." Air quotes included. Clearly, we were helping some poor, terrified someone who had no idea what was happening.

I cracked my knuckles as I followed Gooding across the deadened field, down the dirt road, and up the creaking porch to number seventeen, Postoak Road. Petunia-filled planters hung from the eaves while charming plaques stating that HOME IS WHERE THE HEART IS and LOVE IS ALL YOU NEED tried to distract visitors from the ancient wood and crooked steps. More than likely, it was all a newlywed couple could afford. Our house hadn't looked much better when Dad moved the twins and me to the United States. If I wanted to be honest, it didn't look much better now.

Something dark moved on the banister of the porch, just at the edge of my peripheral vision. Like a whistle on the breeze, there came a shrill voice. *"Missy!"*

My heart slammed like a piston in my chest. What was a shadeling doing out here? Had one of the boys lit the microwave on fire? No. The little imp would be in a panic if that were the case. Sometimes they followed me outside the house, but if this one crossed Gooding's path, it would end up as a pile of dark goo. I closed my eyes and made a sharp, jerking motion with one hand. I'd have to deal with it later.

Fingers brushed gently against my elbow. Even though I knew who it was, I jerked away.

Gooding held up his hands. "It's only me," he said. "Are you all right? Will you be able to focus tonight?"

"You know it," I muttered, crossing my arms. "Just love killing me some Tinkerbell."

Gooding pulled one of his "God is disappointed in you" faces, but before he opened his mouth, the door cracked open to reveal a plump woman in a floral top. Her bloodshot eyes flicked uncertainly to me, then to Gooding as if to ask, *What the hell?*

"Father," she breathed. "I thought . . . Well, I thought we agreed to be discreet about this."

"Miss Johnson is my assistant, Mrs. Barnett," Gooding assured her. "Trust me, she's a very capable young woman. Why, she even helped with Mrs. Clegg's trouble."

Mrs. Barnett's lips twisted into a pained grimace. It took everything I had not to shift from foot to foot like an anxious toddler. I knew exactly what I looked like: dark hair, dark clothes, dark eyeliner, and let's not forget the charming moniker of "Crazy Man's Kid" courtesy of Dad's reputation around town.

I bit the inside of my cheek and stole another quick glance at the banister. Lucky for us both, the shadeling had disappeared.

Mrs. Barnett nodded and stepped aside, gesturing us in. "It started a few weeks ago," she said in a hushed voice. "I thought it was colic. But he was hungry all the time and . . ."

She led us through a pink-carpeted living room packed with the same kitschy cheer as the porch. I wrinkled my nose at a smiling porcelain fairy, holding a mushroom as an umbrella and beaming up at me like it was so innocent.

As Mrs. Barnett led us down her tidy hallway, I turned the fairy to face the wall and followed her to the door at the end. A bright blue plaque reading ARTHUR had been glued to the wood, surrounded by paper cutouts of a smiling sun, fluffy clouds, and plump little airplanes. Mrs. Barnett paused at the door, her fingers hovering over the handle.

"Sometimes . . . sometimes he doesn't even look like himself." Mrs. Barnett's voice trembled as the words tumbled out. "I don't know how to describe it."

"Does your husband know what we're doing here?" Gooding asked.

Mrs. Barnett's breath hitched. She swiped at her eyes with an unsteady hand. "That's why he's not here. We agreed he'd only be in the way. He couldn't sit still, knowing we were having an . . ."

"It won't come to that," Gooding assured her, resting one hand on her shoulder. Like magic, Mrs. Barnett's hands stopped trembling. She looked, if not exactly sure of herself, at least a little less terrified. That was Father Gooding for you, a real Catholic Yoda. He offered a little smile and nodded at the nursery door. "Let us have a look, and we'll go from there."

Mrs. Barnett pushed open the door and recoiled, folding her arms across her chest, as though the doorknob might just bite. Gooding and I stepped inside and, of course, Mrs. Barnett closed the door behind us. My common sense screamed at me to pull it open again, but this wasn't exactly a job where common sense prevailed. After all, common sense generally told someone to stay the hell away from demon babies.

If the situation bothered Gooding, he didn't let it show. He strode over to the yellow crib in the corner and peered down at the baby inside. I peeked in after him.

Little Arthur Barnett stared up at us, squirming in his bright blue footie pajamas. He was about as baby-like as it was possible to be. More baby-like, in fact, than most babies actually were. When they'd been born, Jake and Ash had been cute, too. Of course, they'd also had baby acne; that's how we knew they were real.

Gooding reached in and pulled Arthur's legs straight. One stretched out longer than the other. "I thought so," Gooding murmured. "Bryn, look closer."

Here was where I got paid the imaginary bucks. I gripped the side of the crib and let my shoulder relax, then my neck, then the muscles in my face—just like Gooding had taught me. The world narrowed down to just me and the creature in the crib. Soft, delicate baby skin turned hard and leathery. Nails sharpened. Sparse hair grew coarse and wiry. Its eyes darkened and sunk into its haunted face. The sight made my stomach churn. It was like a baby Crypt Keeper.

"Changeling," I muttered. "With one hell of a glamour to hide that face."

"A newborn, too, judging by its proportions," Gooding sighed. "I'll bet it doesn't even speak yet. Which means we can't just ask it to leave."

"As if it would," I snorted. I couldn't tear my eyes away from the horrible little face. I'd seen pictures of more attractive mummies.

"Patience and optimism are valuable tools," Gooding chided.

I had to roll my eyes. "So are caution, paranoia, and an iron fire poker."

Gooding gave me the peeved-priest look before smoothing his features into his teacher-priest look. "Well, it's a living changeling, not a doll or a golem," he summarized. "And it has a very good disguise. What does this tell us?"

I took a deep breath. "It was put here by a more powerful Fae. Probably from a court. Means we can get Arthur back." Even as I said it, my heart skipped a beat. But there was nothing to worry about. We didn't get the court Fae here. They worked through others and never stepped foot on American soil . . . right?

"If we play our cards right," Gooding murmured, pulling a small bottle from his duffel bag and popping the top off. The room flooded with a sharp, herby smell as he sprinkled a few drops onto the creature. The changeling's monstrous face twisted into an awful grimace. It screamed, writhing in Arthur's crib.

"I think you just pissed him off." I dug through my own pockets for my handy tube of rock salt, perfect for angry fairies and the occasional bland pretzel in the school cafeteria.

"Saint John's wort almost always works," Gooding muttered thoughtfully. I shoved the salt at him and, just to be safe, retrieved the little packet of rowan ash I always tucked away in my jacket. Gooding emptied both over the crib.

The changeling's wails grew louder with each unwelcome substance we dumped on it. I clapped my hands over my ears. Every cell in my body seemed to vibrate. Usually by now the offending fairies just hissed at us, maybe got in a good bite or two, then disappeared.

"Our Father who art in heaven, hallowed be thy name," Gooding boomed over the screeches.

Crap. The Lord's Prayer was the Hail Mary of fairy hunting, the equivalent of throwing a flare in a bear's face. Gooding had given up all pretense of knowing what else to do with this little beast.

Someone pounded on the door, but the baby's inhuman screeches smothered the sound.

"Thy kingdom come," Gooding shouted. "Thy will be done—"

The changeling cries beat harder, like a subwoofer at a metal concert.

Maybe we'd been wrong. Maybe this was a banshee, not a fairy. Bright blood trickled from one of Gooding's ears, standing out against his tanned skin. With one shaking hand, he touched the blood and gaped. Gooding whirled around and yelled out something that was lost under the screeches. I couldn't possibly hear him, but I *could* read his lips.

"Fire."

My favorite way to dispatch a little hellspawn. Of course, the Barnetts didn't have a fireplace. So scarring Mrs. Barnett for life was officially on the agenda.

I pulled my hands from my ears and almost lost my balance as the full force of the little monster's cries crashed into me like a tidal wave. I snatched the ugly thing up from the crib, eardrums throbbing. The changeling kicked and clawed at my arms, ripping right through the black denim of my jacket as I kicked the nursery door open and stormed past an alarmed Mrs. Barnett. The glass picture frames in the hall quivered from the monster's piercing cry.

Gooding must have figured out where I was going because he raced past me into the kitchen, threw open the oven door, and spun the temperature knob to the highest setting. Here went nothing. Even though I knew it was a fairy and it was just going to end up back where it came from, part of me still felt like I was going to hell for this.

I hurled the changeling inside and slammed the oven door shut. The muffled screams sounded more like a wild animal than a child. The lights flickered around us.

Crack!

I jumped back as a jagged fracture appeared in the glass of the oven door. If this didn't work, we were going to have to evacuate Mr. and Mrs. Barnett . . .

The screaming stopped. For one horrible second, I thought I'd gone deaf. I held my breath, waiting. The Fae had to take it back now. It wouldn't leave the changeling to die just to keep a human baby. Even *they* wouldn't do that. Well, I had to check sooner or later.

Preparing myself for the very real possibility of baked fairy, I cracked open the oven door. The changeling was gone. My legs wobbled like jelly, but in a good way.

The door to the kitchen flew open, and in burst Mrs. Barnett. "What's happening?" she gasped, her eyes wide and red. Yeah, this wasn't going to help my reputation. "I-I heard a screaming . . . Where's Arthur?"

A loud, shrill, *human* cry rang out from the nursery. Mrs. Barnett whirled around to stare down the hall.

Gooding swiped at the blood trailing down from his ear, somehow smiling. "I believe your son wants his mother."

Mrs. Barnett turned and rushed down the hall. Within seconds, the child's wails dissolved into distressed hiccups, then, at last, blissful silence. It was a happy-ending sort of night. Those were the best ones.

I stretched and rubbed at my scratched arms. I was going to have to put antiseptic on them. God only knew where that thing had been before it ended up in baby Arthur's crib. At least I wasn't as bad off as Gooding.

"How are your ears?" I asked.

Gooding glanced back at me and smiled incomprehensibly. "Good work tonight," he said, patting my shoulder with his bloody hand.

Maybe I was a little punch-drunk, but I couldn't help grinning up at him. "Think I'll stop by the church on my way home," I said, jerking my thumb at the door. "You know. Switch out the holy water with the tap. I doubt anybody'll notice."

"Yes, I think we both earned some good rest," Gooding replied.

"I may also superglue all the hymnals to the backs of the pews. Nobody reads the words anyway."

"I think so, too. And a cup of tea would be just the thing. You should make one, too, when you get home."

He probably wouldn't be good to take confessions for a while, but he was no stranger to injuries on the job. Sometimes I suspected he kept me around because I had an uncanny knack for avoiding little things like broken noses or split eardrums.

"I'll get on that," I said, slapping his arm cheerfully. "Take it easy."

"Bryn." Gooding caught my arm, his thin lips twisted into a grimace. "This activity's been picking up. Soon it may spread to the rest of the town. You need to tell your family. Especially your brothers."

The lingering adrenaline dried up, leaving behind a sick feeling. Of course. Gooding was never going to let that drop.

"When Jake and Ash demonstrate that they can change the toilet paper rolls, then maybe I'll decide they can handle fairies."

Gooding watched me, brows furrowed. Then, he pressed a hand to one of his bloodied ears.

"What?"

Two

While Gooding returned to his rectory above the church to tend to the minor issue of his bleeding eardrums, I headed home to the only house on Gosling Road.

On this side of town, everything was within walking distance. Ten minutes from Postoak to the church, another ten to my house, twenty to the school if you power walked. Hell, if Dad didn't work out at the oil site an hour away we might not even need a car. Of course, most of the town beyond our cheap patch was big and sprawling and spread out. It was almost like the thirty thousand residents who could afford to live away from the creepy, haunted woods did just that. Whatever. Gooding and I took care of the poor souls who had to live near the fairy-infested trees.

The shadeling met me halfway up the hill to my house.

"Missy," it squeaked, popping out of a shadow like an impish jack-in-the-box, its wide, orange eyes shining in the dark. I spared it a glance and adopted my well-practiced annoyed face. In truth, every step away from the Barnett house left me feeling a little more drained, but the annoyed face tended to intimidate the little buggers, which meant less mess for me to handle.

"I told you never to show yourself to other people," I reminded the shadeling as it scampered next to me, looking like nothing so much as a wingless, two-foot-tall bat with wiry limbs. The sight was almost enough for me to go easy on the creature. Almost.

The shadeling puffed out its ink-colored chest. "Never!"

"I also told you not to show up while I was out with Gooding."

"But Missy—"

"If Gooding saw you, he'd assume you were a pest," I interrupted. "He'd have hit you with iron, you know. You've got to be more careful!"

The shadeling stumbled in the grass, wringing its overlarge hands. "It was important!"

I sighed and ground to a halt a few yards away from the wrought-iron gate that looped around the house. No sense in letting my dad or one of the boys hear me arguing with something they didn't know lived in our house.

"What was so important that—"

"Fae!" the shadeling squeaked. "Fae kind, Missy. Unkind, unthinking, *Unseelie* Fae. They've come all the way here to the wild lands."

"Wait, wild lands?" I had to rub my temple. "You mean here? America?"

"It's only wild fairies here, Missy. No courts. No rules. But now *they've* come!"

The poor thing had worked itself into a tizzy. I sighed and

knelt down, not exactly eye to eye with the little imp but at least not towering over it anymore. "Look, if this is about the changeling, they pop up all over the world. Doesn't mean the Unseelie court found us. Father Gooding keeps us safe from them. That's why we came here, remember? To keep away from them."

The shadeling stomped its feet and grabbed its ears, its wide eyes shining in the darkness.

"No! The old mistress told us to keep you safe!"

"You do," I said. "You guys do a good job, okay? And when I go to college, you're going to listen to the boys. And the Fae aren't going to find us. Not you, not me, not—"

Pain exploded through my head and my chest as I hit the ground. For one bizarre moment, I thought, *I'm being mugged.* As if something as simple as a routine mugging ever happened to me. I blinked, sucking in a sharp breath when I saw it. Barely humanoid, stretched and bone white, too-large eyes boring into mine. This was my bogeyman. This was the monster under my bed. The horrible Faeish *thing* loomed above me like every nightmare I'd had since my family fled Wales nine years ago.

Its white lips pulled up over its blackened teeth. Purplish foam frothed at the corners of its too-large mouth. When a glob of that murky saliva touched my cheek, I snapped back to reality. Court Fae!

The creature swiped at me with its clawed hand. Without thinking, I blocked with my scratched arm as I ripped one of my necklaces free—my trusty iron nail.

I thrust the nail up with everything I had. A jagged gash

bloomed across its pale chest. It screeched as its skin sizzled into bulging, purple blisters. Good old iron.

I rolled onto my knees and tried to scramble away. *Gotta get home.* Beyond the iron gate. Within the protection of the old rowan trees inside the perimeter. Just a few meters away—I could make it!

The Fae threw itself on my legs, pinning me to the ground.

"Agh!" I cried out and turned, slashing at it with my nail. With a wet gurgle, it grabbed my hand. *Crap!* I tried to pull back, but the creature ripped the nail from between my fingers. Its skin hissed as it popped and blistered. With a snarl, it tossed the nail away and leaned forward, bringing its jagged teeth centimeters from my nose. Its fetid breath stank of rotten meat.

"I haaaave meeeessaaaage," it croaked, digging its claws into my shoulder. I bit back a scream as fire shot down my arm. The creature cocked its head to the side, doglike, and twitched its lip. "My queeeen—"

"Shadeling!" I shrieked, but the little imp was gone. Damn little coward!

"—waaaantsss what waaaaas withheeeeld—"

Well, this queen's just going to have to suck it up.

I ripped the silver ankh from around my neck and pressed it to the Fae's purple wound. It shrieked and jumped back, clearly expecting a blistering pain that wouldn't come. I scrambled out from underneath it and raced for the house. My heart threatened to burst out of my chest. My vision blurred at the edges. I just had to get inside the fence. Their kind couldn't pass it. I'd be safe if I could just get inside.

I jumped onto the iron grate and reached for the lowest hanging branch of the rowan tree. The second my fingers closed around it, my necklaces jerked back, tightening around my throat. The Fae howled with fury.

"What waaaaas withheeeeeld!"

Crrrrack!

The rowan branch splintered. I tumbled back. My wounded shoulder slammed into the ground just outside the fence. Stars danced in front of my eyes. The taste of copper filled my mouth. Red rowanberries littered the ground around me. I gripped the branch until my knuckles turned white, struggling to hold in my scream.

Don't let him hear. Don't let him hear. Don't let him know he's winning.

The Fae grabbed the front of my jacket and lifted me from the ground. Dark spots filled my vision as I stared down into its inky eyes.

"Whennnnn the veeeeeeil thinssssssssss," it snarled, its discolored spittle dripping down its white jaw.

I sucked in a sharp breath, gripped the branch with both hands, and swung.

Crack!

The Fae's hands loosened on my coat as it staggered back, those dark eyes suddenly unfocused. I landed on my feet and before I even knew I had my footing, I swung with everything I had. Over and over the wood smashed its skull, purple blood spraying the ground around it. Finally, it crumpled and fell backward onto the hill.

My arms shook as I swung again, with every ounce of strength I had, right at its head. With a final *crunch*, blood spread out like a wine spill along the ground. The Fae spasmed, its limbs going rigid. Then it didn't move again.

I stared down at the mess. There was that unnatural purple blood on my steel-toed boots. An acrid taste filled my mouth.

I let the tree branch fall to the ground. The thud vibrated through my boots, but I didn't hear it. Only a weird buzzing in my ears. The shadeling appeared at my side, nattering away in that squeaky little voice, but the words didn't make any sense in that moment.

The smell crept on me slowly, like a gas leak filling a room. Sharp, metallic, unnaturally sweet. Oh God.

I caught myself on the iron fence as my stomach turned itself inside out. It burned up my nose as tears sprang to my eyes. With each hammer of my heart, the reality of the situation beat into my brain. That was a full-grown court Fae. Not a wild Fae, not a shadeling or a changeling or any of the garden-variety nuisances Gooding had taught me to fight. These things weren't even supposed to *exist* in the United States.

"Sh-shadeling!" I called, but I couldn't see a body. The Fae hadn't gone after my shadeling. It was okay.

"How did you find us?" I wheezed, but the Fae didn't answer. I pressed my cheek to the cool, comforting, *safe* iron of the gate. Iron and rowan. It couldn't get to me anymore. I breathed deeply until my jelly legs could move. The shadeling scuttled along beside me, wringing its spindly hands.

"Missy, I was only trying to warn you. Never wanted—"

"I know," I muttered, pulling my keys out of my pocket. They jangled loudly in my shaking hand. I blinked, staring down at them, willing them to still, but they didn't. Damn.

"Missy—"

"It's fine." Which was pathetic. I liked to consider myself a pretty good liar. Had to be. But I sounded about as fine as a fork in the garbage disposal.

The house was quiet when I slipped in. More likely than not, the boys were up listening to music in their rooms, pretending to sleep. Dirty dishes caked with dry bits of a dozen different foods piled high in the sink. I didn't even want to think about why two adolescent boys needed so many dishes or, for that matter, why they were conversely incapable of cleaning them up. Strangely, my hands stopped shaking when I took in the mess. This was normal. I understood this.

A fly buzzed over a smear of jam, only to be caught by a dark, grimy fist. I started back, my heart hammering all over again.

"Want us to clean it up, Missy?"

My hand flew to my throat, but I couldn't find my nail. It was out on the hill, hidden in the grass. A soft, snuffling sound and a squeal of joy rose from the kitchen table as a mossy-green, bright-eyed shadeling found a forgotten crust of bread on the floor. Just a shadeling. I took a deep breath, willing my heart to still. I was home. These were just the shadelings.

They were probably the closest I'd ever come to having sidekicks. I liked to remind myself of that anytime I developed the unhelpful desire to bring something cute and fluffy into the house. More likely than not, the little imps would try to put a saddle on it. Or try to eat it. We had a certain arrangement in the house. Apparently, Mum asked them to stick around the family back when we lived in Wales. Help out around the house. Act as watchdogs. In return, I kept them fed and safe. They were mine. They were safe. There was nothing to be afraid of.

Six pairs of glowing eyes gazed expectantly up at me. That was six shadelings who had kept out of danger, more and more crawling out of the shadows. The fat one teetering on the counter even had a quivering lip. It sort of made me want to deny them right then and there, but my temples were starting to throb and the jam would only be that much more difficult to deal with in the morning.

"Yeah, th—" I had to cut myself off. First thing the shadelings had told me when they revealed themselves to me. They didn't like to be thanked. Some sort of weird shadeling rule. I sighed. "Just the jam, okay? And the crumbs. Do not touch the utensils. Do not touch the dishes. If I find out one of you so much as looked at the fridge funny . . . Look, just don't. Okay?"

The fat one scowled and scuffed one grimy toe against the seat of the chair.

"Missy's mother would have let us eat the scrumptious dish food," he grumbled.

"Well she's not here," I snapped. *Crap.* The things you wished you could unsay. I needed to be nice to them, but my nerves were a ragged electrical wire, ready to spark at any second. I took a deep breath, counted to three, then let it out. "Sorry. All right. I want half of you cleaning up the counters. The rest of you . . ." I took another breath. One. Two. Three. Let it out. This had to be done. "Th-there's a bit of a mess outside. Take care of it."

The shadelings blinked up at me. Maybe they'd heard something in my voice that set them on edge.

"What sort of mess, Missy?"

I swallowed. My hands started trembling again. Tucking them under my armpits, I clenched my jaw. "It won't hurt you. I made sure of it." My words came out too soft, too ragged. I needed to go. "And you can eat it if you want."

The shadelings needed no further instruction. Like an ant hill disturbed, they burst out, six, then ten, then thirteen of them, lapping up every semi-edible scrap in the kitchen or else bounding outside to what was sure to be a nasty surprise.

"Quiet!" I hissed, my heart jumping up into my throat. I sucked in a sharp breath, curling my hands into fists. I just had to keep it together a little longer. Just until I wasn't being watched.

The shadelings on the counter shot me a baleful look before they returned to their gorging, slurping loudly all the while. For all that they called me their mistress, we all knew full well that I really wasn't unless I was holding a fire poker, and even then I didn't do more than wave it for emphasis. Just this once, I didn't grab it.

It started with the tremble in my hands worsening, like my body was trying to warn me of what was coming. I had about thirty seconds until the meltdown.

"I'm going to bed," I wheezed, my heart hammering. "Don't wake anyone up. Don't let anyone see you."

There was a chorus of grumbles at that. Not one of the shadelings appreciated being kept secret since technically they were here for the whole family. But it was my room they first appeared in ten years ago, and I was the closest thing to a matriarch the family had.

"Good night, Missy," a couple of shadelings chorused glumly.

Well, that was progress. I'd civilize them yet. One of these days I might even coax them into a bathtub.

I dragged myself down the hall. With each step, every bruise and cut ached a little worse. That horrible metallic smell burned in my nose, making my stomach turn. My head pounded. Two of the shadelings scampered down the hall after me.

"Are you . . . hurt?" one squeaked, then yelped as the other yanked on its large, batlike ear.

"Of course Missy is hurt. The nasty big courties hurt everyone."

"Want a cup of tea?"

"I notice you have a brand-new bottle of lavender lotion, which is almost completely still there. Would you maybe like a foot rub?"

I heaved a short sigh and chose, very diplomatically, in my opinion, not to ask why my brand-new bottle of lavender lotion was only "almost completely still there." Or if shadelings even knew how to give foot rubs. It was just trying to be nice. I needed to be nice back. But the air around me was thinning. The shaking spread up my arms until it reached my spine and turned into shivers. I needed to go. I needed away from all of them.

"No. I'm all right. Just make sure that thing out front is gone by morning." I darted into my room and shut the door behind me before either shadeling could follow. I was alone in my own little sanctuary.

I peeled off my boots and grimy socks and ruined jacket, dropping them all on the floor amidst my school books and knitting supplies. The smell was still in my nose. That awful too-sweet metallic stench. I snatched a box of matches from my desk and broke two as I tried to light a sage candle. My throat clogged up. Black spots danced before my eyes. Oh God, they'd found me. They'd found me. We were an ocean away and they knew we were here. I couldn't breathe. I couldn't *breathe.*

My knees buckled and I crashed to the floor, sobbing and hiccuping and struggling to suck in a single breath of air, but all I smelled was that monster's blood and all I felt was where its blood and saliva touched me. I knew it was all in my mind, but it burned like acid on my cheek and my arms and that only made me sob harder. I grabbed a bunched-up hoodie off the floor and buried my face in it to muffle the sound.

My brain kicked in and I remembered what Gooding had told me three years ago, after our first job together. It had been a goblin tucked in the church basement, snarling and snapping at us. I'd almost bolted until Gooding had grabbed my shoulders and locked eyes with me.

"Focus on right now, Bryn," he'd said, and at the time I'd been so grateful that he was so calm and priestly. *"I want you to focus on where we are. Engage all your senses. Where are you now?"*

I sucked in a sharp breath and tried to do that. Where was I? My room. *My* room. My safe haven in the storm. How did it look? Organized, mostly, except for the school books and dirty clothes on the floor. Half-finished college applications I'd been so excited to fill out. Purple sheets. Glow-in-the-dark stars stuck to the ceiling. How did it sound? Quiet, except for my own sniffling. Even the shadelings managed to keep quiet as they went about their work. How did I feel? Cold. Snotty. I wiped my face on the hoodie. What did I smell? Sage. The candle wax had finally started melting, chasing away the reek of the Fae's blood. What did I taste? My stomach churned. Probably a bad idea to focus on that one.

The tears weren't exactly gone, but I could breathe now. Which meant I could think.

A court Fae had arrived in the flesh. This wasn't a changeling or other mischief sent from afar. This one came for us . . . but it wasn't like the last time. This wasn't a *courtier*. Those things were beautiful, quite literally enchanting. The Fae outside had been anything but. Clearly it wasn't the sort that usually went out and messed with humans.

"What waaaaas withheeeeeeld!"

I buried my face in my bunched-up hoodie. It wanted something for its queen, whoever she was. Something it hadn't gotten before. My heart started to pound at the thought. I squeezed my eyes shut. Sight: the dark of my eyelids. Sound: the throb of my heart. Feel: sore muscles. Smell: sage candle. Taste: something awful. But I'd be all right. I just needed to get some sleep. In the morning, everything would make more sense. I'd have to talk to my dad, probably, which was going to be about as fun as clearing out the disposal. Gooding, too. But he would know what was happening. He had to.

I pushed myself to my feet. Sleep. I needed sleep.

I stumbled forward and collapsed on the bed. Somewhere between one breath and the next, the dark behind my lids got darker, and a shrill voice whispered, "Good night, Missy."

Three

My bare feet rested on the mossy forest floor. Dappled sunlight shone down between the trees, dancing over my skin in a strange, mottled pattern that made me feel otherworldly. I knew these woods, right down to the sprites that hid inside the yew and the hawthorns. This was the Before. Before the United States. Before we lost Mum. Before the Fae.

A wet wheeze shattered the sweet morning birdsong. I crept forward and there he was, leaning against a tree. He looked exactly like the sort of tall, handsome Fae princes I'd read about in my dad's fairy-tale books. He had to be six feet tall and white as bone, but he was easily the prettiest thing I'd ever seen.

His too-big, too-sweet eyes flicked up to me and he opened his mouth. A sickly sweet, metallic scent filled my nose as mauve blood flecked his lips. This was wrong. This wasn't safe. I needed to run, tell my parents, lock the door, and hide in the nursery with the boys.

"Do you need help?" I heard myself saying, my voice rolling with a Welsh lilt. I'd had one of those, once. When did it go away?

The fairy-tale prince held out his hand to me. His nails had been filed to points, like cat claws. They didn't have so much as a speck of dirt under them. I could never keep my nails so clean.

"I can help you," I said. "My mum's got all sorts of things at home. Like a doctor. Only she's not a doctor."

The prince didn't say a word. His eyes widened as he reached just a little farther and snatched my hand in his. His grip tightened around mine. Too fast. Too painful. I yelped and tried to pull away. No. No, this wasn't what had happened.

"Stop!" I cried, squeezing my eyes until the pressure pulled away, leaving me gasping, shaking, waiting for it to come back.

"Ssh, sweetheart." A familiar voice. One that made me feel like sunlight and sundaes inside. I blinked as a face swam before mine. Not the prince. Dark curls and human eyes. My heart nearly stopped.

"Mum." I reached out to touch her cheek. Mum. She was here. She would help!

Mum smiled, even as she pulled away before I could reach her. "Sweetheart," she said again in that odd accent of hers—the one that wasn't Welsh or English or Irish or anything I'd heard from anyone other than her. It was like a song that nobody else knew except for us. "I need you to keep a secret for me."

"I can." I couldn't. I knew better. This wasn't what happened. This wasn't how it went. But the prince was gone now, and I was safe. Everything would be fine.

She reached into the front pocket of her crisp, button-up shirt and pulled out a brochure, tattered and folded up and read a thousand times already. My heart skipped at the sight of it. It was the ad for Penn State I'd picked up months ago. My chance for a life away from all of this.

"I want you to go," she said. "But you can't do it if they won't let you."

"Who won't let me?" I asked. Soft lips pressed against my temple.

"You can take care of it yourself," she whispered. *"You know how your father worries. And I worry over him."*

"Me too." I touched the edge of the brochure. *The waxy paper had gone soft from too many readings. But it didn't belong here. I was in the Before. This was in the After. I was forgetting something. Something important.* "Mum, what happened to the Fae? The one from the woods?"

She smiled at me. *"You grew up so lovely, sweetheart."*

"But Mum—"

THE SHRILL SCREECH of the alarm jerked me back into my room. I gasped, staring wide-eyed at the ceiling. The glued-on stars still glowed in the dim, pre-dawn light. My heart began to slow and, little by little, reality sank back onto me like a boulder. This was no longer my room. It all looked right, but this was no longer a world that offered safety from my childhood monsters. The Fae from last night was dead. The Fae prince from years ago was dead. There was no way he could have survived his wounds that day. But that didn't mean the threat was gone.

I slammed my hand on the alarm clock and kicked the covers off. Dark shapes scuttled along the walls, blending back into the shadows. A small, vulnerable part of me wanted to call for them to come back, but I swallowed the impulse. When Mum disappeared and the shadelings first revealed themselves to me, I'd wake up in the night screaming. Seeing those wide eyes staring at me in the dark? Well, they weren't reassuring for a traumatized eight-year-old. Wet the bed for about six months. Now, though? They were my keepers. Or they were supposed to be. But they couldn't exactly take on a court Fae, could they?

I gritted my teeth and finally rolled out of bed with a hiss. My back was on fire. Perfect. I forced myself to my feet and shuffled into the biohazard that was the kids' bathroom. I had to walk along a plush, mildewed layer of middle-school-boy clothing to get to the sink. I turned on the faucet and splashed some cold water on my face. The water washed away purple with Fae blood. My hands began to shake again. Frantically, I scrubbed at the bits of it that had flecked around the edge of the sink, leaving it cleaner than it had been in years.

The reflection in the mirror made my heart stop. Amidst the spatters of snowy toothpaste residue, purplish-brown smears marred my cheeks. *Shit!* I'd fallen asleep with that stuff on my face. My stomach churned. I took a deep breath. One, two, three . . . I could handle this. I had to handle this.

I wetted a washcloth and scrubbed at every inch of the grime, trying not to look in the mirror. Trying not to notice the color the washcloth turned. It was only when my skin began to burn that I stopped. My cheeks, my hands, everything the Fae's blood had touched were now a bright, human pink. Rubbed nearly raw. I threw the now ruined cloth in the garbage and headed back to my room.

It didn't matter that my skin had been cleaned of that filth. It didn't matter when I was dressed in fresh clothing for the day. The memory, the knowledge that it had found me, still clung to me like polluted air. Every twitch of my fingers summoned the feel of its claws on my throat. Every sound was a dull echo of the crunch of its skull under the rowan branch. My raw mood must have filled the room with some kind of greasy, anti-shadeling funk because not one of them appeared as I got dressed.

My stomach lurched, but I swallowed it down. I needed help. More help than a shadeling could offer.

I went for the loose floorboard under my bed and the precious shoebox within. Admittedly, it was probably a little paranoid of me to stash it the way I did. It wasn't like I was hiding anything really dangerous. At least not to humans. But it was better than having to explain to my nosy brothers why I kept rowan twigs or Saint John's wort in my bedroom.

Tucked in the box were a plastic bowl, a bottle of honey, and a half-empty flask of holy water. Maybe it was a little sacrilegious to use holy water for something like this but, hey, whatever worked. I dumped the holy water in the bowl, added a few gloopy squeezes of honey . . . and there it got a little fuzzy. Technically I needed greens. But these things were really about intent and confidence and I didn't feel like wasting any of my herbs. I dug through an old pair of jeans and found a box of Altoids. Minty. Mint came from a green plant. Ergo, an Altoid counted as a green. And Gwen had always liked mint, anyway.

I dropped the Altoid in the mess, too. When it began to dissolve, I leaned over the bowl, close enough for my breath to touch the water, and whispered.

"Gwen. I need your help." Hopefully there was someone on the other end listening in. The Altoid cracked, and the honey-mint scent washed over my face, pushing back some of the pollution. I smiled. "Thank you. I'll be by this afternoon. I need you to look into—"

"Oh my God, Bryn, that looks gross!"

I jerked back. Ash stood in the doorway, still in his pajamas, his nose wrinkled as he stared down at the bowl. My instincts screamed at me to shove everything back in the box, but that would pretty much convince him that I was up to something weird. So I put on my best Big Sister face and crossed my arms.

"Ash, shouldn't you be getting ready?"

Ash's dark brows furrowed. "Is that some kind of freaky diet?"

"Get ready for school, you little Martian. I won't ask again."

Ash shrugged and picked at a hole in his pajama bottoms. "I don't feel like it. Jake's going for me today. Not like the teachers can tell us apart."

Breathe in. One, two, three . . . "Then Jake will get in trouble."

"Please. He's got, like, a perfect record."

"What's Jake got to say about that?"

Ash pointed at the bowl. "Seriously, Bryn, are you going to drink that?"

I like to think of myself as an honest person. When I told him I wouldn't ask again, I didn't. Kids needed consistency like that, and it felt good to fall back into an old routine. I rose slowly. Ash darted off. I followed. Like a good sister.

It was only in the living room when I had Ash in a headlock that I saw Jake half dressed and inspecting his hairless chin in the glass of our old grandfather clock. His gaze drifted to me, then to Ash. With a huff, he rolled his eyes.

"You're an idiot, Ash."

Ash wriggled free from my arms and, for just a moment,

looked like he wanted to shove me. Or Jake. Or both of us. But he adopted his new too-cool preteen attitude and sniffed.

"You can't blame me for trying." He sauntered back to his room with all the swagger of a bowlegged poodle. I glared after him before turning to Jake.

"You aren't really trading places with him, Moonman?"

Jake snorted and turned back to his search for the as-yet-uncharted chin hair. "Come on, Bryn. Like I'm going to give up my perfect attendance record so he can goof off."

Well, that was one less thing for me to worry about. I hoped Jake would never go full irritating preteen on me. I couldn't handle Ash without him.

"Good," I said, grabbing a blanket from the couch and tossing it at him. "Now go put a shirt on."

Jake rolled his eyes. "Why don't you tell me how to comb my hair, too, Miss Priss?" He shoved past me, but paused just in front of the hallway, brows furrowed. "Hey, how come you got in so late last night?"

"Bible study," I replied automatically.

Jake stared at me for a long moment, enough to make my heart pick up the pace, before he huffed. "You're such a liar. I'm gonna tell Dad you've been smoking in the graveyard."

"I haven't."

"Right, and Ash and I have never done each other's homework."

"Careful or I'm going to tell Dad you said that."

Jake held up his hands. "Whatever. Hey, I need to borrow your shampoo tonight. Ash used mine up."

"Ash has his own."

"Yeah, but he was too lazy to get more soap, so he used mine as body wash."

Little weirdo. I shrugged. "Whatever. Just don't use it all up. I'm not going to the store until this weekend."

Jake half saluted and disappeared into his room.

My stomach clenched and, just like that, whatever sense of normalcy I'd regained in the last ten minutes was gone. I counted to ten. When neither boy emerged, I rushed back to my room where . . . Yikes. I must have managed to spill half my stash when I went for the bowl and honey. Little bottles of Saint John's wort, verbena, and dried daisies littered the floor, positively screaming, *Look at me, I'm playing with fairies!*

I dumped the bowl out the window and stuffed everything back in the box, then the box back under the floorboard.

When I finally re-emerged from my room, Dad sat hunched over the kitchen table, breathing in the java steam that curled up from his mug. He looked like a man just coming off of a long, difficult night, and his day hadn't even begun. Once again, I was a little girl, staring up at her father, ready to ask him to make everything better. The words danced on the tip of my tongue.

Dad, a Fae found us. It attacked me last night.

But then there it was. A faint twitch at the corners of his crow's-footed eyes, the sort he tried to control. The words died on my lips. I tried not to stare as I filled my own mug.

"How are things?" I asked, my insides squirming. It was our code. "Things" meant "hallucinations."

Dad frowned into his coffee and took a sip. "Slept rough."

"Rough" meant the hallucinations were getting mean. Probably meant in the next few months he'd have another visit to the doctor to try out yet another medication and hope this one lasted longer. But they never did. This wasn't your garden-variety schizophrenia. This was just a curse in a schizophrenia Halloween costume.

After Mum went missing, Dad had tried to confront the Fae and demand that they give her back. Fae didn't much like being told what to do, so when Dad returned, he was half starved and terrified, seeing Fae everywhere. The doctors called it the weirdest case they'd ever seen. I called it one more reason to hate the monsters that took Mum. Dad's condition wasn't natural, so there wasn't much the doctors could do long-term. Lord, what would he do when I left for college? What would he do if he knew about what had happened last night? The *things* that had done this to him were back. And Dad couldn't tell a real Fae from one of his hallucinations. He'd never even know if he were really in danger.

Shit. What if them being here made him worse? Was a fairy curse worsened by proximity?

Dad drained his mug and pushed himself up out of his chair, looking like a rusted tin man in a button-up shirt. "It might be another late night at the oil rig," he grunted. "Make sure the boys eat something green."

I forced myself to smile, even though my stomach wanted to turn itself inside out. "Lime sherbet. Got it."

His lip twitched in not quite a smile, but it was okay. He'd be in a better mood after he was up and working. He dropped a kiss on my forehead, his large, calloused hand resting on my shoulder. "Good girl. Have a good day." And then he left, the door creaking shut behind him.

A pair of luminous eyes peeked out from behind the

toaster. So much for my anti-shadeling funk. The little creature crept forward, holding the chain with my nail on it at arm's length.

"We see what he's seeing, Missy. The Unseelie nasties are getting uglier for him."

Well, hell. I crossed my arms. "Watch him today. And the boys. But—"

"Keep secret. Yes, Missy."

Four

After I walked the twin headaches to the junior high, I had to crowd into a musty auditorium with every jackass who'd ever called me "Crazy Man's Kid" and every jackass who'd ever let them. On a logical level, I knew that school was not a waste of time, that high school would end, that sooner than later I'd be out of here. But some mornings, it was pretty hard not to stand up and walk out of the building.

"I know many of you have heard of senioritis," the vice principal said as she gestured at an eye-stabbingly bright PowerPoint. "But remember, colleges will still see your senior year GPA. Now, who here is thinking of applying to Penn State?"

Hands shot up in the air. My stomach sank. There was Brooke Tanneman, who'd put white seed beads in my hair and told everybody I had lice last year. And Owen Cope, who'd spread the rumor that I was a devil worshipper back when we were both freshmen. And Dennis Holtzmann, who wasn't awful, but who did spend all of freshman year walking around with a lacy bra outside of his shirts to protest . . . something. He'd never been clear what, exactly. These were the people trying to get into my college. So much for high school ending.

"Good, good. Make sure you don't let those GPAs slip; they could make the difference in your acceptance. Now, Penn State doesn't have a minimum GPA requirement per se, but that doesn't mean they don't take it into account . . ."

A few groans rose up in chorus across the auditorium, hopefully a sign that not all of them would be getting into my college after all. Near the front row, a boy shifted, resting his feet on the empty seat in front of him. Clearly not someone planning on Penn State. Who was that?

I sat up straighter—quite a feat in those creaky old seats—and leaned forward. It wasn't Dmitri or Lance or . . . or anyone I'd ever seen before, actually. *Oh, crap.* In a podunk little town like Easterton, it was kind of impossible not to know everyone. The timing couldn't be coincidental.

The strange boy leaned over and whispered something to Jasika Witters. I gripped the armrests on my seat. Jasika was good people. Possibly the nicest, most genuine person in this whole rotten school. She and her family lived on Postoak. She took care of her kid siblings like I did, and after they got a nasty case of redcaps in their master bathroom, she'd kept it secret. She'd been volunteering at the hospital since June, for goodness' sake! How much more good-person could you get? And he was . . . what? Targeting her?

The boy grinned at something Jasika said and glanced back. Right at me. My heart jumped into my throat and, for just a moment, I was eight years old staring at the Fae prince who'd destroyed my home. This guy wasn't pale by a long shot, and he had dark hair and dark eyes and skin like an acorn, but something about those high cheekbones, the smooth skin, the wide, expressive mouth. Oh God. Ice flooded my veins.

This was not a coincidence. A new student couldn't just happen to show up right after a court Fae. One of *them* was in the school. Maybe even the same one from before. How? The whole building was made of reinforced steel. The catwalks alone stretched above us like a big, anti-fairy barrier. He ought to be shivering, panting, sweating just being near it. Were the more powerful court Fae somehow able to tolerate it?

". . . Okay, lots of you thinking about heading to Pittsburgh. So, let's talk about those SAT scores," the vice principal said.

A band tightened around my chest. I sucked in a shallow breath as I slipped out of my seat, stumbling across the aisle. There were a lot of *hey*s and *watch it*s as I bumped into knees on the way out. The dark-eyed boy watched me, his brows furrowed. I clenched my hands to stop them from shaking. I wanted to scream. I wanted to puke.

I slipped into the restroom, my heart racing. My control frayed at the edges like an old piece of rope. I had to compose myself. I had to *think*. What would Gooding say at a time like this? Probably something annoying about keeping calm. But he'd also tell me to figure out what I was up against.

I took a deep breath, then another, and ran my fingers through my hair, mussing it into a heap. Usually, I could just look past a glamour. This one was different. It was too powerful, too human-looking. I needed a detection spell, then. Gooding would have a heart attack if he knew I was practicing this without him. Well, he'd never know.

I needed fire, and some sort of herb to burn. I glanced

around the sparse restroom. Toilet paper came from plants, but I doubted that would be very effective.

My eyes fell on a little cardboard box poking out from behind the eternal out-of-order sign on the tampon dispenser. Of course. Everyone knew someone hid a pack of cigarettes in here, but nobody knew who. I pulled it out, and eureka! A little plastic lighter to boot. I fished one of the cigarettes out of the box and, after a few flicks, got a flame going in the lighter. I took a deep breath and let the new guy's face swim to the front of my mind.

"Show me the truth of the boy. Show me his face. Show me the truth of the boy. Show me his face," I chanted as I lit the cigarette. The paper caught easily, turning the tobacco and chemicals inside into bright embers. The acrid stench burned my nose. I angled it away and stared into the smoke, praying that whatever laws of magic or physics governed these spells decided I was doing it right.

"Show the truth, dammit!"

For just a hair of a second, something shifted in the smoke. Something that looked like it might be a face. Was I just imagining it, or was it working?

Creeeeak!

I whirled around, the cigarette still perched between my fingers. Brooke Tanneman stood in the doorway, holding up her cell phone. Before I could drop the cigarette, I heard the *click!* Her eyes sparkled with wicked glee.

"Busted, freak."

Five

I rolled my pencil across the desk in front of me, mentally counting each tick of the clock, my leg bouncing five times faster than the second hand.

At the front of the classroom, Mrs. Dinophre—who had to be around 200 years old—nibbled at a tuna sandwich that smelled almost as old as she was.

"You know, Bryn," she said around a mouthful of tuna, "when you stay out of trouble, we both get to go home on time."

"Or you could just let me go," I pointed out. "This early in the year, it's just the two of us. Nobody has to know."

The bell finally rang, piercing the silence loudly enough to make my eardrums ache. Mrs. Dinophre clicked her lunch box closed and gestured to the door. "Go."

I jumped out of my seat, slinging my backpack over my shoulder before taking off. Gwen would be waiting for me. I whipped out my phone, shooting off a group text to the family.

> **Bryn:** Popping out to study group tonight. Will pick
> you up a little late.
> **Bryn:** Jake's turn to make dinner. No casserole.

The hallway was empty as a ghost town. Only the newly posted flyers for basketball tryouts and the Halloween Haunt town dance suggested anyone had been here all day. Well, those and the lewd little hot dogs Dennis Holtzmann had drawn on the corners of the flyers. Judging from the citrusy scent of cleaner, even the janitor had come and gone. I was like the lone hero in a horror film, but that didn't mean I was alone. Now that I'd seen *him*, I could picture Fae around every corner. It made my skin crawl.

"Bryn?" a voice said.

"Gah!" I whirled around, my hand already closed around the nail hanging from my neck. Jasika Witters started back, hands raised.

"Easy, girl. I come in peace."

"Dammit." I let go of the nail and heaved a sigh. Jasika bit her lip, a warm, sunny smile spreading across her face. Everything about her radiated warmth. This close, I could see the little sunflower clips in her hair and the gentle brush of gold glitter over her eyelids. My pulse raced, but it wasn't so unpleasant this time. Compared to a Fae, Jasika was a nice surprise.

"How is it that you aren't scared of things that'll actually kill you but little old me gets under your skin?"

Big talk from someone whose family had needed rescue from a pack of redcaps not so long ago. Or maybe that's why she *could* talk big. She'd come into close contact with those things and she was still so remarkably *normal*. She was the kind of normal I liked to dream about when I showed up at home in the middle of the night covered in some kind of fairy goo. Except she was real.

"I *am* scared of those things." I ran my fingers through my hair and breathed, willing my heart to slow down. "What are you doing here? You weren't in detention." As if detention ever had or ever would be possible for her.

"Tutoring." Jasika shrugged. "And . . . I sort of wanted to talk to you."

That sentence seldom ended with anything good. My stomach clenched.

"To me?"

"Yeah. I mean. You know about, well, all the *stuff*." She raised her brows at *stuff*. "And nobody else in town does."

"That's because Father Gooding and I do our jobs well."

"I know." Jasika fiddled with the hem of her shirt. "And now I know, I kind of get it. But everything I know, I've had to figure out myself. Alone. For a long time."

Everything she knew? The idea of Jasika anywhere near any of that made my skin crawl.

"You're not looking into this too much, are you?"

"Of course I am." Her brows twitched. "Look, I've always known there was a . . . thing going on. And now I know what it is. So what's the point of us doing this separately? I figure if I were to join you and Father—"

"No." The word was out before I even realized it. Sort of a knee-jerk response after years with the twins.

Jasika's sunny smile faded. "No?"

"It's dangerous."

Her brows twitched with something between hurt and anger. "So you get to decide who does and doesn't get to do anything about all of this?"

"Come on. Isn't it better to just pretend it never happened? Go back to your life and pretend you never saw them."

Jasika drew in a sharp breath. For a long moment, she glared down at the floor until, at last, she looked up at me. The sharp glint in those eyes hit me like a sucker punch.

"Look, I don't need your permission. I just figured you might welcome a little help."

I could. I really could. It was tempting. But the thought of Jasika coming close to that sort of danger made my ears ring. No. This was my battle, and she was staying out of it whether she liked it or not.

"You don't want to get any closer to this than you are," I warned, but my gut began to squirm with something that might have been an emotion similar to but not necessarily guilt. "I appreciate it. I do. It's good that you want to help but it's also really dangerous. The best thing you can do is keep your eyes open and call us if anything else happens on Postoak."

"So you want me to be your watchdog." She shook her head. "You know, when you bench people, they feel it. And it doesn't feel great."

Jasika got this look on her face, one that looked like she'd swallowed a lemon. I probably should have been glad she didn't say whatever she wanted to say out loud. This was enough to make me feel like an asshole. Time to shift focus.

"Who was the guy sitting next to you at the assembly?"

"Who? Wait, you mean Dom?" Jasika knitted her brows. "This has nothing to do with—"

"Humor me." I crossed my arms. "Who is he? Where'd he come from?"

Jasika crossed her own arms, mirroring me. "He just moved in with Ms. Helen down the road. Foster kid. He's nice."

"So he moved in on Postoak."

Jasika frowned, searching me for a few long seconds before her eyes widened. One hand flew to her mouth.

"*No*, Bryn. You can't mean . . . Bryn, he's a sweet guy. He's not one of, you know . . . *them*."

Nice to know she was squeamish about saying *fairies* in public.

"I'm going to find out," I told her. "Listen, there's been more happening around Postoak lately. Some new guy happens to move into Fairy Central right when everything's getting crazy?"

She shook her head. "You're paranoid."

"I have a right to be." I took a breath and forced myself to straighten. "You could stand to be a little more paranoid yourself. If you see bad guys everywhere, you catch the ones that really are there. Just promise me you'll keep away from him until I figure out what his deal is."

Jasika sighed like I'd asked her to carry an anvil up Mount Everest. "Fine. But when you determine he's not one of them, you let me in on your next job with Father Gooding. Deal?"

Well, it wasn't exactly like I was bringing her in on the fairy hunting. I was just going to teach her to protect herself. And, in return, she would . . . protect herself. So why did thinking about that make my stomach all squirmy and fluttery? Somehow, it felt like I was getting the raw end of this deal.

"Fine. Meet me during study hall tomorrow."

"Deal." Jasika grinned and winked. "And don't worry, the boy's all yours. You could have just said you liked him."

Hilarious.

Six

The walk home with the boys was a long one, largely because they'd had to stay in the after-school program while I served out my detention sentence.

"Do you know what it's like there?" Ash demanded. "I'm pretty sure Mrs. Horton thinks we're all, like, six or something."

"No, she treats *you* like you're six because she knows you lied about getting your homework done in class."

"Yeah, well, she's not my math teacher. It's none of her business!"

I checked my phone for the time as we crunched our way up the gravel path to the house. For all the griping and dramatizing from Ash, I was still going to be on time to meet Gwen. She didn't like coming out if I showed up after dusk.

"Hey, did you pick up more soap?" Ash demanded.

I rolled my eyes and pocketed the phone. "Why, get bored of using shampoo?"

He shot a glare at Jake and kicked the iron gate hard. It swung so hard it clanged against the fence and bounced back, smacking him right in the foot.

Jake burst into loud peals of laughter while Ash fell back, spewing profanity. Dad would have had a cow if he'd heard.

I dropped to my knees and checked his ankle.

"You're fine," I announced, and rose, holding open the gate. "Okay, both of you inside. I've got to get to my study group."

"Since when do you socialize with actual people, Miss Priss?" Ash climbed to his feet, not even bothering to dust himself off as he traipsed inside with Jake on his heels.

Once I made sure the boys were home and sufficiently occupied, I pulled the half-full bag of bread out of the pantry.

"Behave," I called over my shoulder, both to the boys and the shadelings. The shadelings, thank goodness, stayed hidden. The boys, on the other hand, lounged in the living room. Ash doodled in the corner of his geometry book while Jake played some sort of game on his phone.

"Fine, but if you're home too late it's tuna fish casserole."

I glowered at him. "Nobody likes tuna fish casserole."

"Yeah, but nobody hates it more than you," Ash pointed out. "That's what you get for making us wait in the after-school program."

Jerks. It might have sincerely irritated me more if it wasn't so familiar. Familiar was good right now. I glanced at them one last time, just to make sure all was well before I headed out the door. There was still a nasty, dark stain on the ground just outside the gate. The sight filled my mouth with a sour taste. I looked away, focusing on the cool iron beneath my fingers, the creak of the gate as it opened and closed. This would be over soon. I'd take care of it.

Nine years in this town and countless trips through the

trees, and the woods still sent shivers down my spine. The cloying scent of pine clogged my senses. My steel-toed boots crunched the underbrush so loudly I could barely think. Every creature in the woods knew I was there. The wild, courtless fairies tended to give me a wide berth, but every flicker of movement in the corner of my eye, every snap or rustle in the distance made my hand tighten around the bag of bread. I just had to count the number of steps between here and the safety of the pond.

When at last I broke free of the treeline, I sucked in a long, deep breath of freshwater air: all mud and wet plants and the faint odor of fish. Gwen's pond stretched out in front of me, the water glimmering like diamonds in the evening sun. I let myself relax, first my head, then my shoulders, then the rest of me as I knelt at the edge of the water, the moist earth squishing under my knees as I knelt.

At first glance, it looked like any other pond. Then, among the brown river stones and the intermittent flicker of movement from minnows, tiny houses shimmered to life, swaying in the gently windblown current. Feminine laughter drifted in on the breeze, accompanied by a smell like honey. The village of the Gwragedd Annwn. The water wives. Probably the only fairies besides the shadelings whom I could honestly claim to like.

"Gwen," I called, dangling the bag of bread over the water's surface. "Brought your favorite."

"Bryn, you know half a dozen of us are named Gwen," a sweet voice said from behind me. "You're only lucky they know it's me you call for."

For just a second, my heart skipped a beat, but only for the one second. At this point, it was just a physiological reaction my body seemed to have to her, one I doubted I'd ever really outgrow, no matter how long we stayed split up. There would always be the lingering sensation of fireworks inside of me where the smoke hadn't quite cleared. My lips curled up in an automatic smile. The whole world could be burning around me, and somehow Gwen's presence would always make it better. "That's the second time someone managed to sneak up on me today," I pointed out. "I must be losing my edge."

Gwen looked like a figure in a classic painting who'd had all her color washed out. Milk-white hands poked out from the full, gauzy sleeves of her pale shift. Ash-blond curls tumbled down to her waist like a blank canvas. The only real specks of color on her were her lily pad–green eyes that sparkled with delight.

Of course, the fireworks were always chased with the throb of a little shard of glass that had embedded itself in my heart the day I downgraded us back to "just friends." Once junior year had ended and the summer began, it had hit me. I'd be going off to college in a year. I'd be chasing that normal, human kind of life, but I couldn't really accomplish that if I was still dating a water fairy. So, I'd ended it like one of those old, nostalgic rock songs. *I'll love you forever, babe, but I've got to be moving on.* Maybe it had been cowardly. Maybe it had been the wrong choice and I was just impulsive. But, right or wrong, I was back here begging for her help. Like an asshole.

Maybe Jasika was on to something about my personality.

Gwen, at least, was too good to act smug about me being back here. Maybe it wasn't even an emotion she was capable of feeling. She held out her dainty hands for the bread. As soon as I handed it over, she bit gleefully into a slice and sank down to the ground, her shift ballooning around her.

"Gwen," I said. "Something's happened."

Gwen froze, those lily-pad eyes locking onto me. In one graceful motion, she set the bread down and moved to my side, her hands on my back, right on top of my bruises. I bit back a hiss of pain, but Gwen already knew. This wasn't exactly the first time she'd had to patch me up. It was how the thing between us had started in the first place.

Warmth trickled across my shoulders and down my back, pooling in every scrape the Fae had left. I couldn't help the little sigh of relief.

"Thanks."

Gwen pulled back, her delicate features set in a frown. "It is no wild one who did this to you," she murmured. "There was a touch of the court in them."

Well, she cut right to the chase, huh? "Yeah, looks like a Fae wandered over here by accident."

Gwen arched a brow. "We are all Fae, Bryn."

Semantics. I shrugged. "It's easier to think of courts as Fae and the rest of you as fairies." Because deep down, the thought that Gwen and the shadelings were in any way related to that *thing* made my skin itch.

Gwen pursed her lips. "We are what we are, Bryn. The Unseelie are the dark. The winter. The Seelie are the warmth. The summer. Even we in the wild align with them or between them. It is a balance."

"Wouldn't mind throwing that balance off a little," I muttered. But trying to argue about balance and nature with a water wife was like trying to convince a river to flow backward. "Anyway, it said its queen had a message, but I was a little busy trying to stay alive. Have you or your sisters heard anything?"

Gwen tilted her head and gazed out over the water. Her words came out slowly, like ice melting. "This is Unseelie doing. Mischief-makers and death lovers. Stirring things up in the woods. The Seelie would never resort to such violence. Not without a call for war."

I figured as much. In all my short life, I'd never actually dealt with the Seelie court. Pity. Apparently that court was all midsummer dances and sunshine, about as far from the Unseelie as Gwen was from the Postoak changeling. I picked at a blade of grass and worried it between my fingers.

"Dad said . . . well, implied his hallucinations were getting worse."

Gwen nodded. "It was an Unseelie courtier who cursed him," she said. "His visions will be tied to them, if it is their will that he should suffer."

A band tightened around my chest. "But the doctors will still be able to help, right? I mean, this curse acts like a real disease."

"An amethyst and a quartz may resemble each other, but one shatters more easily than the other."

"And which one does my dad have?"

Gwen ran her fingers through her pale hair, brows furrowed. "It is hard to say. But if the Unseelie retreat, I believe his condition will ease to something he can manage again."

"So I just need to push them out of my territory."

Gwen touched my cheek. Her fingers felt like still water.

"You broke with me because you wished to leave this place. Now it seems you intend to root yourself here."

Perfect. Now she was trying to feel sorry for me. Why couldn't she just be pissed? That would be easier to deal with. I batted her fingers away, perhaps a bit more gently than I might have with anyone else.

"I'm still going to college," I insisted. "I just need to take care of this first. Make sure Dad and the boys are safe."

Gwen reached over, plucking another bit of bread to chew thoughtfully before she spoke. "Bryn . . . you have grown up with my kind. You know our ways, the wicked and the good."

"I know the wild fairies," I snorted. "The court Fae might as well be from another planet."

"You know them better than you will admit," Gwen pressed. "If the Unseelie will be this bold, then they seek some advantage. You were a child when first they approached you, but your brothers were newly born. Newly *known* to the world."

"What are you—" But the realization crept into my chest, closing its icy claws around my heart. I caught my breath, ears ringing. "You think they're after the boys."

"What mother would not sacrifice herself for her children?"

The world began to swim. I buried my head between my knees, but it didn't do anything for the frantic beat of my heart. Of course. Twins. Twins were said to have powerful magic, right? And Mum hadn't exactly been ignorant about magic. What could she have gotten herself into? What had she gotten *us* into?

Why had the Fae prince even been in the woods that day?

My head spun. Before I realized what was happening, my

back was on the grass. In seconds, half a dozen water wives swarmed above me, all frowning and tutting like a gaggle of hens. One clasped my wrist, checking my pulse, while another wrung water onto my forehead with the hem of her shift.

"Stop. Hey, quit it." I waved my arms, batting them away as best I could. The water wives hesitated, but one by one, they disappeared back into the pond, leaving only Gwen crouching beside me. I pushed myself back up, wiping the pond water from my forehead. "You know, you and your sisters don't have to coddle me every time I get a little dizzy. I'm . . . fine."

"I apologize," Gwen murmured. "Perhaps I was too bold."

"No, no . . . It's a good theory. I'll look into it." Just saying that made me feel like maybe I really would pass out. I took a shaking breath and bunched my hands into fists. Nope. I could do this. Nerves of steel, that was me. Steel nerves, steel boots, steel . . . whatever. "Thank you, Gwen. If, um . . . if you and your sisters could keep your eyes open for me. Let me know if you catch wind of anything else . . ."

"Bryn." Gwen reached out to squeeze my hand. Her skin was cool on mine, like water on a hot day. I tried not to let it reassure me. Steel heart, too, apparently. Gwen's eyes widened with concern. "What else is there?"

She could always see through me. That's what I got for letting someone come too close. Or maybe it was a water fairy thing.

"There's a boy at my school," I admitted. "I think he might be a Fae spy. Probably Unseelie, if it really is them after us. I tried that detection spell you taught me, but I didn't get a clear image."

Gwen nodded and straightened. With the finesse of a Las

Vegas magician, she plucked a smooth, brown stone out of the air, perfectly round, with a hole worn right in the middle.

I snorted. "A fairy stone? Gwen, I can look through glamours on my own. That thing's for kids and beginners."

"And difficult glamours," Gwen said, holding it out to me. "Try it on the boy. If he is Unseelie, there will be darkness about him. If he is Seelie, there will be light."

"Fat chance one of the Seelie will lift a finger to help us," I muttered, but I took the stone, instantly rubbing my thumb over its sleek surface.

Gwen smiled. "You once said something similar of me," she pointed out. "And who alive has since taught you more of my kind?"

"I let Gooding believe it's him." I pocketed the stone and pushed myself to my feet. Gwen rose beside me, her hands folded in front of her. Always so stinking elegant. Sometimes, I had to wonder if the water wives knew how awkward they made us humans look. I reached out to pat her shoulder, feeling a little clumsy doing so. "Thank you, Gwen. I get the feeling I'll probably ask for your help when . . . if I find out that your theory about the Ash and Jake is true."

Gwen gave a little curtsy. "Of course, Bryn. You know you need only ask."

"Right," I chuckled weakly. "And be sure to share that bread with your sisters."

Gwen scooped the bag off the ground and held it close to her chest like a child who wouldn't let go of her teddy bear. My lovely Gwen. She positively pouted as I made my way back into the woods and home.

Seven

When I arrived home, a pair of mud-caked sneakers sat just next to the door. Apparently, one of the boys had decided to take a little outdoor trip but hadn't bothered to clean up. The smelly sludge of what was probably supposed to be tuna casserole sat on the stove while a box of baked goods waited on the table with a note from Gooding. Apparently, the ladies from the church knitting group had heard that Dad was working late hours and sent over a care package. It looked like there might have been chocolate something in it at some point, but it was long gone. By the sound of the muffled punk rock music from the boys' room, I didn't really have to guess what had happened. At least there was still a bag of what looked like lemon bars and a couple of summer sausages tucked into the basket.

"Nice of you to leave something for me!" I called.

The music grew pointedly louder. I frowned. It wasn't like them not to even show their faces. Was this how Dad had felt when I'd entered high school?

One by one, the shadelings appeared, bright eyes in a

dozen shades of ink, all hiding in what little shadow the kitchen afforded. They'd been my secret companions for years . . . and suddenly the sight of them made my skin crawl. Gwen's words echoed in my mind. All fairies had to align themselves to a court. What court had they belonged to before they decided to protect my family? Why had they given us their loyalty?

One of the shadelings scrambled onto the table, its little claws skittering against the wood. "The boys are doing homew—ack!" It jerked back as another grabbed its large, batty ear.

"Mister Jake does the homework, Missy, but only him. Not Ash," it corrected, eyeing the casserole. "We can—"

"Yeah, yeah." I gestured toward the sludge. "Just leave some for Dad."

With bright, wicked smiles, the shadelings descended on the dish like a pack of wild dogs on a steak. For one horrible moment, I imagined them biting into human flesh, hot blood trickling down their chins . . . I swallowed and reached into my pocket, fingering the fairy stone. One peek. I took a deep breath, steeling myself for whatever I might see, and brought it up to my eye. Through the hole in the stone, the shadelings gnawed on bread, fat globs of goo and crumbs falling from their lips to the table. No dark or light surrounded a single one of them.

One of the shadelings glanced up at me, its bright yellow eyes shining like lamps. It was hard to miss the surprise on its face. Or the betrayal. The shadeling set its scrap of pastry down and wrung its long fingers together.

"Missy?"

"Nothing," I said, stuffing the stone back into my pocket. My hands shook. The shadelings weren't Unseelie. Of course they weren't. But I could have cried. They were still on my side. Whatever happened, they were still mine. I shouldn't have doubted them.

"Don't worry about it," I said, grabbing the milk jug from the fridge and a bowl from the pantry. Milk sloshed onto the counter as I tried to pour, but they'd clean it all up.

A dozen pairs of eyes stared at me in disbelief. One piped up, its big ears twitching. "Is . . . is that for us?"

I offered them a little smile. "Sure. Just make sure you clean up after yourselves this time."

"So, let me get this straight." Jasika crossed her arm and leaned back against the worn old library chair. "You want me to put a bowl of milk out on the porch every night?"

"It'll pacify any you-know-whats that try to come by," I insisted.

Jasika wrinkled her nose. "Sounds like all we'll get is a bunch of stray cats. I don't want to catch ringworm."

"I'm serious."

"You're overreacting. Besides, I doubt any of the really dangerous ones are going to go 'Oh look, milk! Better not do anything nefarious now. In fact, I think I'll change my whole outlook on humans.'" She sighed and rubbed her temple. "Sorry. That was rude. I was up late last night."

I hesitated a moment and looked her up and down. Her usual sunny glow had been dampened just a bit, like light blocked by a rain cloud. She still had her makeup and hair clips and a nice floral body lotion that made her smell like a spring garden, but the bags under her eyes didn't quite fit. "Is, um, everything okay?" I offered lamely.

"I was just up late practicing is all."

"Practicing . . ." I waggled my fingers in what I hoped was a universal sign for *magic*.

Jasika gave me a Look and folded her hands in front of her. "Maybe. Maybe something a little more reliable than putting milk out and praying the right ones respond to it."

Touchy. She really wasn't going to let this go, was she? I wanted to retort, but a voice that sounded suspiciously like Father Gooding echoed in my head. *Try not to be an asshole.* Great. Now my subconscious had decided he needed to be involved.

I leaned in close, dropping my voice low. "Well, the milk can't hurt. And maybe it'll get some of the nice ones on our side after I expose the one in school."

"Fine. I'll pick some up on the way home." Jasika held up both hands. "But are you sure you want to do this? Like, here? There are more subtle places to check up on someone. We could try scrying or something."

My mind flashed to the fairy stone in my pocket, heavy as a brick. I curled my fingers around it, focusing on its comforting weight. All I had to do was confirm that he was, in fact, Unseelie. That was the only goal today.

"The school's full of iron," I whispered. "He'll be weaker here than if I meet him out in the open."

"Well, he looks pretty healthy to me." Jasika pointed over my shoulder with a grimace. "Here he comes. Please don't be weird."

The last thing anyone was ever supposed to do at a time

like that was actually turn around and *look*, but I was far from super-spy levels of cool and collected. I whirled around, my heart in my throat. There he was. Tall and dark and seething with inhuman charm as he grinned and waved at the assistant librarian, who smiled and waved back. Why was everyone so apparently comfortable around him? Was it some sort of spell? How many people would be in danger if I didn't get rid of him, and fast?

"Yeah, he looks like a real menace." Jasika's sunny smile really was too bright for the situation. "I bet he wants to steal my soul right now."

"Fairies don't steal souls," I pointed out.

"No, but the point is I'm making fun of you because I think you're wrong. I think he's a nice guy, and if you aren't careful, you're going to scare the hell out of him."

If that was our worst-case scenario, I could probably live with myself. I watched as he selected a book and checked it out. The librarian laughed at something. He gave her a little half salute. I pulled the fairy stone out of my pocket and took a deep breath. Even if he saw me, even if he got angry, he wouldn't know Jasika knew. "I guess it's time to settle our bet."

Jasika's brows knitted together as she folded her hands in front of her. "Hey. In case I'm wrong, and I'm not saying I am, just be careful, all right?"

I nodded and tried to give her a reassuring smile, but it came out feeling like kind of a queasy grimace. All I was doing was getting close enough to get a good look at him. The getting-close bit was going to be the problem.

I tightened my grip around the stone as I followed him

out into the hall. Predictably, nobody spared me a second glance as I wove through the crowd. Good. An uncomfortable warmth crept up my neck, and it only worsened with each step I took near him. I brought the fairy stone to my eye, focusing it on Dom.

The would-be spy laughed and even fist-bumped Body Spray Blake. Through the hole in the fairy stone, he looked like an unsuspecting target in the scope of a rifle. Crooked smile, bright eyes . . . and no aura of either light or dark. Nothing at all. My stomach sank. Was this thing busted? Even if he was from a lesser court, this stupid rock was supposed to show me his real face.

Body Spray Blake went on his rank, merry way, and Dom turned, his dark eyes locking with mine. Shit. My face burned. I fumbled with the stone, trying to shove it back in my pocket. It clattered to the ground, skittering across the tile. I scrambled after it, but within seconds, it was lost under foot traffic. Dom strode toward me, his expression open. Positively sweet. That's how their kind always were.

At least, that's how the prince in the woods was.

I turned and pushed my way down the hall. I'd screwed up. Now he knew I was onto him. The bell screeched overhead, and the storm of footsteps picked up, all rushing toward their classrooms. I swallowed the sour taste in my mouth and veered toward the girls' bathroom.

"Hey. Bryn, right?"

He knew my name. My heart hammered in my chest. The prince in the woods. *He* knew my name. What if . . . Oh God. My vision swam. I couldn't breathe. He was following me. He knew, and he was *following me.*

"Hey. You dropped—"

A hand fell on my shoulder. White-hot panic burst in my chest. I grabbed his hand, jerking him off-balance and dragging him through the swinging door into the girls' bathroom. The overpowering stench of antiseptic washed over me, making me gag. I shoved the Fae against the wall and popped my nail off the chain on my neck.

"Holy—no no no, stop, I am very sorry, geez!" The Fae bastard pressed himself against the wall, his dark eyes fixed on the little spike of iron in my hand. "Look, you obviously don't know this about me, but I-I'm really not a big fan of violence."

I held the nail an inch away from his throat. "What do you want with my brothers?" I demanded. By some sort of miracle, I managed to keep the tremor out of my voice.

The Fae took a deep breath. "All right. I—I can see you are very upset here, uh . . . but I really don't think there's any call for uh, for bloodshed—"

"What do you want?" I pressed the side of the nail to his tan skin, gritting my teeth in preparation for the hiss of heat and the bubbling of blistered skin. It never came.

"To say hi! Geez, that's all. It's a thing people do when they want to meet someone." The nail shifted as he swallowed, his Adam's apple bobbing. Sweat beaded on his forehead. "Oh my God. Okay. Look, clearly we've had some kind of misunderstanding," he said, like some kind of professional damned negotiator. "But if you would move the nail just a little farther away from my jugular, I'm sure we can talk about this like rational people."

I stared at his perfectly smooth, healthy skin, free from

burns or blisters despite the iron. The queasy realization of it crept into my stomach. There was no Fae in existence who could stand iron. Not one. I had a human boy, *Dom*, pinned against the wall in the girl's bathroom with a nail to his throat and no good explanation.

My mouth bobbed open, but for the life of me, I couldn't form a word. He stared back, a bead of sweat running down his temple. This poor guy had no idea what was going on.

"Missy!" The shrill voice pierced the quiet of the bathroom, and just like that, Dom wasn't staring at *me* anymore.

"Holy fuck!" Dom jerked so fast, the nail drew a thin line of blood across his neck, but he didn't seem to notice. He stumbled back into the corner, pinned between the sink and the hand dryer, his eyes fixed on the dark form perched atop the stall.

In the harsh, fluorescent light of the bathroom, the shadeling looked violet. Perfect. Abso-freaking-lutely cheese-and-cherry-pie perfect. I pointed the nail at the shadeling.

"I told you never to show yourself!"

"Oh my God, don't talk to it!" Dom's voice shot up an octave.

The shadeling hopped from foot to foot, clutching one of its large ears like a security blanket. "Tân. Brysio," it squeaked.

Welsh. Always a bad sign. For about half a second, I tried to translate, but my frantic mind wouldn't have any of it. "What are you—speak English!"

The shadeling released its ear and sprang down onto the ground, landing with a soft *pat*. "Fire!"

Eight

All I could think of was that annoying question everyone was asked sooner or later: If your house was on fire and you could only grab one thing, what would it be? What would I grab? The boys were in class. Dad was at work. My knitting? My stash? Mum's jewelry?

The shadelings. *Oh God, some of them might still be in there!*

That snapped me back to reality. I was standing in the girls' bathroom while my home burned. The shadeling stared up at me with wide, yellow eyes, gnashing its needle teeth.

"I have to go!"

"Stop!" Dom grabbed my wrist. "What the hell is going on?"

What was going on was my house was on fire and this guy was between me and getting to it. In that moment, caution could go screw itself. I had to get home!

"I thought you weren't human!" I snapped. "And I don't have time for this because the not-human things are burning my house and they could kill the shadelings!"

So much flashed through his face in that moment, too much for me to read. I think I spotted some fear and shock and anger and possibly bizarre fascination, but I couldn't say for sure. Maybe I'd get lucky and he'd just brand me crazy and leave me the hell alone.

His eyes flicked back to the shadeling, bouncing from foot to foot, tugging at its ear in terror.

"Is that thing in danger?"

"What?"

Dom let go of my wrist to point at the shadeling. "Are there innocent things in danger here?"

What the hell did he care? But I couldn't stop myself from blurting out, "Yeah."

He took a deep breath and straightened. His eyes were still wide. There was still a bit of tremor to his hands, but when he spoke, his voice felt like the only steady thing in the world. "Are we going to do something about this or what?"

Nothing like a crisis to snap a guy out of a justified panic. I'd have to explain things to him. Later. When the crisis passed and he remembered how pissed he was. At the moment, he wanted to help. I had to try to be grateful. I nodded and pulled away.

"Right. Okay. Let's go."

I took off down the hall, boots thudding like hammer blows against the tile.

As soon as I charged through the double doors and outside, the acrid stench of smoke washed over me like a wave on the air. My stomach turned. All I could picture was a smoking heap of embers where my home had been and God, oh God, another home ruined because of those monsters.

Dom veered off toward Grey Elm, where most of the nicer houses in town were. I could have just let him go. Clearly he had no idea where I really lived. Probably would have been better to handle this alone. But the shadelings were in danger. I could use all the help I could get. I grabbed the back of his shirt.

"This way," I barked as I charged down the road to the edge of town. Dom jerked back and ran close behind, huffing and puffing. I should have been tired, too, but I couldn't feel it. It was like my whole body was made of lightning. As I ran, I dug my ancient cell phone out of my pocket. My fingers shook, making it impossible to dial.

991 . . . 992 . . . 891 . . . 911!

"911, what's your emergency?" came the well-rehearsed greeting.

"My house is on fire," I gasped. "7 Gosling Road. I-It's the only house, it's on the hill at the end near the woods."

"All right, miss. Are you inside the house?"

"No, just . . . just get there."

"Miss, please don't hang—"

The phone slipped from my grip when I saw it. Atop the hill, my house burned like a bonfire. Black smoke billowed from the windows, orange flames dancing within. The wind blew sparks away, right into the rowan tree at the gate. Here and there, tiny fires lit our protective tree up, its red berries falling like fireballs onto the ground.

"Yes ma'am . . . yeah, no, of course," Dom said, holding my abandoned phone to his ear. He must have picked it up. With a sharp whistle, he gestured to me. "Uh, the emergency lady says we need to stay outside and wait for—"

Like hell. I raced up the hill, through the iron gate, and grabbed the water hose from the side of the house. The old iron handle was warm to the touch as I twisted it. Water spewed out, turning the dirt beneath my boots to mud in seconds. Dom nearly dropped the phone.

"Are you kidding me?!"

Well, as long as he was around. "Take this. Break the windows, spray inside," I said, shoving the hose at him.

Dom scrambled to take the hose and succeeded in spraying himself in the face. He sputtered. "What? Okay, where are you—are you crazy?"

Well, couldn't call the boy dumb. I tore off my jacket and shoved it under the spray.

"Just spray it inside whatever room looks worst," I ordered. "I need to get everything living out of there."

Dom gaped like a fish on land, and for a second I thought he was going to bolt. But he snapped back to scared-but-functional. Hopefully, the notion of living things in actual danger would be enough to keep him from turning heel and running while I was inside. And if he did? Well. He probably should have already, anyway. I charged inside, the wet jacket pressed to my face. It was easier if I didn't really think about it. One step at a time.

Step one: Don't touch the doorknob. There might be fire on the other side.

Crrrack! The doorframe splintered under my boot as I kicked it in.

Step two: Get low. The number one threat in a fire was smoke inhalation.

I dropped to the floor, still holding the jacket over my face. The tile was warm against my bare hand as I shuffled across the floor. It was hard to see anything through the clouds of black smoke. Dimly, I could just make out the misty forms of shadelings shuffling back and forth, carrying anything and everything they could find to toss out the windows. One scrambled across the living room holding a loaf of bread, only to drop it in favor of the remote control, only to drop *that* so it could grab a throw pillow.

"Get out!" I cried, then choked as my chest began to burn. The shadelings squealed, swarming around me. I waved at them, shouting through my damp jacket. "Go, go."

"Missy, the worst of the fire's in your room."

"We tried to throw water on it."

Then a lot of Welsh I couldn't follow. Crap, I'd really let the language slip, hadn't I? My head began to spin. I didn't have much time. I pointed at the door and waited until the first couple of them disappeared before I scrambled forward. Smoke swirled above me, sucked out through the open windows. No. Not open. Under each one was a smattering of glass. Broken.

At this point, step three might have told me to get out of the house . . . too bad personal safety rules only went so far when you had fairies on your ass. I crawled forward, eyes locked on the shards. There had to be a clue.

There, right in the middle of the mess, were the remains of a broken bottle. Brown. Not window glass. Looked like the Unseelie were familiar with Molotov cocktails. Lucky for me, the one intended for the living room lay in flameless pieces. A dud. I snatched a blanket off the back of the couch and gathered as many shards as I could in one hand.

The world went hazy at the edges. I had to get out. Not much air, but . . .

If you could only grab one thing, what would it be?

I shuffled along the hall to my room. Fire licked the walls. Through the haze of smoke, a spray of water peppered the floor. Whoever this Dom guy was, he was reliable. But it wasn't enough. My room wasn't safe. There went everything I had.

What would you grab?

No time to think. Thinking would slow me down. I stumbled forward, hands full, and charged into Dad's room. He kept Mum's jewelry in an old wooden box under his bed, doling out bits and pieces to me for important milestones. Her opal earrings on my thirteenth birthday. A gold chain on my sixteenth. Those would be lost, now, but the rest of it would be there in that box. A lifetime of memories to save or to lose.

Dad's room was farthest from mine and, as such, the coolest in the house. I almost dropped the jacket from my face. No. Keep to the rules. No sense in saving something if I couldn't live to enjoy it.

I set the blanket with the glass shards aside and dug single-handed under the bed. Amidst the half-used tubes of wrapping paper and old shoes, I felt it: polished wood with delicate carvings in the grain.

I sucked in a sharp breath, then hacked as the hot air singed my lungs. Black spots danced in front of my eyes. I shoved the box in the blanket with the glass and tied the whole thing like a satchel. Couldn't go back the way I came. Too hot. I wouldn't last.

I glanced at Dad's window, the buggy one he kept complaining that he could never open on nice nights. Possibly the one window in the house that hadn't been smashed open.

Well, what was one more busted window? I took a deep breath and kicked. Glass shattered outward as fresh air rushed inside, *whoosh*ing against my skin like a kiss from the fresh air itself. I gulped in a deep breath and scrambled out, careful not to touch the jagged bits of window with my bare hands.

The second my feet touched the ground, my knees buckled. I crashed down into the yard, pressing my cheek against the grass, sucking in fresh, clean oxygen. Distant sirens wailed. Looks like the authorities finally bothered to show up. I took another deep breath, then wheezed. Well, maybe I could take just a couple of minutes to catch my second wind. I'd earned it, hadn't I?

"Bryn?"

So much for my second wind. With a groan, I pushed myself to my feet, leaving the jacket on the ground. A pair of Doms stood over me, their faces the color of soot. Right. He'd been close to the fire. I blinked up at him, waiting for the two Doms to become one.

"Leave the hose in the window," I wheezed. "Firefighters'll take care of the rest."

"You are out of your mind," Dom accused, but there was a glimmer of something like exhilaration sparkling in his eyes. "I saw more of those things come out of the windows. Was that all of them?"

He was a bleeding psycho, that's what he was. Raging fire and all he cared about was the safety of a bunch of creatures he didn't believe in an hour ago. Of all the guys in school I could have attacked . . .

"I have to go," I said, taking a step forward. Okay. No. Maybe not such a good idea. I wobbled and might have fallen back down if he hadn't caught me. Boy, he was strong. Or maybe he just seemed that way, since he was the only thing keeping me from the ground.

"Hey, impulse control! You're in no condition to go anywhere," he insisted, holding me tight. "Seriously, what was so important that you had to stay in there?"

Mum's jewelry box.

"I needed to know who caused the fire." That was the smart answer. That was the one I had to work with, anyway. It was an answer I could move forward with.

"If you think I'm going to let you just take off after—"

"Fine, then come with me," I huffed, clutching the blanket to my chest. "Just don't get in my way." I pulled away and managed to stagger to the back gate without falling flat on my face. I probably should have felt bad about not being able to save anything else. Later, when it really hit me, I probably would. For now, this was easier.

"Well . . . w-what about the fire trucks?"

"They're professionals," I snapped back, my heart pounding. I needed to get out of here. Get answers. Breathe. "But please, feel free to hang around someone else's house and try to explain how it caught on fire. I'm sure they'd love to hear it. But I've got to go."

"Well, I'm not letting you wander off to get yourself killed!" He tromped behind me. "I don't want that on my conscience. Did anyone ever tell you you're completely insane?"

"All the time."

For once, the woods didn't feel like some kind of malevolent force out to get me. Maybe it was because, for once, I wasn't alone. The rich smell of earth and pine fought the lingering smoke in my nose. The shade and the damp air were like a cool balm on my hot face. I probably had burns. Couldn't be too serious if I still felt them, right? The serious burns didn't hurt. This pain meant I still had nerve endings.

"This doesn't feel right. Where are we going? And who would even want to do that to someone's house? And what was that thing in the bathroom? And why were there so many of them in your house? They just disappeared when they got out. Where did they go?" Dom babbled, lumbering down the path like an elephant at a tea party. Was there a single twig or branch he'd left unsmashed?

I tried to whirl around to tell him to shut up, but apparently smoke inhalation wasn't good for whirling. The world pitched sideways. I stumbled, catching myself on a tree. Usually this was the point when the shadelings would pop out of nowhere and demand to know what was wrong. Except I'd told them not to show up if anyone else was around.

Dom was on me in a second, hovering like a persistent fly. "Oh my God, you need water. I don't have my water bottle. Uh . . . berries. Those have liquid in them. How do you tell the poisonous ones from the safe ones? Shit, should we get you to a hospital? Hey! Don't pass out on me!"

He was more suffocating than the smoke had been. I set the blanket down on the path so I could shove him away. Dom stumbled back, his eyes wide. Now he looked like a wounded puppy. Great.

"What the hell?" I snapped, sagging against the tree.

Dom blinked, and the wounded puppy was replaced with an irritated cat. "I think that's more my line right now."

"No, seriously. What the hell?" My head began to spin, and

Dom went blurry. I groaned and sank down to the ground. Pine needles crackled underneath me, sounding just like the fire. I swallowed back an ashy taste. "There was a fire at my house, and you just ran toward it. No questions asked. *After* I threatened you and . . . and you saw the shadeling and now you're in the woods with me. Seriously, what is wrong with you?"

Dom's dark eyes were unreadable. He looked so much like the prince I wanted to cry. My throat tightened, and my eyes began to sting. Just trying to hold it back and the lingering smell of smoke made me want to puke. Maybe I did need water.

"You know," Dom said at last, "most people would either say 'Thanks' or 'Sorry' at a time like this. So maybe the real question is: Why are you being such an asshole right now?"

Wait. What now? I blinked up at him. It was like Jasika and Gooding were speaking through his mouth. "That's . . . that's not even the right insult. Shouldn't you call me a bitch?" Was the smoke inhalation getting to me?

Dom shrugged and crossed his arms, looking like a kid who'd been stranded halfway between embarrassed and terrified, and there was no adult to tell him which direction he ought to go. "No, cause you seem like an asshole. You're clearly arrogant, you project the problems onto someone you can yell at, and after I just followed you to apparently *not* try to save your house, I think I deserve a little less attitude. I mean . . . seriously."

Crap. If that wasn't right on the money, I didn't know what was. I'd already attacked the guy. Now I was giving him hell after he'd helped me save the shadelings, for no reason other than the fact that they needed help. I took a deep breath, not liking the squirm of guilt in my gut. "Okay. Sorry. It's just . . . It's been a stressful day."

Dom didn't exactly look satisfied, but neither did he look completely pissed. "Yeah, Jasika warned me your social skills were a little on the rocky side. She just didn't warn me it'd be like this."

I knew it.

"You two have chitchats about me?" I grumbled.

Dom snorted. "You came up now and then. When she talked to me." He wrinkled his nose. "You know, I find it a little funny that she suddenly stopped yesterday. Just completely avoided me."

Typical. Maybe I shouldn't have tried to boss her around. Just made me that much more of an asshole, in retrospect. "I must have seemed pretty crazy."

"Jury's still out. But it's definitely a different kind of crazy." Dom crouched down, balancing his elbows on his knees. "I'm going to try really, really hard not to freak out because obviously you're having kind of a day, but I need you to tell me what happened. What was that thing in the bathroom? Why was your house full of them and, you know, on fire? You said it was something not human that you thought I was." He froze, his breath hitching. His eyes grew wide. "Oh my God. Is . . . is magic real?"

It wasn't funny, but for some strange reason, that innocent question sure sounded hilarious. I started to laugh, but my breath caught in my throat. It felt like I had a giant rubber band tightening around my chest until my lungs burned. I hacked again. This was bad.

Dom reached out to help me sit up straight, which really wasn't all that helpful, but I suppose it made him feel better to do something.

When my chest stopped trying to squeeze itself into nothing, I almost shoved him away, but stopped myself. I needed to not be an asshole. I waved him off.

"Go get Gwen," I called out to the shadelings, who had to be eavesdropping just out of sight. Where else would they have gone but the woods?

"Who's Gwen?" Dom demanded. "Shit, are you hallucinating? How many fingers am I holding up?"

And, helpfully, he shoved his entire hand in my face. "Back off," I growled, very nicely pushing his hand away. Not slapping it. I could at least try to be a nice person. "I'm talking to the shadelings."

A pair of lights flickered in the trees, just for a second. Either I was seeing things or that was a shadeling letting me know it had heard me.

"Shadeling? Wait, you mean one of those things we saved?" Dom glanced over his shoulder. "Bryn, we're alone."

"They're always around." I shifted and reached for the glass-filled blanket. "They're . . . not exactly servants. More like volunteer help, only they won't let you send them away or tell you why they hang around. They're shadow creatures, I think."

There it was. The blood drained from Dom's face. Ask the guy to take on a house fire, and he was fine. Give him a bunch of *Labyrinth* rejects, and he got squeamish.

"And they're . . . what?" His voice cracked. "Demons? Did we just save demons?"

I pictured the drooly little boogers stuffing baked goods in their faces while serving Lucifer, and couldn't help the loony smile that worked its way onto my face.

"You know, I read somewhere that they're descended from fallen angels or something." Another giggle threatened to bubble up. I had to take a deep breath to stop it. "But whatever. No. Fairies are fairies."

"Fairies." Dom stared at me for a few seconds, brows raised. Oh. He was waiting for me to say I was joking. How adorable.

I grinned. "Yeah. Fairies."

"Like . . . like the little girls with the butterfly wings who live in flowers?"

That mental image was almost as absurd as them serving the devil. Now I was picturing evil demon shadelings with butterfly wings. It was like Halloween had come early.

"I have actually never met a fairy like that," I said. Well. Slurred. It was getting hard to speak. I licked my lips. "It's . . . more like a . . . a folklore thing. Those fairies are like Shakespeare and . . ." And it was getting hard to focus. It was amazing how fast the exhaustion was crashing into me.

Dom said something, but all I heard was a soft whooshing sound, like water rushing through grass. Couldn't be him. Dom's mouth stopped and he turned, his expression twisted in nothing short of pure astonishment. It was a funny expression. I almost giggled as my eyes finally slid shut. The last thing I felt was a cool hand on my forehead. Gwen.

Nine

Gwen's lips were as cool and soft as I remembered, pressed against my forehead. All things considered, it wasn't the worst way to wake up.

I opened my eyes and blinked away the gummy sensation of sleep. Gwen smiled down at me. Her perfect lips formed a heart on her too-pale face. She always smiled at me like that. Like I was the only thing in the world that made her happy. In that quiet moment, I wanted her lips to touch my forehead again. I wanted her to give a little comfort and tell me everything would be all right. If I asked, she probably would.

For one queasy moment, I let myself wonder if I broke her heart at the beginning of summer. If I had, why was she still so kind to me? Why were any of them?

I huffed and pushed myself up, expecting to feel like hell, but I didn't. I could breathe, for a start. I touched my cheeks. No sting, either. Gwen must have patched me up while I was sleeping. She really was too good for me.

Dom sat at the edge of the pond, deep in conversation with a pair of water wives. He had this big, goofy smile on his face, like he had just found out that not only was the tooth fairy real, but she also shared his taste in music. Nothing like a pond full of beautiful women to distract a guy from the insanity of the day. The water wives didn't look the least bit annoyed that he was there. If anything, they looked as interested in him as he was in them. The one in the water whistled a lilting tune, which Dom tried to whistle back. Poorly. A shadeling curled up at his side, not quite touching him, but regarding him silently. Maybe they realized he'd helped to save them. Well, crap. He really was the kind of guy to jump into danger to help strangers and make friends with people the second he met them . . . And I'd just held a nail to his throat.

He was right. Hell, everyone was right, lately. I was an asshole.

Gwen hummed that musical hum of hers and glanced over her shoulder.

"It has been many years since a human male has come to our home," Gwen observed. "But your friend is . . . pleasant. He demands nothing of us." The corners of her eyes crinkled as she smiled. "His is a rare sort. You were lucky to find him."

Find him. Threaten him. Expose him to the Fae. Real lucky. Poor guy had no idea what I'd just dragged him into. I ran my fingers through my hair. They came out smeared with soot.

"Bryn," Gwen said, resting her cool hand on my forehead. "What happened?"

"Fire. Nothing," I muttered. "I got here as soon as I could."

"Liar!" Dom snapped. I shot him a glare as he hurried over, all gangly limbs and judgment. "She went inside. Nearly got herself killed." He shot me back a glare of his own. Right. Maybe I wasn't entirely forgiven.

Gwen's gaze sharpened to two chips of jade as she turned to me.

"Is he telling the truth, Bryn?" she asked, but didn't wait for me to answer. Water wives couldn't always catch a lie, but they could always catch the truth. "This is most unusual from you." Gwen turned back to me. "What happened?"

"I . . . Well, the house was on fire," I explained. "I had to look after the shadelings. Here, where's my . . ." I glanced around. There, just within reach, was my blanket, still bundled up. The fibers were singed here and there, but it looked more or less whole. "Apparently someone threw a few Molotov cocktails in through the windows. I think when they couldn't get through the house's defenses they had to get creative. This is the only bottle that didn't ignite. Can you tell us who threw it?" I tugged the blanket open to reveal the bottle shards. Mum's jewelry box sat on top of them. Some of the wood was scratched and torn. A sudden knife of panic stabbed through my chest. I had to take a deep breath. A little sandpaper and stain and I could fix it.

Gwen reached for the box, but I snatched it away before she could touch it. My palms stung as tiny shards that had embedded themselves in the wood pricked my palms, but I didn't let go. "No. Just the glass."

Dom's eyes widened, his eyes glued to the box. "Is it magic?"

"It's my mum's," I snapped.

Gwen glanced sidelong at me, then down at the remains of the bottles. Her pale hand danced over the glass shards for a moment, like she was feeling the temperature, before she brushed the pads of her fingers against one.

Her scream sounded like the shriek of metal being rent apart. Gwen flew back from the glass, holding her hand up in front of her, fingers spread wide. I jumped to my feet.

"Gwen, what happened? Did you cut yourself?"

"What's wrong?" Dom demanded, starting back. The other water wives gasped and dove back into the lake without so much as a splash.

Gwen swerved past him, plunging her hand into the water. Her chest heaved. Sweat beaded on her forehead. Her eyes were so wide I could see the whites all the way around her irises.

"Gwen," I gasped, reaching for her.

In the same moment, Dom knelt down next to her, his hand hovering over her shoulder. "Just breathe, you're going to be okay. She'll be okay, right?" He stared down at her like a doctor on the battlefield, desperate to save a soldier. Like he even knew her. How the hell did someone care so freely?

I wanted to snap at him to back off. He didn't know her. He shouldn't be the one to comfort her, but I smothered the selfish urge and turned my attention back to Gwen. She needed me. I squeezed her shoulder. On her other side, Dom did the same. With both of us supporting her, Gwen's breathing slowed. She closed her eyes. Her lips shook, then moved with silent words.

"I can't hear—" But maybe I didn't need to.

The water shimmered in front of her. Within seconds, the stones and little fish and the faint outlines of the homes disappeared as a pale, inhuman face swam into being. An ashy taste filled my mouth.

"Shit." Dom's hand flew to his mouth. "What *is* that?"

"An Unseelie Fae," I muttered, swallowing hard. I knew it. I held the box just a little closer, as if it could chase away the image of that horrible face. Oh God. This was really happening, wasn't it?

Gwen pulled her hand out of the water. It shook so badly, it sent droplets flying everywhere, rippling the surface of the water like a rainstorm. Her cheeks took on a strange, greenish hue.

I grabbed her hand, giving it a squeeze. "I'm sorry I asked you to do that."

"What was that thing?" Dom demanded again. "It's . . . You said it's what burned Bryn's house? That's the bad guy? How many of those things are there in this town?"

Gwen gave a little chin jerk as she stared down at the water. "A drone," she murmured. "So few are kept. Most are traded for changelings at a young age. I have never heard of a grown drone warrior being sent against a human before. They're too wild. Rest easy, Dom. They are rare. But that one would come close to you, Bryn—"

"It's one of them that attacked me the other night," I told her. "So this makes two of them."

Gwen's head whipped around, her mouth wide. "Bryn, only the reigning monarch of the Unseelie court may command these wretches."

I stared down at the box in my hand. The one Mum had treasured so much. Was that what had happened to her? Had she been taken before an Unseelie king or queen?

"I don't get it," Dom insisted. "If they're fairies or . . . or Fae or whatever, then why the firestarters? Can't they use magic or something? Or, like, is there some way to keep them out?"

I traced my fingers over the intricate patterns of the box. It felt like my mind had been split in two. Half of it was back in Wales on a rainy day when Mum told me stories and kept me safe. The other half was anchored to the darkening present.

"Our house is too well protected," I explained. "The gates are iron. No Fae can touch it. And everything we planted in there is supposed to repel them . . ." My heart slammed like a sledgehammer into my ribs. I took a few deep breaths to calm it before I could speak. "I think they were trying to force us out of the house."

Now that I'd said it out loud, it seemed so obvious. They couldn't touch the boys so long as we lived behind the iron gates and the rowan tree. The only remarkable part was that they hadn't tried it sooner. We needed to go somewhere else. Somewhere my brothers would be safe.

"Okay, so why are the *Unfeeling* after you?" Dom asked.

Sweet little lamb. He didn't need to get tangled up in all of this. But I couldn't just make him forget everything he'd seen today. He cared too much.

I scrubbed my hand over my face before letting go of Gwen's hand, hugging the box closer. "Family thing," I muttered. "We think it had something to do with my mum. I'm going to have to tell Dad."

"Your dad? Wait, is he the one with the . . ." Dom brought his hand up to his temple, and for a moment, it looked like he was going to make an insensitive gesture. Lucky for him, he seemed to think better of it and lowered his hand. "Um . . . hallucinations?"

"He was cursed," I said. "But yeah. He sees fairies everywhere he goes, so much that he's just learned to ignore them.

This is only going to make it harder for him." And now that court Fae were trying to get to the family, he was as good as unprotected. He could be standing right in front of a drone and wouldn't know it was real.

"Your family cannot protect themselves if they don't know the threat," Gwen pointed out. "Today only proves that you cannot do this on your own."

"I wish Mum had taught me about this."

This would all be so much easier if I knew what she'd done. How she got us into this. I gazed down at the box and let the memories take over. The ugly floral rug in the living room and the rain *pat-pat-patt*ing against the windows. Mum's powdery perfume as I curled into her side for warmth, as I ran my fingers over the wood, trying to find pictures in the patterns the way I might find them in the clouds.

"Was that box hers?" Dom pressed. "Maybe there's a clue or something inside."

"No, it's just her jewelry. Dad kept it to remember her." And would he be happy to know I'd saved it? Maybe that would soften the blow. I took a deep breath, clicked the latch, and swung the lid up.

Mum's jewelry. It was like being sucker-punched with a memory. I caught my breath. There was the armband that looked like a snake. She'd worn it the day we went to the beach and I got sand in my ice cream, back before the boys were born. And the heavy pendant with the love knot in the middle. I think Dad gave that to her.

I pulled out the pendant, focusing on its weight in my hand and—

"What's that?" Dom blurted out.

Just under the layer of gems and precious metals was an old, leather-bound book. I pulled it out and waited for some memory. Nothing. Had I ever seen Mum with this book? A few long seconds passed, but my mind remained blank. If this was Mum's, then she'd never had it out around us.

I opened the front cover. The old pages crackled softly as they moved. They weren't paper. They were something thicker, like what they made books out of in the Middle Ages. Vellum, maybe? It was the sort of thing I probably needed to handle with gloves. Gently as I could manage, I turned the pages one by one. Scribbles in half a dozen languages littered the pages. Nordic runes. Celtic ogham. Others I didn't recognize, all forming what looked like poems and recipes and spells.

Had Dad known this was in here? He had to. He'd had it for years. He'd known about this and he'd kept it from me.

Dom's eyes widened. I might as well have held the Holy Grail in front of him. Much more excitement and his eyes were going to pop right out of his head. Gwen reached out, her pale hand hovering over the pages as it had over the glass.

"A grimoire. Some of the contents are certainly human," she said, then wrinkled her nose and hissed. "Much is not."

"What do you mean not human?"

Gwen withdrew, burying her hands in her voluminous skirt. "Fae magic. But every word in that book was written by the same hand that once held that box."

"You mean my mother?" I held the book out, a sudden hunger gnawing at my insides. This could be my first chance to see Mum in nine years. "Can you do what you did with the shards? Touch it and show her picture in the water?"

Gwen grimaced and shook her head. "No, Bryn. It's been enchanted to repel any Fae kind who attempt to touch it."

I tried to imagine my mum doing that, but it felt wrong. She was the one who'd taught me to look for the nymphs and sprites in the woods. Anti-Fae enchantments didn't fit the picture of her that I still had in my head.

"Gwen, I'm sure it's safe."

"No!" Gwen's green eyes burned. "There is Unseelie magic there, Bryn. I will not touch it!"

"Unseelie? No, Gwen, it's my mum's. She was human."

"Maybe," Dom suggested, "maybe she experimented with fairy magic."

It was like a slap to the face, but he couldn't know what he'd just said. He'd only found out that fairies existed an hour ago. Except . . . except a little voice in my head had to question all of it. Dad must have known about this. And he'd never told me. Why wouldn't he tell me?

"It would explain a great deal," Gwen said. "Why your family's being targeted. Bloodlines are powerful things. If an ancestor of yours made a deal with the Unseelie—"

I slammed the book shut. "My mum didn't do dark magic," I snapped. "Neither of you knew her. She was a good person."

Dom looked like he wanted to say something, but he held his tongue. Gwen, on the other hand, had no such reservations. "Good people make mistakes," she insisted.

"You just don't get it. You . . ." I needed backup. I jumped to my feet and turned to face the trees. "Shadelings!"

There was a flicker of movement somewhere amidst the dark branches. A bright pair of eyes blinked to life, flicked toward Dom, then vanished again. Right. Him. It would be easy to send him away. Except he'd dropped everything to save them. With no good reason at all, he'd jumped into action to help me. Gwen liked him. He was this light, gentle kind of good I only ever saw in the water wives, the kind everyone needed more of in their lives.

Maybe it was time to learn how not to be an asshole.

"Standing order," I barked. "This human is with me. It's fine. You can show yourself around him."

The shadelings shuffled out from the shelter of the trees, all watching Dom with open suspicion. It was strange to see all of them out of the shadows at once, but there they were. Twenty-seven dark forms, inky black to plum purple to forest green, all two feet tall, huddled and leery of the sunlight.

I knelt down, showing them the book. "Do you recognize this?"

I waited for them to shake their heads. Maybe the Fae who'd taken her had dropped it. Maybe Dad had picked it up when he was still trying to figure out how to get her back. But, one by one, the shadelings nodded.

"Missy Mistress always had it. Wrote in it all the time, she did."

"What? I've never—" I protested, but the purple shadeling with the yellow eyes interrupted me.

"Not you, Missy. Your mother, our Missy Mistress."

I could feel Gwen's and Dom's eyes on me. I probably wouldn't get any obnoxious *I told you so*s from them. Somehow, knowing that didn't do much to make it better.

"She wrote in it herself," I breathed, and it made my stomach turn to see the shadelings nod. My mum had practiced fairy magic. My dad hadn't told me.

"It's why we're here, Missy," the shadeling squeaked. "Human magics can't summons us like fairy magics can."

Mum played with fairy magic. Lawless magic that didn't require ritual or practice or care. That's why our whole family was in this mess. This was all her fault. And for the last nine years, I'd thought it was mine. And Dad had just let me. But it was her all this time. She'd dealt with them. Something in me felt hollow, like a place that had always been too full was cleared out, leaving behind a chilly emptiness. Memories fought for a place in the front of my mind, every one of them tainted like that nail polish you could never quite scrub out of the carpet. Every hug, every kiss, every lullaby had come from Mum. The one who'd brought them to our doorstep.

"Mum's the reason all this happened," I breathed. How was I supposed to feel? Betrayed? Relieved? Scared? My whole body jumped into overdrive. Hands shaking. Cold sweat. Heart trying to pound its way out of my chest.

My head began to spin. I sank down onto the ground and focused on breathing. Breathe in. One, two, three, four, five, six, seven, eight . . .

"Here, I think it may help to get that out of the way," Dom said, tugging at the book. After a fraction of a second, I let it go. There was a clatter of beads on wood as he settled it back in the jewelry box, then the faint *clack* as he closed it up. Nobody said anything. Not that there was much of anything to say, anyway.

The purple shadeling padded forward and curled up in my lap. It smelled like dirt and smoke. I rested my hand on its back.

"Eeerp!" it squeaked, squirming away from my hand. A

bright burn stretched from its shoulder to its lower back. How had I missed that?

"I'm sorry," I sighed as I gathered it into my arms. "Gwen, can you and your sisters help me with the shadelings?"

The water wives never really needed much encouragement to offer their healing to anyone or anything. To their credit, the shadelings must have been more bothered by the events of the day than the prospect of a bath. For the most part, they let the water wives usher them to the shallows of the pond without a fight.

I'd let the information about my mum simmer. Better to think about that later. For now, I would solve the problems right in front of me. I rose, carrying the shadeling in my arms to the pond with the others.

Ten

Dom walked with me back out of the woods like some sort of gangly watchdog. To his credit, he didn't ask any questions, though every couple of seconds his hands twitched, tugging at his shirt or cracking knuckles. Any little noise to fill the silence. He didn't know how to handle any of this.

When we finally reached the edge of the woods, I sighed. "Look. Thank you for helping me. But maybe it would be a good idea to pretend it didn't happen. Fae stuff is pretty chaotic."

Dom all but tripped on his own feet as he whirled around to stare at me. "What? Are you kidding me? Bryn, magic is real!" His eyes sparkled brightly. Christ, he wasn't scared—he was excited!

"Yes, and it's dangerous!" I tightened my grip on the blanket holding my precious cargo. "My father has hallucinations because one of the Fae decided to play ping-pong with his brain. My house just burned down because of them. Their magic plays by rules I don't even think our brains can comprehend! This isn't fun or games, Dom."

Dom's hands twitched again before burying themselves in his pockets. He licked his lips, his gaze fixed somewhere over my shoulder.

"Do you have somewhere to go?"

"Huh?"

Dom sighed. "Do you have somewhere to go tonight? Do you need a place to stay? I can talk to Helen. I'm sure she'd be more than willing to put you and your family up for a couple of days. I mean, it would be crowded but doable. I know she wouldn't want to see anyone without a place any more than I would."

I blinked. It was such a mundane, normal thing to say that I almost worried he hadn't even heard me. And I was too damn tired to press the matter.

"No. We're fine. I know where we can stay tonight, at least." And, not for nothing, but if our house wasn't safe, nothing on Postoak Road would be.

Dom grimaced but nodded. "If you're sure." He reached out to squeeze my shoulder. "It's going to be okay. And if you ever need anything, I'm at the end of the road. We can, you know. Talk about all of this stuff."

He was just so stinking earnest. I had to avert my eyes before he blinded me with that overbright puppy-dog look.

"I just attacked you in the bathroom today."

"Yeah. I'm still working on that." Dom pulled a face. "But I think I sort of get why you were scared. If this sort of thing was after me, I guess I'd be trigger-happy, too."

Right. I forced myself to nod. "Bye," I muttered, and of course Dom didn't turn to go anywhere. "Seriously. I know where I'm going."

"You're sure?"

I took a shallow breath, wincing at the faint itch in my lungs. "Yeah. Go. Don't want you to miss dinner."

Another squeeze to my shoulder, and then he finally peeled off. Probably toward Postoak.

I pulled out my phone and speed-dialed the middle school. The receptionist confirmed that, yes, both Ash and Jake were in class, and was I calling about Ash's recent string of absences? The twerp had been playing hooky after all. Typical.

"No," I said. "But could you tell both of them to go to the after-school program? We're . . ."

We're homeless? We're under attack? What could I say without starting a panic?

"We're having a family emergency. Someone will be by to pick them up later. Uh . . . either me or my dad or Father Gooding. We don't want them walking home alone today."

"Well, I'll be sure to tell them. I hope everything works out."

Me, too. I pocketed the phone and took a deep breath. Time to set the Fae world aside and deal with the very human consequences of all of this.

The familiar door to Gooding's office loomed over me like an entry into the underworld. A gust of the early evening wind swept down on me, biting at my bare arms. Gooseflesh rippled across my skin. In that instant, I was a scared kid again, standing on the steps of a strange church, ready to ask a strange man for help. I wanted my mum to knock for me. I wanted my dad to squeeze my shoulder and promise me it would be okay like he did all those years ago. But I was the only one here.

With one hand, I clutched the blanket and its precious contents. With the other, I knocked.

Several long seconds passed before the door creaked open. Gooding poked his head out, his eyes bloodshot. Working without his glasses again.

"Bryn, why aren't you in . . ." He trailed off, looking me up and down. I could only imagine what he saw. His brows furrowed. "You're covered in soot. What happened?"

"My . . ." My voice came out sounding strained and thin. I swallowed. "My house was on fire. I managed to save—"

I didn't get to finish that thought. The instant I said "fire," his arms were around me, pulling me close. I stiffened and almost dropped the blanket, but I relaxed just enough to wrap one arm around his middle. It was a strange fit. Gooding and I didn't hug. But it fought off the chill of the wind and the pervading sense of aloneness, and I wasn't about to turn that down.

"You foolish girl," Gooding said. "What were you thinking? You could have been killed! *Nothing* is worth your life, Bryn!"

For just a moment, his words had a bite to them, like he was truly about to scold me, but he didn't let go. Tears welled up in my eyes, and the second they seeped through his shirt, he pulled away.

"I'm sorry, Bryn. It's going to be all right."

I scrubbed my face, shoulders hunching against the return of the cold. Trying to organize my thoughts felt like grabbing for dust motes in the air. "I tried to find out what caused it. There was broken glass in the living room. Don't worry, I called for help, too. The fire trucks are already there."

I gave the blanket a little jerk, making the bits of glass clink against one another. Hard to say why I was even still holding on to it since I'd already let Gwen see it. By this point it was probably half ground to sand.

Gooding took a deep breath. I could just hear the lecture he probably wanted to unleash, but after a couple of seconds, he pursed his lips and nodded.

"Come inside," he instructed. "Tell me everything."

He took my shoulder and steered me out of the office, down the hall, and into the cramped church kitchen.

"Sit," he instructed, letting go of my arm to point at the table currently covered with clothing donations. I slumped down in a rickety folding chair and pulled the blanket into my lap. The box and glass shards shifted under the fabric in the horrible, screeching way that made me want to grind my teeth.

Gooding puttered around the kitchen as he prepared tea. There was something distinctly comforting about the normality of it. Even if he did prepare it in the microwave.

I probably should have tried to explain everything then, when his eyes weren't on me. But if I was honest with myself, all I wanted to do was grab the least hideous muumuu from the pile, take a shower, and curl up anywhere with a pillow. Not that I was going to get that chance anytime soon.

Gooding set a steaming mug of chamomile in front of me and leaned against the table. "What, exactly, happened?" he asked. "And what on this good earth were you thinking?"

Here came the time to edit the story a bit. He wouldn't approve of the shadelings or the water wives.

"I had a bad day. Needed some air, so I cut class. I saw the smoke, and I just sort of ran into it." There. Only half a lie. Well, if I counted all the parts I was leaving out, it was

90

probably seventy-five percent a lie. But I was telling him some truth. That had to count for something.

Gooding sighed and pulled up another chair, gesturing at the charred blanket. "What's in there?"

I set the blanket out on the table and flipped it open. There, on top of the remains of the glass shards, sat Mum's box. *Mum's book.* For one horrible moment, I saw his hand twitch toward it. He'd want to look inside. He'd find the book. He'd see what was in it, and . . . oh God. He'd never let me see it again. He'd hide it or burn it because, in his mind, that would be the safest thing to do.

I felt something squeezing around my heart. Before he could touch it, I snatched the box up from the pile.

"Gnngh!" I nearly dropped the box as pain shot through my hands.

I ground my teeth together, setting the box back on the table. Tiny shards of glass glittered under the fluorescent light, ground into the now thoroughly beaten wood of the box. And my stinging hands. Gooding jumped up from his chair, going right for the first aid kit under the sink.

"Give me that," Gooding instructed, reaching for my hand. The pain in my palms settled into a steady throb. Gooding pulled out a pair of tweezers, plucking out the glass shards one by one. Each pluck felt like a stab right into my palm. I glowered down at the table, trying not to make any sound. I did pretty well until he splashed the rubbing alcohol on the cuts. Fire washed over my hands, and Gooding definitely didn't appreciate the word that came out of my mouth.

"Bryn, you are in a church," he pointed out before pulling out a long, thin strip of gauze.

I shot him a dark look. "I think the big guy will forgive me. It's been kind of a long day."

Gooding opened his mouth, then closed it and nodded as if to say *Touché*. Score one for me, then. As he finished bandaging my first hand, he nodded toward Mum's jewelry box. "Of all the things you could have taken, why that?"

"Mum's jewelry," I answered automatically. "I just wanted something of hers. That's all. And if I have the glass, maybe I can show the police what happened. In case the rest of the evidence is gone." Okay, that was a little bit more of a lie than the last one.

Gooding pursed his lips and started on my second hand. "You should have trusted the authorities."

"Right, because they know what we're up against." I took a deep breath and focused on the gauze as he wrapped it around my palm, the soft feel of the cloth against my cuts. It was easier to focus on that than everything else. "I think it's time for me to tell Dad. About everything."

Gooding's hands stilled. There was a long silence as he stared at me, his expression unreadable. Shouldn't he be cheering me on? Scolding me for taking too long? My heart jumped into my throat. What, was he going to make me beg now?

"Father Gooding, this wasn't just some prank. They couldn't get past our gates, so they forced us out of our home. Dad needs to know."

Gooding took a deep breath before he finished wrapping my hand. After what felt like an eternity, he reached forward to squeeze my shoulder. "Drink your tea," he said. "I'll call him."

* * *

WHILE GOODING MADE THE CALL, I curled up in the chair and held the mug of chamomile until it started to go cold. I felt like a buoy after a storm—one more big wave, and I'd be done. Little by little, the light outside the window faded into the buttery yellow of late afternoon. There were voices. The church secretary and Gooding explaining to her precisely why I was in here. I stopped listening around the word "fire" and focused on the table. A small spider crept along the laminated wood before disappearing under a faded hockey jersey. I couldn't help wondering if some poor guy was going to receive it and get a nasty surprise. I blinked down at it. Without really thinking it all through, I grabbed Mum's box and slid it under the pile. Out of sight and beyond question.

My phone shrieked. The name *ASH* lit up the screen, just above a picture of him on his eleventh birthday with chocolate frosting on his nose. I stared at it, trying to decide whether or not to answer. After a minute, the ringing stopped, replaced by a text beeping across the screen. From Ash.

Ash: Wtf Bryn?! Why can't we go home????

I stared at it, trying to process the words.

The door flew open. I barely had time to look up before Dad was in front of me, his hands on my face as he forced me to look up and into his terrified eyes.

"My baby girl, what happened?" he sputtered, rubbing his thumbs across my cheeks, half cleaning, half smearing the soot that still clung to them. Before I could say anything, he pulled me into a rib-crushing hug. Something wound up tight in my chest and squeezed until tears pricked at the corners of my eyes. A few slipped out, and I didn't even bother to wipe them away. I bunched my fingers in his coat and breathed in the spicy, sweet smell of his aftershave. It felt like a lifetime since my own dad had comforted me like this. And if I wanted to look at the ugly truth of it, it was the first time in a long time that I had let him.

It took me a couple of seconds to even realize that he was still talking.

". . . insurance company. Figure out what started it."

An involuntary flinch shuddered through my arms. I let go of him and took a step back, wiping at the tears and soot on my cheeks. "It was the Fae, Dad."

His shoulders sagged like I'd just dropped a bag of bricks on him. Worse, he looked at me with those sad eyes that every school counselor had given me when they had to talk to me. Like he could pretend I was making this up. Like he didn't live with a psychological condition *they'd* given him because he tried to go after Mum. Like he hadn't kept her book of spells under his bed for almost a decade.

"Sweetheart, I'm sure there's a perfectly human explanation for what happened today."

"Dad." My voice came out in a hoarse wheeze. This wasn't how I wanted to do this. I should have been standing up straighter, chin raised, shoulders squared. I should have had a nice speech ready. But I didn't. It was all I could do to string one word after another. "I know it was them because I *know* them. I fight them with Father Gooding."

Dad's brows twitched. His eyes flicked to Gooding for the barest second before returning to me, filled with just a little less pity than before. "Bryn—"

"There was a changeling on Postoak a week ago." I curled my hands into fists to stop them from shaking. This was wrong. This was raining-frogs wrong. He still saw me as the scared little girl who'd just lost her mom. And, deep down, he was still the guy who'd just lost his wife and suddenly had three kids to look after alone. If I was ever going to tell him about what I was doing, it wasn't supposed to be like this. Dad had enough on his plate . . . but now that I'd started, I couldn't stop the words from spilling out. "And a month ago, the Witters family had redcaps. And . . . and I saw one of *them*, too. From Wales."

The color drained from his face. He flinched, the same jerking tic that came when things were going wrong in his head. I wanted to reach out to him, to draw his focus away from whatever he was seeing, but Father Gooding beat me to it. He stepped forward, his hands folded in front of him. Business as usual. "I've been teaching her to protect herself, Tom."

Dad turned to stare at him, and in that moment, I honestly thought he was going to punch a priest. He flexed his hand, rolling it in and out of a white knuckled fist. "You put her in danger?"

"Knowledge is dangerous, yes. But not half as dangerous as ignorance."

Dad wasn't a big man, but he looked like a bear ready to strike. "I came here to keep my family *away* from all of this!"

"Dad." I reached out, resting a hand on his tense arm.

Dad jerked away as though I'd burned him. It only took a second for him to realize it. His expression crumbled. When he spoke, his voice wavered. "Bryn, sweetheart . . ."

Sweetheart. I couldn't unsee the pain and fear in his eyes. The whole point of working with Gooding was to keep anyone in my family from ever looking like that again. Guess I'd screwed that one up, hadn't I?

"It was my choice, Dad." Yeah. That felt right. I squared my shoulders and took a deep breath. "It's my choice. I decided to do this." That was what you were supposed to say, wasn't it? The strong statement that felt true. The sort of declaration that was supposed to make you sound independent and confident and hide how small and scared you were under the bravado.

Dad's expression didn't change. If I stared at it too much longer, I'd start to feel it. I wouldn't be able to keep this up.

"Why did you keep this a secret?" he rasped.

Shame curled in my belly. I wanted to force it down, but it was hard to ignore the hurt in his eyes. The square of my shoulders collapsed, and it was all I could do to keep from giving up entirely. Just sitting back down and blocking it all out because, hell, I really could have just dropped my head down and passed out for a week.

"You had enough to worry about," I mumbled. "This was something I could do. And up until now, it's gone pretty well."

Dad sagged down into one of the folding chairs. All the energy seeped out of him, leaving someone who looked as beaten and defeated as I felt. I suppose, if nothing else, we could commiserate. There wasn't any reason to it. There wasn't any logic. This was Fae. It was otherworldly and ineffable and so, so damaging. I reached out to rest one hand on his shoulder. This time, he let me.

"No more," he said in a soft voice.

"Tom—"

"And how dare you," Dad growled, shooting Father Gooding a withering glare. "Putting her in harm's way. I trusted you. We moved here because you were supposed to be able to protect us. You promised!"

"Dad." I squeezed his shoulder. "We were only trying to protect you and the boys."

"I know what you were trying to do." He glared down at the linoleum. "I know how hard it's been on you and the boys. But this ends." He leveled his finger at me. "No more. You go to school. You do your homework. You get into a good university half a continent away from this mess. But I never want to hear that you've been seeking it out."

It all sounded so normal. It was exactly the sort of thing I'd been barreling toward. Had things gone my way, I would have been planning nothing else. But things didn't go my way, did they? Monsters attacked. Houses burned down. Battles would just keep happening until the war was over.

My eyes flicked back to the untouched pile of old clothes. Until now, we'd been on the defensive. It hadn't worked. Stopping wouldn't work. Pretending we were normal and life was normal wasn't going to work. But, in that moment, I just needed the pain to leave my dad's eyes. If he and the boys were okay, I could be okay to carry on with what I needed to do.

"Fine," I muttered.

The lie didn't taste all that bitter.

Eleven

It felt like there was so much to do. But Dad had gone to pick up the boys. For me, there was nothing more important than a hot shower, clean clothes, and figuring out where I was going to live now. The bathroom was clean, but worn through with age. The pajamas were soft, if threadbare. It all felt sort of like getting a hug from my surroundings. Things wouldn't be perfect, but they would be okay, for now.

The convent cell was about two-thirds the size of my old bedroom, but the tall, white walls somehow made it feel too open. I dumped the armful of clothes with Mum's box on the bed, adding a splash of color to the dull, porridge-colored bedspread. I don't know what I was expecting. Gooding wasn't running a bed-and-breakfast here. Most of the time, the old convent served as storage space. Well. When they weren't housing people down on their luck. *People like us, I guess.*

"We want to go to the house, Dad!" Ash called from down the hall.

"Not tonight."

"Why not? It's our home, too!" Jake, that time. It was probably the first time he'd ever raised his voice to Dad. If this was how they behaved in the church, I shuddered to think of how they'd behaved the whole ride here.

"Boys, please . . ." Dad sounded so tired.

I sank down onto the bed and closed my eyes. If I could ignore how thin the mattress was, how the room smelled like mothballs instead of lavender, I could almost pretend I was home, sitting on my bed, looking out at my own room. There, to the right of the bed, was where I kept my textbooks. Over in the corner was my knitting basket. And the loose floorboard where I hid my stash. Had it survived the fire? I couldn't imagine it did. Half the things in that box were made of wood.

Tap tap. Tap tap.

I opened my eyes and turned. One of the shadelings stood in the window wringing its hands. I stared at it, my brain too fuzzy to really connect to what I was seeing for a few seconds. Then it clicked.

I rose and pushed the window open, stepping aside for the shadeling to enter. It hopped down from the windowsill and scuffled across the floor, tugging at one of its large, batlike ears.

"We . . . live here, now?"

"Yeah. For a while." I sank down onto the flat mattress and patted the spot next to me. The shadeling hopped up beside me, grabbing at the pile of clothes to fold them. Or, well, try to fold them. This was probably the first time one of them had ever willingly tried to help with laundry. Lots of firsts tonight.

"Don't worry about that," I sighed, taking the wads of hand-me-downs away. "Come on, put it down." The shadeling gripped a bright purple windbreaker until I finally tugged it free and added it to the pile. "Hey. Leave it be, I'll take care of it later."

I shoved the mound of clothes to the floor, but the shadeling wouldn't be stilled. It scrambled to the head of the bed, where Mum's box still was, and started picking bits of glass out of the wood. I grabbed the shadeling by its torso and dragged it off the bed, dangling it over the trash bin next to the door. "Drop it before you cut yourself."

The shadeling glanced over its shoulder a little resentfully but opened its thin hands, letting the tiny shards tumble into the bin. Satisfied, I set it down on the ground.

"Seriously, I don't need any of you helping me right now . . ." I blinked. Usually by this point a couple more shadelings would have showed up to make trouble. "Where are the others?"

"In the woods, Missy," the shadeling said. "They don't like the church. They say it's too clean, and Mister Priest makes the shadows hard to swim through here."

Of course. Gooding's defenses around the church would be different from home, where ours were tough on powerful Fae, but not designed to repel something as tiny as a shadeling. I knelt down in front of the little creature, folding my hands in my lap.

"Why are you here, then?"

The shadeling shrugged, scuffing its foot against the stone floor before reaching into the small shadow it cast on the ground . . . and pulling out a well-folded brochure, singed at the edges and reeking of smoke.

"I thought you might want this, Missy." Like a zookeeper

trying to feed a testy leopard, it dropped the brochure in my lap. My heart skipped a beat as I stared down at the saccharine smiles of the students on the front under the bold title, PENNSYLVANIA STATE UNIVERSITY.

"We're living there next, right?" it asked in a small, squeaking voice.

"You want to come to college with me?"

The shadeling tugged on its ear again, nodding. Somehow, the notion that any of them would actually want to come to college with me had never occurred to me . . . and how could I say no? With everything else going up in flames, this shadeling was still here. A lump formed in my throat and, dammit, the tears were coming back. The shadeling squeaked in alarm and scrambled to the pile of used clothes, grabbing an old pair of shiny granny panties to shove at my wet face.

I couldn't help it. In spite of everything, a startled laugh escaped me. It felt like the worst possible time to be laughing, with everything going on, but it was sort of like grass growing through the cracks in the sidewalk. I couldn't stop it, and it only made the cracks bigger, and soon I was laughing and tears streamed down my face. I bit down on my knuckle to quiet it all before Dad or the boys heard, but it was hard when the shadeling scrambled into my lap and pressed the satiny fabric of the panties to my cheeks again, mopping clumsily at the tears. I wrapped my arms around its tiny frame and hugged it close.

I almost let a small "thank you" slip out but stopped myself. I had to remember their rules. Instead, I dropped a kiss on the top of its head. It reeked like old cheese coated with the algae and earth that lingered around Gwen's pool. Maybe the others were still there right now. I sighed and stroked its violet head. "You should go meet up with the others."

The shadeling shook its head. "No. I'm staying here."

It was staying. Relief flooded through me. This place felt just a little more like home now. I nodded and set the shadeling back on the ground before grabbing the pillow and sliding it under the bed where the shadows were darkest. For the barest of seconds, I wanted to pull it back and invite the little creature to share the bed with me, like they had when I was a kid. At the time, it had been so nice to have what felt like living, albeit smelly, imaginary friends . . . but the shadeling had already scrambled under the bed, curling up on the pillow like a cat. It looked as comfortable and at home there as a water wife in the pond. After everything, it deserved to be comfortable.

I folded up an old hoodie to make a new pillow, slid Mum's box under the bed next to the shadeling, and turned off the light. If I closed my eyes, I could pretend I was home. There was no accounting for the poor padding the hoodie provided under my head, or the itchy blanket, or the cardboard-thin mattress, but maybe, just maybe, if I pretended hard enough . . .

The door creaked open and light streaked into the room. I cracked my eyelids just enough to see Dad silhouetted against the light of the hall. He stood for a few seconds, then nodded and left, shutting the door behind him.

I couldn't sleep after that. It was stupid. I was exhausted. Sleep should have come as easily as closing my eyes, but it hovered forever out of my reach. With a huff, I reached under the bed, flipping open the latch on Mum's box and digging through the necklaces and bracelets for her book.

Maybe it was in my head, but it almost felt like the covers thrummed with energy, like touching a power cord plugged into the wall. I flipped through the pages, but the dim light from the window wasn't enough to read the scribbled words. But there was so much here . . . Mum had written so many different spells. Something had to help us. *All* of us. I couldn't leave for school until this mess was cleaned up. Maybe Mum couldn't do it . . . but I had fresh eyes, didn't I?

Reluctantly, I closed the book, but I couldn't bring myself to hide it in that box again. I slid it under the hoodie and rested my head on it. It felt like resting my head on a brick, but that was fine. In a bizarre way, I felt stronger. I had Mum's book now. I'd make sure the Fae never took anything from us again.

The charred hull of the house sat listlessly behind the iron gates, shivering in the wind like a cicada shell clinging to a wall. Any moment it might blow away. I walked up the path, so worn down over the years that the grass seemed to grow sideways. The gate was warm under my fingers, but it swung open without so much as a creak. The front door swung open before I even had to touch it. In a single step I was across the yard and inside the house.

Broken dishes littered the floor. There wasn't a single smudge of ash or soot in the house. Just destruction. This was the Welsh house now, not the American one. The couch cushions had been ripped open, their fluffy innards spilled on the floor. Family photos lay ripped in shattered frames, hurled against the wall. I blinked, stepping into the living room. Mum's favorite rug had a bright purple stain in the corner that made my skin crawl. I staggered away from it.

"Mum?" I called in a small voice, turning around in a full circle. Deep rents in the floral wallpaper exposed the wood beneath.

A tall, dark-haired figure flickered in the hall, her dove-gray gown fluttering on the breeze. Behind her flapped a red banner with a golden dragon.

"Mum!" I called again.

I charged down the hall, but the door to the bedroom stretched away like a rubber band. The faster I ran, the more blue congealed on the walls, fading into purple before settling into a thick, dripping red that seeped into the carpet, sticking to my shoes. And then I could smell it. Like copper and meat. I tried to breathe through my mouth, but I choked on it. My lungs burned as I swung my arms out, the red seeping into my eyes, painting over everything I could see.

My fingers touched brass. The door swung open.

I fell to my knees. Red turned to green. The stench faded into moss and earth as the house disappeared around me, replaced by the wild woods. I clung to the decaying leaves that coated the forest floor, sucking in air until my head spun.

"Mum?" I wheezed, blinking against the bright sun. It was midday, but my skin still felt chilled. I scrambled to my feet, my heart in my throat. There was nobody here. Not a bird or a bug in sight.

Words floated on the breeze, the lilt of old Welsh, older than I'd ever heard. Dove-gray silk fluttered between the trees. A face peered around the tree, and for a second it looked so like Mum that I almost ran to it. But no. Her nose was too straight. Her hair too long.

My heart jumped into my throat. I needed to go home. I needed to find the boys. I turned around and . . . and there he was.

The prince leaned against a tree, his chest heaving. Blue blood pooled around him and dripped from his snow-pale lips and the jagged tear in the side of his armor. His sparkling eyes locked with mine. My stomach flipped. He stretched out a hand.

No no no no don't take it don't take it he isn't safe he isn't a friend—

"I have bandages at my house," I offered, slipping my hand into his.

White-hot pain exploded in my gut. The air hissed out of my lungs. The world blurred black at the edges until all I could see was the red-stained hilt that sprouted from my stomach, right through the worn cotton of my nightgown with the silly mouse pattern.

"Thank you," my Fae prince whispered in a voice like velvet.

The ground pounded into the side of my head. I watched the Fae's bare, bloody feet retreat, his blue and my red mingling on the green grass.

I closed my eyes and sucked in a slow, shuddering breath. The pain faded to a dull ache. The grass under my cheek thinned and stiffened, scratching against my cheek. I forced my eyes open. The green forest had withered into grays and browns, dead and listless and so unlike the forest I knew from my memory. Unnatural lights flitted from the trees, paired with laughs that sounded as though they were being played through a tinny old radio. The air crackled with a thousand tiny electric sparks. And in the middle of it all, Mum knelt over her book, flipping through the pages frantically. Her favorite floral-print dress pooled on the ground around her. My heart jumped into my throat. Tears stung at my eyes.

"Mum," I wheezed.

"Ssh, sweetheart," she crooned, her eyes wild as she stared down at the pages. "I don't have much time with you."

I started to push myself up, but the dead grass and moss stung my palms like needles.

"Stay where you are, Bryn. Don't let them—" Mum stiffened, glanced over her shoulder. Dove-gray silk flashed between the trees. Sometimes nearer, sometimes farther. Mum gasped and shoved the book toward me. "Quickly, dear. I don't . . . There's no time."

"For what?" I blinked hazily, reaching for her hand, but she pulled away before I could touch her.

She stared back at me, her dark, bloodshot eyes filling with tears. "Stop them for good. Keep our family safe." She bit her lip. "I'm so sorry I couldn't protect you from this, my darling girl. But I know you have the strength to finish where I left off."

I opened my mouth to protest, but the words wouldn't come. Mum shoved the book into my hands. I blinked.

All I could see was the dark scrawl across a vellum page.

GWELLA

GWYBODAETH

FREUDDWYTH

I JOLTED AWAKE, my heart fluttering like a hummingbird. It was just a dream. Unless it wasn't. I hadn't dreamt about Mum in forever, and now I'd had two dreams in three nights. Maybe she was reaching out from wherever the Fae had taken her.

I dragged the book out from under the hoodie and took a deep breath. Gwella, Gwybodaeth, Freuddwyth. Dad hadn't bothered to speak Welsh in the house since we came to Pennsylvania. It took me a second to process the words through my head, like starting a car that hadn't been touched in ages. Gwella, Gwybodaeth, Freuddwyth. Healing, Knowledge,

Dreaming. She couldn't have possibly given spells and rituals such simple names. Right?

The spine creaked as I opened the book, the must from the old vellum filling the room like an ancient perfume. I couldn't read most of what she'd written. Some was English. Some was the rudimentary Welsh I'd learned as a kid. Then there was definitely Gaelic, something in Futhark, and everything else was too foreign for me to interpret. Something warm bloomed in my chest as I flipped through the pages. These were Mum's. She'd written these words, drawn these little diagrams. Maybe, if she'd been around, she would have tried to teach all of this to me.

"I told you!" Jake spat.

I started. Out in the hall, the twins hissed like a couple of snakes at each other, their voices too quiet to hear, save for when Jake got really emotional. It sounded something like a radio going in and out.

". . . never listen to me . . . everything . . . Dad . . . should have told me!"

Whatever Ash said in return, it must have been exactly the wrong thing to say. A door slammed.

I shut the book and shoved it under the thin mattress. Two seconds passed. Then three. Nothing came to the door. I ought to crawl back into bed and pretend to sleep, but something told me I needed to at least try to comfort whoever was still out in the hall.

When a full minute had passed, I padded to the door and pushed it open, peering out into the dark hall.

Ash sat hunched against the wall, a smear of soot across

his cheek, clutching a grimy box full of charred belongings he must have scavenged from the house. At the top was that pair of headphones he'd begged Dad for last Christmas. The foam peeked out in places where the thin rubber had been burned. They probably didn't even work anymore.

Ash stared down at the ground with glazed eyes. As quiet as I was trying to be, there was still no way he hadn't heard me. But he didn't even glance up.

I knelt down next to him and waited for the words to come, but what could I say? Nobody had told me what I needed to hear yet. Nobody had made me feel safe. I didn't even know what it was I needed to hear, much less what would help him.

Ash beat me to it. "Jake says it's *them*." He spat the word out as he looked up at me, cheeks red.

My stomach flipped. We didn't talk about this. We'd never talked about this. But the boys weren't stupid. They knew exactly what had taken Mum. They deserved better than a lie right now. "We think so, yeah."

For just a moment, he looked like he was ready to throw the box across the hall. His cheeks burned red. Tears pooled at the corners of his eyes. "I always wanted to see one of them. I thought if I could meet one it'd make sense why they took her."

I reached out to rest my hand on his shoulder, but he jerked away, holding the box to his chest as he scrambled to his feet. He stormed into his room, slamming the door behind him.

I stared at the closed door. It felt like all my energy drained out of me . . . but there was nothing else I could do for him now. At least, nothing beyond what I was already doing.

I dragged myself to my feet and trudged into my room. The little purple shadeling sat on the bed, gnawing on something I didn't really want to identify.

"Still just you?" I asked, unloading my textbooks and binders onto the bed.

The shadeling glanced up and nodded.

"The others don't like it here, Missy. I told you."

"But they're safe, right?"

The shadeling nodded. "They're clever. They'll be fine."

It was a strange sensation. For so long, I'd wished they'd go away and stop stealing my cosmetics and tangling up my yarn and knocking over the trash can. Now I just wanted them back. I wanted to see with my own eyes that everything was okay. I'd have to satisfy myself with being able to look after this one. For one crazy moment, I considered telling the others about them. Father Gooding wouldn't be too pleased I was allowing a Fae in here past his protections, but the boys could keep a secret. And wouldn't it be better for Dad to know that one fairy out there was trustworthy?

Was it worth the risk that they might make me send it away?

I hesitated, then rested my hand on the shadeling's head.

"Well, th—" I had to stop myself before a "thank you" slipped out by mistake. The last thing I wanted to do was offend the little creature. "I know it can't be fun to be away from all the others."

"It's okay, Missy. I've got you."

"Yeah." I forced myself to smile. "We've got each other. And the boys've got you, too."

"Of course, Missy."

Twelve

In a town this size, the gossip spread like an oil spill. I felt
weirdly exposed in my borrowed clothes, the secondhand
sign that I'd lost everything, including the clothes off my
back. I didn't look like me. I didn't *feel* like me. I didn't even
bother with makeup or any jewelry besides my nail. None of
it felt right now. People looked at me differently, and unfortunately nobody had invented an armor for pity.

As I opened my locker, two cards tumbled out and onto
the floor. The first one had a drawing of me and what looked
like Jasika Witters, both of us in bright blue capes, signed
by her little sister, Jade, in clumsy cursive with a note that
read *I'm sorry about your house.* Just one of many that shared
the same sentiment, most of them from the Witters clan.
Three or four came from well-meaning teachers or student
council representatives who didn't otherwise take note of
me. On top of them all was a simple card with Jasika's careful
script.

Bryn
I'm so sorry about what happened. If there is anything I or my family can do for you, please don't hesitate to ask. Remember, you're not alone in this.

J. W.

I glanced over my shoulder, but Jasika was nowhere to be seen. Of course, she'd probably tucked these into my locker well before I arrived. Why that made my heart twinge with disappointment, I couldn't quite say. I tucked the cards into the back covers of my government and health textbooks.

My morning classes were a buzz of chatter and the uneasy sensation of eyes on the back of my neck. I'd somehow sprouted a shining neon sign hovering above my head: SEE THE INCREDIBLE HOMELESS KID! MARVEL AT THE GIRL WHO LIVES IN THE GLORIFIED STORAGE UNIT! Worse, they weren't looking at me the way they usually did. Nobody, not even Brooke Tanneman, so much as glanced with anything more than gut-churning, gag-me pity.

By lunch, all of the silent judgment had eaten through my limited patience. I didn't even bother taking my paper sack into the cafeteria. The librarian shot me a warning look but didn't stop me as I curled up at a table in the far corner, nibbling at my sandwich while I tried and failed to not feel sorry for myself. It was hard, everything considered. I tried to focus instead on the three words itching in the back of my brain.

Gwella, Gwybodaeth, Freuddwyth

Healing, Knowledge, Dreaming. Mum had said them when she'd told me to stop the Fae for good. Right after I'd found her book. Was she telling me those were the spells I needed?

The thought made my heart skip. Human magic was one thing. It had rules. Ingredients and candles and incantations. It came from your intent and your mind-set. Fae magic came from somewhere else. It would be like a Roman centurion fooling around with an atomic bomb. Then again, maybe it was just a dream. I could have been scared and just wanting to dream about my mum. For that matter, who was the woman in the gray gown? Nobody sensible, that was sure. I was definitely assigning too much meaning to a dream.

I was halfway into a decent sulk when I saw him. A stack of fantasy books in his arms. All gangly limbs and wide mouth pulled not into a pitying frown but a smile of relief. He was probably the first person all day who hadn't looked at me with pity. I blinked.

"Dom?"

"Found you." He sprawled in the chair beside me, dropping his backpack on the floor and the stack of books next to it. *A Midsummer Night's Dream, Sir Gawain and the Green Knight, Le Morte d'Arthur.* How traditional of him. Looked like he was taking the revelation that magic was real very well.

"I see you've been doing a little light reading," I mused.

"I see you showed up at school. I thought for sure you weren't coming today."

I wrapped the remainder of my sandwich in foil and stuffed it back into the paper bag.

"I didn't want to just sit around the church all day." Because, really, what better way to remind yourself that you didn't have a home than to sit in your shelter and feel sorry for yourself? I took a deep breath. "I hope I didn't get you in trouble at home yesterday."

Dom shrugged. "Helen didn't even notice. But I couldn't sleep last night. I think I was up till two researching all this . . ." He waved his hand indistinctly. ". . . stuff."

"You mean the Unseelies?"

He nodded, his expression grave. "I had no idea that fairies were . . . I mean. It's a lot to take in, isn't it?" He shook his head. "And magic. Apparently ingredients don't matter? But maybe that blog was just written by a lazy witch."

"Human magic's got a lot to do with your personal belief and intent," I explained. "But maybe. I dunno."

"And fairies! All the stories, and so many of them disagree. Don't you think it's nuts?"

Honestly? I wouldn't know. I'd been raised on the idea that fairies existed. As soon as I'd learned to walk, I'd learned how to look for sprites in the woods. But if finding out magic was real was anything like watching your home go up in flames . . . I nodded.

"All the fairies yesterday, um, the shadelings. They were so scared of them." His brows twitched as that wide, expressive mouth of his pulled into a frown. "I never thought of fairies as trying to hurt each other."

Sweet thing. He didn't need to be around all this violence and ugliness. Not if his heart was this tender for a collection of creatures he'd barely met.

"Yesterday was an unusual move for them. You're not seeing normal behavior from their kind. They're adapting to the defenses my dad and Father Gooding put up."

"Right. But some of them are good. See, I found out a lot about the water wives, too, but your little goblin friends . . ."

"The shadelings? No. You won't find anything about them

anywhere, except a Dungeons and Dragons manual. And that's not the same. I think they're . . . unique."

"And you're sure you can trust them?" Dom's brows furrowed. "I mean, they move through shadows. Aren't shadows kind of a dark, bad-guy thing?"

The notion would have seemed absurd, had I not briefly considered the same thing myself not so long ago. Suddenly, the idea that I'd ever doubted the shadelings made my stomach turn. They'd been with me for almost a decade and look how quickly I'd doubted them.

"The shadelings are fine," I promised him. "They were loyal to my mum. Not sure why. They won't say. But they hang around us."

"So they're like your servants?"

Yeah right. I snorted. "No. Not really. They try to help out around the house. I think they want to earn their keep, but otherwise, they're just sort of there. Eating any food we leave out. Keeping an eye open for the Unseelie. Trying to keep me alive. I think because they know I'll protect them." But now they were all gone. All except for the one last night. The purple one. My stomach flipped. Maybe there was a little bit more to why they hung around after all.

Dom chewed his lip and drummed his fingers against the table. "Right. And they were in danger, yesterday. Do these Unseelie want to go after them, too?"

The suggestion stung unexpectedly. I'd always worried about other humans getting involved in this nonsense. If I'd thought about it from a fairy's perspective, yesterday might not have happened. Leave it to someone with a gentle heart to see what someone like me couldn't.

"You know, you don't need to be involved," I reminded him. "I mean, thanks for your help yesterday, but I never asked you. Probably better if you just keep a wide berth."

Dom arched a brow and shrugged. "If I'm going to live in some crazy town with killer fairies, I just want to make sure I understand everything I'm up against."

"It's probably safer if you don't."

"When I didn't know, you almost stabbed me with a nail, and I wound up running headfirst toward a house fire. Yeah. Real safe." He ran his fingers through his hair. "Look. Magic is real. Fairies are real. You can't expect me to see all of that and just ignore it. I mean, this is huge!" There was a sparkle in his eyes like . . . well. Like he'd just found out magic was real. No shoving that rabbit back in the hat.

It was Jasika all over again, but I still had just enough guilt about the nail incident that I couldn't quite say no to him.

"Well, I doubt you'll find much in those books," I sighed, nodding at his little stack. "I'm pretty sure Merlin wasn't a real guy."

"Yeah, but he was from Wales," Dom pressed. "Just like you. Just like the water wives. That can't be a coincidence!"

Yeah, and I'd thought a new guy in town couldn't be a coincidence, either. Live and learn.

"You're getting excited over nothing."

"It's not nothing. Fairies are real." Dom leaned back in his chair and crossed his arms. "And I want you to help me with one."

I frowned. "What? Do you have one in your house or something? I'm pretty sure Helen would have called Father Gooding by now."

Dom shook his head. "No. She's fine. It's nothing in the house. But, see, since I moved here, I've seen something in the trees. I thought it was like a coyote or something, but since yesterday, well, I think you might be able to figure out what it is and how to, you know . . ." He made a shooing gesture with his hand. "Make it go away. Or at least keep away from Helen. I don't know how to talk to them and the internet says they get offended really easily."

"What makes you think it was something I can take care of?"

Dom dug into his pocket and pulled out . . . my fairy stone. *Well, son of a bitch.*

"This is a fairy stone, right? Well. I looked through it, and, well, whatever I saw, it wasn't human. Now, I'll give this back to you if you at least come and check it out."

He wanted me to go to work. Without Father Gooding. Of course, he didn't know about Father Gooding. He was new and totally ignorant about the way things worked here. He didn't know about redcaps or brownies or any of the Fae. And he was trusting me. Well, nice to know that somebody still did. For all the good it did. I reached forward, snatching the stone from his hand with a scowl. Dom didn't even try to fight for it.

"I'm not exactly invincible," I pointed out. "You saw that yourself yesterday."

Dom leaned forward, his expression sober. "Maybe this thing has something to do with the ones that are after you. Or maybe it doesn't. But Helen's old. I don't want her getting caught in the crossfire, you know?"

I thought back to Mum's book. How many spells were in there? How much might it help if I could use them? Catch a

Fae right there in the woods before it could hit me? My insides squirmed at the thought.

"I'll take a look. But you stay in the house. That's the deal."

Dom shot me a crooked grin. "Aye aye, captain."

The bell rang. Dom grabbed his bag and straightened, once more serious.

"Meet me in front of Helen's house," he said. "I'll show you where I saw it. And . . . thanks. Seriously." He smiled, offered me a little half salute, and spun around to saunter out the library door. Weirdo.

IT WAS DISORIENTING walking to Postoak during the day, unaccompanied by Father Gooding. The eerie quality of the homes faded away without the shadow of evening to cast a dark tone over everything. Cheerful flower beds and tinkling wind chimes actually managed to give the whole place a pleasant facade. Even so, I clutched my backpack's straps a little tighter, feeling the weight of Mum's book inside. There was a good chance more than a couple of nosy creatures watched me from their hidden perches.

Helen Grady, and consequently Dom, lived in the single most protected house on the street. Gooding had brought me here years ago to teach me how to place wards. Every little lawn ornament and hummingbird feeder was in some way inundated with anti-fairy protections. No surprise. Helen Grady lived right next to the woods at the very end of Postoak Road. Had things gone the way they were supposed to, it's entirely likely that Dom could have made it all the way through the school year without noticing the trouble so many of his neighbors had with the creatures.

As I came to the line of landscaping rocks at the edge of Ms. Helen's iron fence, I saw Dom kneeling at the gate, setting out a bowl of milk. He was a quick study. When he saw me, he jumped to his feet, wearing the biggest smile I had probably ever seen on a human being. Somehow, beyond all reason, he looked positively thrilled to see me.

"Hey." He looked like he might just hug me. I jumped half a step back, hand tightening on the strap of my backpack. Dom's wide mouth shrank into a frown, brows furrowing as he looked me up and down. Damn. Had I offended him? Why did I keep doing that to everyone who seemed to like me?

"Hey," I offered in return.

We stared at each other silently for a few seconds until, at last, Dom cleared his throat.

"So, uh . . ." Dom shoved his hands in his pockets and rocked back and forth on the balls of his feet. Every time he leaned closer, I could smell the same spicy aftershave Dad used: the cheapest brand the store sold. Dom cleared his throat and jabbed a thumb toward the woods. "I've seen something out there. A few nights, now, actually. I figure if we try to catch it during the day, maybe it'll be weaker."

"Not a bad idea," I allowed, and Dom positively lit up. Oh boy. I was encouraging him, wasn't I? "If *I* can find it," I added. "You stay in the house, remember? That was the deal." And the light went out. Sweet boy. Definitely not cut out for this.

Dom chewed on his lip but nodded. At least he could follow directions.

I tugged my nail down. Here went nothing. I crept onto the rough path that snaked between the trees, the light around me darkening under the canopy of the trees. A few meters in, something tucked against the foot of an ancient maple caught my eye. It was a little gathering of sticks and leaves, wilted flowers shoved in between the cracks, forming a tidy arch. Right above it, carved into the tree, was an odd symbol that I couldn't quite place—sort of like a scribble, but there was more to it than that.

"What the hell?" Fairy houses in an actual fairy-infested forest. Dumb kids probably had no idea what they were doing. But whatever this symbol was, it didn't look random.

I tugged a few twigs out of place, effectively dismantling the fairy house, and turned . . .

Right into the face of a shriveled crone. Not a court Fae or a drone. Her hair fell like crinkled straw around her shriveled, mud-smeared face. In one arm, she clutched a crude sculpture of a baby, one leg longer than the other.

In the span of a blink, I knew what she was.

Bendith y Mamau.

The fairy named after the blessing of the mother, or rather, mother of blessings . . . and of changelings.

Before I could so much as raise my nail into the air, she swept her gnarled hand across my cheekbone, sending me crashing against a birch. Pain burst across the side of my face and, oh Lord, how was I going to explain this to Dad?

Something moved in the dark beyond the trees. Ice flooded my veins. Stupid! Of course they'd have lower courts or wild creatures to protect them.

The bendith hissed and swept up to me, her thin lips pulling up over her teeth. I kicked out, my boot catching her right in the chest. She crumpled to the ground in a heap of rags and gangly limbs, but she wouldn't be down long. I staggered to my feet. Whatever was in the woods, it was getting closer. Reinforcements? Did it recognize me? Fine. I could do this. I had my nail, and the shadelings were no doubt lurking nearby. They had to be pissed about the loss of their home, too. Maybe I'd get a little help.

The bendith clambered to her feet, ancient joints popping and squeaking like unoiled hinges. I squeezed my nail tighter. Come and get it, bitch.

"FWEEEEEEEEEEEE!"

The sudden burst of noise made my heart skip a beat. The bendith's head jerked around, eyes widening in shock at Dom, who still held his fingers to his lips.

My blood froze. What in the actual and non-figurative hell was he doing here?

"Uh . . . balls," he swore, taking a step back. "I think we should run now."

"No shit, Sherlock!" I snapped.

The bendith straightened, cocking her head to one side. For some reason, she stared at Dom the way most people stare at modern art. Perplexed, torn between amusement and annoyance. She took a shambling step forward, extending one gnarled hand. Then, between the space of one step and the next, she transformed. The withered crone disappeared, her hunched frame giving way to a beautiful woman with curves that just wouldn't quit. She looked like an exaggerated version of a new mother, with shining, golden hair and perfectly sunbrowned skin. A mother of the earth. I blinked and tried to relax, tried to see the hideous crone beneath the beauty. There wasn't so much as a flicker. This wasn't a glamour. It was as much her as the other form.

"Come with me," she crooned in a voice like honey.

The bendith reached out, taking his hand, a small smile playing on her wide, soft lips. Dom's mouth bobbed open and closed. My stomach churned. This was stupid. This was so stupid. What the hell was he thinking? But if I moved too quickly, I'd spook her. And she was touching Dom.

The bendith stared straight into his eyes as she began to hum. A shiver ran down my spine. The tune was haunting, and beautiful. I could feel my blood chilling, my heart breaking, and my throat aching like I'd just been crying.

Dom stared back at her, his jaw slack, and I knew that whatever I felt, he felt tenfold. He didn't so much as twitch as she swayed back and forth, the haunting melody picking up speed. Shit, it looked like he was mesmerized.

"Get down!" a voice cried over the humming.

I had only a second to drop to the ground as a new figure flew through the underbrush, hurling an iron net toward the bendith. Dom scrambled out of the way, half crashing into the underbrush as the net slammed into the bendith. She hissed and yowled, trying to buck it off. Ugly red welts rose under the poisonous iron netting, an awful sizzling noise filling the air.

"If you stop moving, it'll hurt less!" the new person snapped. No. Not new. I blinked. Jasika?!

The bendith shrieked and kicked out, burning a fresh part of her leg on the toxic iron. Finally, with hatred seething in her eyes, she stilled. I gaped at Jasika.

"When did this turn into a friggin' party?" I blurted.

Jasika jerked a thumb over her shoulder. "Dom called me. Apparently, he was worried you'd get hurt and decided we ought to give you backup. But, of course, we all know the great and powerful Bryn Johnson doesn't need help, right?"

"I'm sorry." Dom pushed himself to his feet, his eyes drifting to the bendith. "I'm sorry, I just . . . I don't want anyone to get hurt."

The bendith's eyes snapped to him, and for a second there was a flash of betrayal there. Then, they drifted to me. When they fell on Jasika, she snarled.

"Not here to kill me?" Her beautiful voice grew that much more eerie coming from such a haunted face. So much about her felt wrong. On instinct, I tugged my nail free. I couldn't think too much about Dom and Jasika being here or what assholes they were for following me. I just needed to make sure they didn't get hurt.

"We'll see." I knelt down, careful not to look right into the bendith's eyes. "You've been trying to steal children in this town, right? You could have been more subtle. That guy over there actually saw you. So, are you doing it for your court?"

The bendith looked ready to spit until a smile stretched her withered features. An acrid taste flooded my mouth. I tightened my grip on my nail.

"Only on the one road," she crooned, her eyes glinting. "Only from the people who live near to the forest. Maybe you'll try and steal from us in return, hm? Thieves! All of you!"

I stepped onto the net, pressing the iron into the exposed skin of her leg. The bendith howled.

Dom grabbed my arm. "That's not necessary, Bryn! We already caught her."

I shrugged off his arm. "Are you stealing children for the Unseelie?"

The bendith sneered. "A pittance. Until I find what my queen and I are looking for."

Ash and Jake. My heart lurched. The bendith had been after the boys on Postoak, until the drone tracked me to our house. "They're safe in the church now. You can't have them."

The bendith's smile widened. She curled her claws into the ground. "You think yourself so wise, girl. So strong. I see your mother in you."

Mum?

Dom's hands were on my arms again, restraining me. I balled my hands into fists, my face burning. "How do you know my mother?"

"Bryn," Jasika said softly. "She's just trying to goad you."

"We all know her," the bendith cackled. "Did you not know? She's famous. The deserter. The *thief*."

I had to bite my tongue, even as my heart pounded. Thief. Deserter. She'd called Mum a deserter. *Deserter*. What did that mean for a human woman with a book of Fae magic? The world tightened around me. I felt like I was breathing through a wet cloth.

The word clanged around in my head over and over until I could barely hear anything else.

Deserter. Deserter. Deserter.

"She's just trying to get a rise out of you," Dom repeated. "Just send her away, don't listen to her."

Jasika cut in. "Are you the reason there's been so much trouble on this road?"

The bendith snarled at Jasika. "You're going to regret this, child. May every baby born in this cursed town be sickly. May they colic and cry until their lungs have no more air in them. May every child in this thrice-cursed town come to serve my mistress and me. The wails of their mothers—"

"No!" Jasika shouted. "We don't have a quarrel with you, we just want you to leave our people alone. How can we get you to—"

"There's no need. The queen will come on Samhain to take what is ours." She shifted and hissed, a fresh spot on her shoulder sizzling as she locked eyes with me. "She will take her vengeance on that bitch who betrayed her own court."

Her court. The echo grew louder. *Deserter. Deserter. Deserter.* My hands shook. No. Mum was human. She couldn't have. No human would have ever allied themselves with *them*. My mum would never have made a deal. She was wrong.

The bendith bared her teeth. "You will all pay for the traitor's—"

My blood boiled. I jerked away from Dom's hold and lunged forward, plunging the nail through one of the holes in the net. Right into the bendith's leathery throat. Sickly blue blood bubbled out.

The bendith flailed, a wet gurgle escaping her lips. This time two pairs of arms locked on me, dragging me back. I hit the underbrush, leaves and berries flying around me. Dom raced forward, his face pale with horror. He ripped out the nail and tore off the net, but even as he pressed his hands to her throat, it was clear that he wasn't going to save the wretched Fae. The bendith gave a few helpless twitches, her eyes wide as her irises darted back and forth for a few seconds before they stilled and went glassy. Blue stained the vibrant reds and yellows and browns of the forest floor.

The cacophony in my head died down as I stared down at her. The creature I'd killed not in self-defense, but in anger. Our prisoner. The back of my throat burned. I tried to look away but I couldn't. I tried to reassure myself that she'd goaded me. That she'd known what she was doing. But that didn't make her any less dead.

Dom stared down at her in horror for a few seconds, his arms covered in Fae blood. Then, slowly, he pushed himself to his feet, his eyes locked on the bendith's still form. Whatever loveliness had been in her had withered away like the dead leaves around her.

Jasika took a step forward. "Dom—"

"This isn't what I signed up for." Dom's hands curled into fists. "She was our prisoner. We had her captured."

My stomach squirmed. I pushed myself to my feet. "She worked for the Unseelie. She was one of the bad guys, Dom."

"So?" Dom turned to me, his eyes red-rimmed. "She was a living thing! I didn't want anyone to die."

"Dom, I—"

"I'm done," he muttered before turning and stalking away.

Jasika stared at me for a moment before she backed away, following him without even retrieving her net. And then, just like that, I was alone with the fairy's corpse.

I probably should have gone after them, but I didn't.

Thirteen

I really didn't like casserole. Who decided that, after tragedy, people needed to Frankenstein whatever they found in their pantry instead of just delivering some groceries? After a miserable day of being an asshole, all I wanted was a pizza. Still, I couldn't let food go to waste.

Ash wandered in not too long after I'd sat down, his eyes glued to his phone the whole time he made his dinner. The fluorescent lights of the church kitchen didn't do anybody any favors, but I was pretty sure the bags under his eyes weren't normal.

"Do you have homework?" I asked, but he didn't answer. He just slapped some casserole onto a plate and shoved it into the microwave.

"Hey, Martian," I said, turning in my chair to face him. "Is school going okay? Do you want to talk about it?"

Ash bit the side of his cheek and flipped through something on his phone. His hand trembled faintly.

"Hey, are you doing okay? Are you sleeping well?"

"No," he ground out, pointedly dropping his hand to glare

forward. When the microwave dinged, he pulled out his food and left without a word.

A few minutes later, Jake shuffled in, his eyes glued to the floor.

"Hey, Moonman. Do you have homework?"

Jake grunted a non-answer and prepared a plate.

I bit the inside of my cheek. "Hey. Is everything okay with you and Ash? He wasn't looking—"

"I don't want to talk about him."

Jake grabbed a bottle of water from the fridge and left without even bothering to heat up his food.

I watched the open door for a while after he left, but I wasn't sure what I was waiting for. They weren't coming back. I forced myself to take a bite of casserole and not think about the way Dom and Jasika had stared at me that afternoon or the fact that my brothers weren't talking to me or each other or, apparently, anyone. But thinking about how much I didn't want to think about it turned the already misguided casserole to cardboard in my mouth.

At a quarter to nine, Dad shuffled in, his shoulders slumped and his eyes half closed, but at least he had the good sense to heat up his food. The hum of the microwave filled the space between us for a minute or so, but soon enough, that was over, and all that was left was him and me and all the stuff we didn't want to talk about.

He took a bite, and I took one. It felt a bit like eating with a stranger, and I couldn't shake the ugly feeling that this was all my fault. It was one thing to have secrets. It was another thing for those to come out, and then to keep more of them.

Dad was the first one to speak. "How're you keeping up with your classes?"

"Fine. Progress reports'll be out in a few weeks."

"Good. I don't want you to fall behind." He cleared his throat. "I know you had your heart set on Penn State. I thought, maybe, we could go tour it over Christmas."

Penn State. It felt a million miles away. It was the sort of life another Bryn got to have. But here Dad was, trying to make sure I had it anyway. My throat tightened.

"I thought, with the house gone, my college fund—"

"Is still your college fund." Dad gave me a tired smile and rested a hand on mine. "I know I've depended on you a lot, especially with the boys. But I don't want you to limit yourself for us. I'll sort out things with the insurance. It's not your job to worry about this."

I bit the inside of my cheek again. I wanted so badly to be the girl who went off to college and had fun.

"I don't even know what I'll study."

"I didn't, either," Dad chuckled. "My first year of college I thought I wanted to be a historian. It was no small leap to go into engineering, let me tell you. That's part of college. It's figuring out who you are and what sort of life you want to lead."

I knew what sort of life I wanted to lead. I wanted the house with the picket fence and the stupid dog who was always happy to see you and the good job that could pay for real family vacations, not the same camping trip or beach visit we'd taken every year since we'd come here. I wanted to feel safe. The question was whether or not I was the kind of person who got to live that sort of life. Maybe everything that had happened had warped me somehow inside.

Dom's and Jasika's expressions wouldn't leave my mind.

I swallowed and squeezed Dad's hand. I wanted to ask how he could keep up so much hope after how badly he'd been hurt by the Fae. I wanted him to tell me that, if he could keep it up after losing his wife and suffering this awful curse and being forced to leave his home, if he could still do all that and still be a good person, then I could certainly get through this. Words had never come easily for me, though, and everything I wanted to say just got caught in my throat. It was a good thing Dad was better at this than I was.

"I just want you to be safe and happy," he said. "That's why we came here. You should get to live your own life. Don't let *them* define you or dictate who you get to be."

And I could hear what he wasn't saying. That was why he'd banned me from working with Gooding the second he'd found out about it. Dad stuff. Maybe part of me was still a little pissed about that. But he was giving me real permission to not have to be the person I'd been in the woods today. Maybe I could be just a bit better.

I wrapped my arms around his shoulders and hugged him close. He smelled like sweat and oil. When he wrapped his arms around me in return, it felt like home.

"Thanks, Dad," I muttered, dropping a quick kiss to the top of his head.

After that, we talked without really having much else to say. Dad told me about some work at the rig and how a new hire was giving him headaches. I told him about what we'd done in science. It felt like the time flew by, and suddenly, our plates were empty. I still had a stone weighing down my gut, but it was smaller now.

When I flopped down onto my bed that night, my phone buzzed.

Jasika: Is your dad off work on Saturdays? If so,
swing by Dom's place around 10 a.m. If not,
we can come to the convent so the boys are
supervised.

Ominous. But it meant that maybe they were still willing to talk to me. Not much of a surprise with Jasika, but Dom . . . I took a deep breath and glanced around. The shadeling dozed on a pile of dirty clothes. It was basically the only real friend I had. Well. It and Gwen. Not a single human seemed to fit on that roster. But Jasika and Dom were willing to be around me, and they were clearly going to involve themselves in this whether I worked with them or not. And Jasika had saved my ass with the bendith. Working alone hadn't been a good idea after all.

Maybe this wasn't the hill I needed to die on. If I worked with them, I could probably stop them from getting themselves killed. And, hey, it could even teach me how to operate like a normal person. Who knew? Maybe, working together, we'd even win.

I took a deep breath and turned back to the phone.

Bryn: I'll be there.

I FELT LIKE some sort of imposter as I made my way to Helen Grady's house for the second time in as many days. This wasn't what I did. This was what other teenagers did while I made sure the boys ate and stopped the shadelings from breaking open the marmalade. But hey, look at me. Going to a classmate's house after school. Maybe I was an asshole, but I was trying.

The bowl still sat by the gate, now empty. Whether by wild fairies or stray cats, it wasn't clear, but Dom was certainly making friends. He was awfully good at that.

I made my way to the door and knocked. The door opened. This time, Dom looked me up and down, his wide mouth tugged into a little frown. Without a word, he stepped aside, holding the door open.

Helen's house still had the salmon-pink walls and worn, beige carpet I remembered from the last time I'd been here with Gooding, and unfortunately, it still smelled like thirty-year-old phone books. But here and there, Post-it notes were stuck to the lamp or the wall or the coffee table, scribbled with "Remember your foot medicine" or "Remember, you can't drive until your new license comes in."

Dom closed the door behind us and swore. "Gimme a second . . . Just go to the kitchen, I'll meet you there." He went to the coffee table and grabbed a pad and pen, scribbling away at something. Ms. Helen shifted in her recliner, blinking at him in surprise.

"Donny?"

"Dom," Dom sighed, ripping the sticky note off the pad and sticking it to the top corner of the TV. "You need to leave these where I put them."

"It blocks my view."

"Your meds are more important, Helen. I don't want you to get sick."

"There's too many to remember."

"That's why you've got the organizer. Here, I'm going to put it right here on the table next to you so you don't forget."

It was like watching some sort of surreal scene. Ms. Helen had always been a little bit batty. Hell, when we first moved here, a lot of people brought us casseroles or cookies in an attempt to casually spy on the weird Welsh family who'd moved into the creepy house on the hill. Helen? She'd brought us a tub of sauerkraut. Even so, I didn't remember Helen being so far gone the last time I'd been here . . . but it had been a couple of years.

After a long minute of staring, Helen reached for the pill organizer.

"You're a good boy, Dom, but you're too old for your age, you know that? You need to live a little. Stop fussing over me. I've lived this long without a nanny."

"You know you love the attention," Dom said with a laugh. "Hey, I've got a couple of friends over. Is it okay if we hang out in the kitchen?"

A hand brushed against mine. I jumped and whirled around to see Jasika, her lips pulled into a little half grimace. Her eyes darted down to my shoulder as she fiddled with her jacket sleeve.

"Come on," she said softly. "Give them some privacy."

I followed, something uneasy curling in my stomach. "How long has this been going on?"

Jasika stepped into the kitchen—which looked like a wall-papered nightmare from a '70s homemaking catalog—and went straight to the cabinet for cups.

"A while. We were all getting a little worried about her until Dom moved in."

"He takes care of her." I glanced over my shoulder, but Dom wasn't here yet. "Is this even legal? I mean . . . Child Protective Services can't possibly know."

Jasika shrugged. "He needs a safe place to live. She needs the money from the state. And, it turns out, she also needs someone to keep an eye on her. He doesn't mind. The situation could be a lot worse."

"And what happens when he turns eighteen?"

Jasika started filling the cups from the tap and arched a brow. "For someone who's usually tight-lipped about herself, you can be kind of nosy."

Touché.

I sat in the chair and jumped back up as something *twang*ed under my bum. It looked like a ukulele, or a cigar box that really wanted to be a ukulele.

Jasika grinned. "Coming into the house, breaking their stuff."

"Oh, like you're so perfect," I muttered, setting the battered instrument on the table as delicately as I could manage. "I didn't know Helen was into music."

"She's not. But she doesn't mind me making a little noise. As long as I don't interrupt *Jeopardy!*," Dom announced, ambling into the kitchen. His expression was carefully neutral as he bypassed Jasika and her water and went right to the fridge, grabbing a beer. I felt like I ought to object on principle, but we were in his house, in the presence of his legal guardian. Jasika, on the other hand, shot him a sharp look.

"You're seventeen."

"Time flies." Dom popped the top off the beer, took a swig, and started rummaging through the drawers until he found a large, yellow pad of paper and a pen. "All right," he said. "So . . . yesterday. I wasn't a huge fan of that."

Understatement of the century.

Jasika shifted a little in her chair to fix me with a look that could have given Gooding a run for his money. Except, coming from Jasika, it managed to feel worse.

Guilt squirmed in my gut and I sighed. "Look. A bendith is dangerous. They plant changelings, they enchant people. She was . . . I was just . . ." The longer I spoke, the harder it became under their scrutiny.

"She could have also cursed all the kids in this town," Jasika pointed out with a frown.

"She could have also been reasoned with," Dom added. "We didn't even try. Not really."

"Did you even hear the things she was saying?" I reminded him. "She didn't sound like she was up to talk."

Dom shrugged. "She was trying to get under your skin and you let her."

"I'm sorry, okay?" I clenched my fists and took a deep breath. "She said some things about my mum. And yeah, I fell for it. I'd take it back if I could. But you called me here, right? I mean, I assume you've got reasons to want to take care of this."

Dom and Jasika glanced between them. Dom drummed his fingers against the bottle before he took a swig.

"Helen's is the first place I've been in a long time where I felt like I belonged. And now magic's real and I can't just go back to a life where I forget that. And it's dangerous, and Helen lives right next to it. I don't want anything to happen to her." He straightened. "I think we could work together. As long as nothing like yesterday happens again."

"It won't," I insisted, and turned to Jasika. "I won't let them get to me again."

She tucked a curl behind her ear, her lips twisting into a half grimace for just a second as she stared down at the table. My chest tightened, and it didn't loosen until she took a deep breath.

"I've got family, too. And I feel like I've always . . ." She trailed off and shook her head. "This is something I've got to do. The way I see it, if we work together, we can check each other. Make each other stronger. Make sure things are done right."

Or, more directly put, she wanted to make sure I didn't screw things up again. I bit the inside of my cheek. I couldn't ignore the conversation we'd had a few days ago. About going at it alone. She didn't want to go at it alone anymore. But teams didn't just share their skills with each other. They shared their trouble, too.

"It's great and all that you two want to protect the town. Really. But do you have any idea what you're volunteering for?"

"We're not stupid, Bryn." Jasika leaned forward, resting a hand on mine. "It's our town, too. We can all work separately, but I'm pretty sure it'll be more effective if we work together. Provided we lay down some ground rules."

Her hand felt like a warm, weighted blanket on mine. If I left it too long, I'd feel too comfortable. Too okay with the idea of them fighting and maybe getting hurt. Reluctantly, I pulled my hand away and crossed my arms, glancing between the two of them.

"Okay. My number one rule is if I decide something's

too dangerous for you two, you stay out of it. No questions asked."

"No deal." Jasika crossed her arms, too, and arched a brow. "That just sets it up for you to run into something dangerous instead. Look, we've all got people to protect, but there has to be a line in the sand. I say we draw it at killing prisoners or suicide scenarios."

"How about we agree not to rush into any situation without you," Dom offered. "And in return, Bryn, no killing them."

Right. I'd been ready for that one. "Deal, unless it's a life-or-death situation. That includes one of them running off to tell the Unseelie queen what we're doing."

Dom drummed his fingers on the table for a long moment before he gave a jerky nod. "Life or death only. Otherwise, I don't know. Try and catch it or cut a deal. I read that fairies love to make deals. Or else use something out of your magic book. Or get the shadelings to help."

Jasika blinked. "Magic book?" Then, "Wait. Hold up. What's a shadeling?"

I shot Dom a halfhearted glare, more out of habit than anything at this point, before turning back to Jasika with a shrug. "The shadelings are . . . Well, they're these sort of imps that live in the shadows. They've been around ever since my mum went missing. Think *The Shoemaker and the Elves*, only they smell awful and all they want is food and a safe home . . ." My gut twisted with a sudden pang of longing. They still hadn't turned up.

Jasika furrowed her brows and glanced between us.

"They're kind of cute in a Jim Henson sort of way," Dom elaborated.

"I guess that's a thing." Jasika shook her head. "So what's this magic book I've only just now heard about?"

I squirmed in my seat. It didn't feel natural, being this open about everything. And Dom had really overstepped, blabbing about Mum's book. I'd have to be careful moving forward with what I told him. But now the cat was out of the bag. I let my eyes dart up to Jasika, down again, and forced myself to explain about Mum's jewelry box, the book, and what we'd found out from the water wives. After all, I was making a distinct effort to play nice with others. And maybe Jasika was right. Working together was our best shot, even if it spread the danger around to all of us.

"So if it's protected by Fae magic, it's probably got that same magic inside," I explained. "I don't want to count it as an asset or a liability until I've had a chance to check it out more. Their magic runs on something I don't understand."

"Wait, so your mom just happened to have a book of Fae spells lying around?" Jasika demanded, drumming her fingers on the table. "Doesn't that feel like a big coincidence to you?"

"I . . . I don't think so." I chewed the inside of my lip and reached out, swirling the water in my cup to watch the little whirlpool form in the center. It was easier to watch than their faces. A small voice in my head pointed out that I really didn't need to tell them. But the words spilled out all the same. Maybe I'd just kept it all pent up so long it only needed a tap to come spilling out. Maybe some small part of me was so desperate to push them away from all of this that I'd tell them everything. "When I was a kid, she taught me all about Fae and fairies. I think she had a past with them." I swallowed and tried to focus on the singular words. Not the weight they carried. "Um . . . so I was eight, and I found this Fae wounded in the woods. I didn't know back then that there were bad ones, so I brought him home to try and help him. I left him in the living room with all the family pictures and went to get bandages. When I came back, the living room was a mess, and he was gone."

Just thinking about it—the shattered picture frames. The rips in the couch, stuffing everywhere, and Mum's face when she came home from the store. She must have known what had happened. What would happen. She must have known it was all a trap.

My eyes burned at the memory. I forced myself to drink some water, but it went down like cement.

"They took her. Dad went out to the woods to try and get her back, only when he came home, he was seeing things. The Unseelie did something to him. Gave him the hallucinations. When he realized what they'd done to him I think he gave up hope of finding her. Packed up. Moved halfway across the world to live in a small town with a man who specialized in protection against the fairies. Only I don't think it was enough. Maybe they, um, they didn't just want Mum."

I could feel their eyes on me, but I didn't want to look up and see it. It felt weirdly like I'd just stripped down naked in front of them. After a few long seconds, Dom cleared his throat.

"I'm . . . shit. I'm so sorry." He tapped his finger against the neck of his bottle. Every little tap was like little bomb going off in my ears. Out of the corner of my eye, I saw him take another swig of beer.

"I never realized," Jasika breathed.

I squirmed in my seat. "I didn't tell you to make you feel sorry for me. You two need to know the stakes here."

"Yeah. The stakes. They're high." Dom cleared his throat. "But if things go wrong, a lot of people get hurt."

"You've gone at this alone long enough," Jasika added. "And I get it. It's made you hard inside. But maybe it's time to accept help from other people with skin in the game." She leaned forward and rested her warm hand on mine. Like a weighted blanket, right when I needed it. This time, I didn't pull away.

"I guess you'll be teaching me all the things you've taught yourself," I said.

Jasika smirked. "I'll do my best, as long as you return the favor."

Dom leaned forward with a grin. "Not to intrude or anything, but there's one other person who can probably teach us a thing or two." His eyes shone, and I didn't even have to ask who he was thinking of.

He was probably right. I turned to Jasika. "Well, if we're going to start our own little Scooby gang, I think there's someone you should meet."

Fourteen

It felt downright sacrilegious at this point, bringing not one but two visitors to the side of Gwen's pond. At what point would they declare enough was enough and ban me for good?

As we broke the tree line, I gave Dom a nudge. He dug a box of wheat crackers and a can of green beans out of his backpack. I blinked at the offering.

"I told you to bring greens and bread."

"Crackers are like bread and these are *green* beans." He gave the can a little jiggle.

I could have smacked my forehead.

"This isn't some little BS phone-call ritual, Dom. This is an actual—" I broke off at Jasika's gasp as Gwen rose from the water. Pond water sparkled like stars in her wet hair as she stepped onto the land, surveying us silently. After a long moment, she folded her hands in front of her.

"My sisters won't come out for so many people, Bryn," she warned me. "But you know that I always will."

I couldn't help smiling at that. "Yeah. Thanks, Gwen."

Gwen's eyes sparkled as she clapped her hands. "So, what have you brought me?"

"Only the best for the pretty lady." With a flourish, Dom handed her his pantry rejects.

Gwen blinked and took a deep breath. "I see. How very . . . generous." She turned, nodding at Jasika. "We have not met."

"Jasika Witters." Jasika stuck out her hand, just like I had when I'd first met the water wives. Gwen stifled a giggle, awkwardly resting her hand on Jasika's.

"I am Gwen," she murmured, looking Jasika up and down. "You have a power about you. You've been educated."

Somehow, the way Gwen said "educated," it didn't sound like she was talking about algebra. It almost sounded like it was spelled with a capital E. For all that Jasika insisted she knew things, I was looking at her in a new light. I knew I'd underestimated her before, but now there was no telling how much.

Jasika caught her breath and nodded. "Self-taught, mostly. I've always sort of . . . known. Then Bryn and Father Gooding got my family out of a scrape. After that, I figured I ought to learn more. There are a few things I think I can do with it."

"Impressive." Gwen glanced at me. "Such interesting friends you've brought, Bryn."

"Yeah, well, I try." I knelt down in the muddy grass and opened my backpack. "Sorry to drop by unannounced again, but Dom and Jasika are going to be working with me. I figured it would be a good idea to lay everything out and let them know where all my cuts and bruises keep going."

Gwen giggled, managing to sound like a gurgling stream

as she knelt in front of me. Very close in front of me. Right in front of the others. Apparently, boundaries and personal space weren't really water-wife things. I glanced at Jasika, but she'd plopped down on the grass next to Dom, hands folded politely in her lap. And Dom? He was laser-focused on the backpack. He might as well have waved a neon sign screaming SOMETHING COOL INSIDE! Gwen could have snogged me right there and I doubt he would have noticed anything if there wasn't active magic involved.

Well, it was time for just that. This wasn't just a social visit after all. "Gwen, the Unseelie didn't just send a drone. The changelings were being delivered by a bendith right in these woods. In person."

Gwen's eyes widened. "Oh, Bryn. That was you, wasn't it?" She took a deep breath and began to play with her long, pale hair. "You killed the bendith. Of course it was you. Did you at least learn her name?"

"I . . ."

"There wasn't time," Jasika cut in. I glanced over. Jasika had smoothed her expression into a stony mask. For his part, Dom wasn't looking at any of us, and there was a faintly greenish tinge to his cheeks.

Gwen narrowed her eyes. "Did she curse the town?"

My stomach sank. "I guess there was time enough for that."

Gwen hissed something that definitely wasn't English under her breath and rose, storming back and forth in front of the pond.

Dom hurried up to her, holding up his hands. "We're sorry. But we talked about it. There absolutely won't be any more killing."

Gwen slowed and crossed her arms. "That death should not have occurred. You've placed the whole of this town in danger."

I sighed and pulled the book out. In an instant, the friendly atmosphere dissolved. Jasika leaned forward, brushing her fingers against the leather cover. Gwen recoiled, eyes wide.

"Bryn, why have you brought that here?" she demanded.

I glanced helplessly to Dom and Jasika, but they didn't offer anything to help. "Gwen, I know it's risky, but—"

"A grimoire of this sort is not to be used lightly."

"My mum used it!" I insisted, and my heart skipped a beat. "This was her book. Maybe it's risky, but if she could use it, then so can I."

"If the town is in danger, then help us save it." Jasika leapt to her feet and grabbed the book. For one knee-jerk moment, I almost lunged for it before I caught myself. We were working together now after all. All the same, my hands itched to take the book back.

Gwen turned to face us. A long, quiet moment passed. I don't think any of us dared to breathe until, at last, Gwen gave a little nod. Jasika tried to hand her the book until Dom stopped her.

"Oh, no, um . . . apparently Fae can't touch it? It's enchanted or something."

"Just rest it on the ground," Gwen murmured.

Jasika did, and we all huddled around as Gwen pursed her lips, watching carefully as Jasika turned page after page.

"This book is very old," she said, and I wasn't sure if she said it to herself or to all of us. "It's far older than any human ought to be. Perhaps your mother was not its first owner."

I rested my hand on hers. "Could you tell us which spells might have been written by my mum, then?"

Gwen bit her lip and threw a glance over her shoulder at the pond. "The Welsh and the modern English spells are most trustworthy. But I don't think any of you should try anything but the English. At least, that way, you'll know what you're saying."

Well, it was a start. I squeezed her hand. "Okay. Do any of these look good to undo a bendith's curse?"

Gwen watched Jasika flipping the pages before she held up her hand. "This one. It's just an incantation. Everyone here should be able."

By "everyone" she plainly meant Dom, who looked like he was about to explode with excitement.

"Wait. Right now? Are we actually going to do this right here, right now?"

Gwen stared at him a moment before her lip twitched. Yeah. Dom seemed to have that effect on people, didn't he?

"Don't we need ingredients? Elements, salt, anything?" Jasika demanded. "I mean, we haven't even secured the circle."

"Secured the circle?" Dom cut in.

"Usually before you do this, you're supposed to make a circle around yourself with a knife," Jasika explained. "It sort of keeps everything unwanted from getting in or out."

"Don't worry, I'm here. Fae magic is a little easier. And a little harder." Gwen crossed her arms in front of her, wrist over wrist. "I can secure the circle, but you shouldn't try without human methods. If you haven't the strength, human magic simply won't work. Fae magic will often work and just keep taking and taking until you've paid for it."

"So better to read the fine print and follow the rules," Dom muttered, flipping his wrists a few times before he was satisfied.

"Better not to try Fae magic without a Fae," Gwen clarified. "Misguided humans have been known to turn to stone."

Jasika and I shared a glance before we folded our hands in the center.

"You need to focus your power into the center of us all. Over the book," Gwen explained.

"What?"

"Just imagine your hands getting warm, Dom," Jasika explained, closing her eyes.

Gwen's lip twitched.

"How long have you been doing this, Jasika?"

Jasika gave an awkward half shrug. "Actively? Maybe a year or so. But I think I've sort of been playing with it since I can remember. This'll be the first time I do it with a group, though."

Gwen nodded in approval. "You'll find it a bit easier."

After a few seconds, something thrummed behind our hands, like the tingling, tightening of skin near a fire without any of the heat. I focused on pushing my own out, but none of us could have matched Gwen's strength. If we were campfires, she was a power plant.

"I will lead in the human fashion. You will follow," she instructed, and her voice dropped lower than I'd ever heard it. "Hail to the water of the west. Guide our sorrow and our joy and purify this place we call home. Be with us and feed our intuition."

The pond began to ripple, little waves slapping against

the muddy bank. Dom jumped, glancing behind him. For a moment, I almost snapped at him to keep still, but with the kind of energy Gwen was putting out, I don't think we were about to throw anything off.

"This isn't the full ritual," Jasika whispered.

"Ssh!" Dom hissed. "I'm listening!"

"Bryn?" Gwen pressed.

I licked my lips and tried to remember how this was supposed to go. That was the thing about human magic. It was so based on willpower and belief that the most certain way to get it done was by following the same rituals over and over until you trusted in them like you trusted the sun to feel warm. If I didn't trust I'd remembered it right, there was a chance it might not work. Okay. Gwen had summoned the west. So I needed to go counterclockwise. Probably.

"Hail to the fire of the south. Feel our love and our rage. Help us to break the curse I sort of might have unleashed on the town. Be with us now to strengthen our wills."

The burn of spice tickled my nose. I could swear a bead of sweat ran down my neck. Hard to tell magic from psychology sometimes.

"Dom?" Gwen pressed. "Air is the element of knowledge and clarity."

Dom positively quivered with excitement. "Okay. Um. Hail to the air of the east. Show us knowledge and clarity. And be with us while we . . . do that."

A tinkling of bells danced on the wind as an unexpected breeze tickled my cheek. I cracked my eyes open, then shut them before someone could catch me.

"Jasika?"

And of course, Jasika tackled it like a pro. "Hail to the earth of the north. Guide us through the darkness that has fallen on this place. Grant us the strength to resist it. Be with us as we seek stillness and wisdom."

The soil itself seemed to thrum under us as we followed, building up to a steady rumble in my chest stronger than anything else. Jasika gasped. Her hands trembled against mine. The whole of nature seemed to be awake and intent on her. And we hadn't actually started the spell yet.

I might have to rethink the balance here. Dom and I were campfires. Gwen was a power plant. Jasika was somewhere in between. How could she stand to walk around with all of that humming inside of her?

Gwen took a deep breath. "Repeat after me, now, but do not repeat after me unless you understand what I'm saying. Is that clear?"

We shared wary glances. Dom was the first to nod.

Gwen took a deep breath and began to mutter something, probably to make sure we didn't try to clumsily mimic whatever she was saying. But, here and there, her voice rose in an English phrase for us to parrot.

"Watch over this town and expel ill will against it."

"Guide us in strength, push us in love."

And something I didn't entirely catch, but it was either "Peace to all life" or "Bees for all time," so . . . I was pretty sure which one I was supposed to say.

The trees creaked behind us and the water churned in the pond. Gwen's power washed over us like a tidal wave until all we could do was hold on. Sweat beaded on my forehead. I tightened my grip, waiting for it to end as Gwen's muttering carried on. Then, with a squeeze of her hands, it stopped. The power receded and I caught a breath I hadn't even realized I'd been holding.

Gwen sighed.

"Water of the west. We thank you."

My turn. "Fire of the south. We thank you."

Then Dom and Jasika, like we'd done this a thousand times already.

"Air of the east, we thank you."

"Earth of the north, we thank you."

Gwen gave a satisfied little nod and let go of our hands. Dom looked like he'd been punched, but judging by that dazed little grin, I didn't think he minded it. Gwen stood, primly brushing the bits of grass from her shift dress.

"Please attempt nothing from this book without me," she instructed.

"Of course," Jasika said, smiling a little too widely. I tried to catch her eye, but Jasika didn't quite meet it. It seemed I wasn't the only one willing to ignore Gwen's advice.

I wobbled to my feet and returned Mum's book to the safety of my backpack. "Thank you, Gwen. I promise we'll keep you in the loop for anything else we do. We'd really appreciate your help if we hit a wall."

Gwen pulled a face.

"Please understand me," she said gravely. "I wish to help you. But if my sisters are threatened, we must retreat from this place. We cannot risk provoking the Unseelie court."

"We don't want to provoke anyone," Jasika said. "We're just going to look after our town."

Gwen nodded and dipped into a little curtsy. "Until I see you all again."

It was awfully formal. Dom and Jasika bobbed in little bows before they turned to head back into the trees. I started to follow, but Gwen caught my wrist. Of course there would be something we couldn't discuss with the others around.

"I'll see you at school tomorrow," I called.

When Dom and Jasika disappeared into the trees, Gwen took my face in both her hands, pressing a cool little kiss to my forehead. My heart fluttered. I had to make myself take a step away.

"What was that for?"

"Something else is troubling you," Gwen stated.

"Something's always troubling me."

"Tell me."

I sighed and glanced over my shoulder. Dom and Jasika were long gone.

"I've been having dreams about my mum." I swallowed. "But there's someone else there. Dark hair. Gray dress." I paused, grasping at ragged edges of the dream. It had felt so vivid when I'd dreamt it, but now it already felt vague and far away. "There was a banner. It was red and it had a gold dragon on it."

Gwen pursed her lips. "Have you dreamt of this person many times?"

"Just a few. I only saw her once. Along with other people. Memories." I pushed back against the image of the bleeding prince before he could fully form in my mind. "But I never saw her or the gold dragon. Do you know what it is?"

"It belongs to a family line that ended over a millennium ago." Gwen shook her head. "They had a powerful witch among them, and she was known for deals with the darkness."

Something in my gut wriggled. It almost felt like hope.

"But if she was a really old and powerful witch then maybe she's the one who made the deal with the Unseelie. Not my mum." I wanted to believe that, anyway.

Gwen gave me a sad look. "Pray it isn't so. She was powerful as she was cunning. If her reaching out to you is tied to the Unseelie, I would recommend not trusting her. Do not speak to her. She was only ever loyal to herself and her ends. We have greater matters with which to concern ourselves."

For the time being, I didn't think I'd have any problem following her advice.

Fifteen

The Fae weren't going to back down any time soon. It was time for everyone to prepare. Of course, that would mean asking a priest to break a promise and resume my lessons. I needed to ask as casually as possible. Perhaps a passing question on the way back from the kitchen with a plate of the seemingly never-ending supply of casseroles that had packed the church fridge since we'd moved in. But as I passed by his office, the door was shut. A voice echoed from inside.

". . . digging around in my garden. Pest control says it's moles, but I know it's not, Father. They're doing things. Causing mayhem. Scaring my dogs."

"You were right to come, Herb. I'll be by to look later tonight. I'm sure this will have a simple solution."

The door opened and Mr. Herbert filled the doorway, his sweat-stained baseball cap folded in his hands. He froze when he saw me, lips twitching like he had to come up with something good to say. Great. Even the adults couldn't swallow their pity.

"I'm . . . glad to see you got the casserole, Gladys was very determined."

I glanced down at the warm plate. Was this one from Ms. Gladys? Hard to keep track of all of them.

"Um . . . yeah. I mean, yes, sir."

He nodded and shuffled past, replaced in a second by a haggard-looking Father Gooding. He'd deny it, but it was clear what sort of strain we put him under. Us living in the church was a perpetual reminder that things were no longer under his control in this town.

I took a tasteless bite of casserole. "Sounds like Mr. Herbert's got gnomes."

Gooding nodded. "It does. I'll be out this evening tending to it."

I frowned. "Okay. I'll go with you and we can talk about—"

"Not after your father forbade it."

"He's working late," I pointed out. "He's *always* working late." Because apparently the oil industry didn't much care if your house burned down.

Gooding took a deep breath and folded his arms behind his back. "All the more reason for you to look after your brothers."

"Gooding—"

"Bryn," he interrupted. "If one of the courts attacked your home to flush you out, do you really think it's wise to intentionally place yourself in their path?"

My protests dried up in my throat. Gooding wasn't going to take me with him. He really just wanted me to sit back and do absolutely nothing. He wanted me to let go of my own fate, just like that.

"You can't be serious," I croaked. Then, with what remained of my endurance, I repeated, "You can't be serious!"

Gooding scrubbed a hand over his face and straightened. "Was there something else I could help you with?"

This wasn't fair. This wasn't right. After years of working by his side, he was just willing to dump me the second things looked sticky. I blinked and shook my head, shoving more casserole into my mouth as I tromped down the hall, skin itching with irritation. Fine. I could do this myself.

I finished my plate and prepared a couple more. At least if I took the food to the boys, I could ensure they actually got a few vegetables. And it was something to do as long as I was going to be stuck here. Maybe I ought to text Jasika and Dom about the gnomes on Postoak, just in case. I wasn't sure what they could do, but I got the feeling they'd appreciate knowing that something was happening.

I went to Jake's room first, but the door was wide-open with no Jake in it. Not that I had to go looking.

"We're supposed to be in this together. You're full of shit if you think you can just cut me out!"

The door to Ash's room flew open and Jake stormed out, looking positively murderous. He stormed past me and into his room, slamming the door shut behind him. A second later, it creaked open and he reached out, grabbing one of the plates of casserole from my hand before shutting it again. Less noisily this time.

"What crawled up your butt?" I demanded. No answer. Apparently, Ash still wasn't talking to Jake any more than the rest of us.

Screw it. I set Ash's dinner on the ground in front of his

room, rapped once against the door, and almost stomped off to my room. But something niggling inside me stopped me just before I reached the door. I was having a crappy day. They were, too.

Groaning inwardly, I went to Jake's room and knocked. When he didn't snarl at me to go away, I tried opening the door. To my surprise, it actually swung inward.

Jake slumped on his bed, glaring down at his feet. He'd already made himself at home, scattering clothes everywhere. It smelled better, though, with only one boy's dirty socks. Each of the twins had his own room. His own mess. For the first time, Jake had his own space. Poor Jake.

"Sounds like you two are having problems, Moonman," I said as gently as I could.

Jake huffed. "Yeah."

"Wanna tell me what's going on?"

His lower jaw jutted out for a second. His fingers tightened on the mattress. Whatever inward battle he had going on, it was a real rager.

"Ash came back with bruises."

"What?" I jerked back and almost stormed over to Ash's room.

"No point. He won't even let me see it." The ultimate insult for twins as close as they were.

"Do you have any idea what happened?"

"Doing stupid stuff, I guess," Jake muttered. "I don't even know what he's been up to since the . . . the fire." His voice broke at the end. I had the decency to look away when his eyes started to go red. This was rough on all of us. I wasn't about to rob the kid of his dignity.

"You know you can always talk to me if things get to be too much. Right?"

A strange, alien silence settled between us. I waited for him to call me Miss Priss. Tell me to get out of his hair and give him some space. But all I got was the rustle of fabric. After a few seconds, I glanced back to find Jake buried under his blanket, his wet eyes fixed on the wall.

I swallowed and retreated back into the hall, tugging the door closed behind me.

Dinner eaten, homework finished, shower done, and no apprenticeship to tend to, I sat on my bed, bouncing my leg up and down. For once, there was actually nothing to do. If I was home, I might surf the internet, read, or knit and watch TV . . . but none of those were options here. I could have checked on the boys again, maybe asked if they wanted to watch one of the DVDs in the media room, but the thought of having to coach them through whatever tiff they were having sucked all the energy out of me. They could deal with it on their own.

I slumped back on my bed, staring up at the dull, white ceiling, my brain looping around in circles. Dom was either out nursing his social life or hanging out with Helen watching *Jeopardy!* reruns or, bless him, trying to research magic. Jasika was probably getting in her community service tutoring somebody. They still had their things to do when they weren't working with me. What did I have?

I had a shadeling and I had a book.

The thought sent an electric shock buzzing through me. Mum's book. Somewhere in there had to be the spells she wanted me to use. Playing it safe and doing things Gwen's way hadn't gone anywhere. I wanted a way to ward off the Unseelies, and I had what might just equate to an H-bomb stashed under my bed.

Lord, it felt like the epitome of teenage rebellion. This was Fae magic. It wasn't for humans, certainly not without Gwen's guidance. Hell, other Fae were scared of it. But Mum hadn't been. I was her daughter.

Just thinking about it made my gut squirm. Mum had used something that scared Gwen. Mum had dabbled in some dangerous stuff, and maybe that had put the rest of us in danger. Maybe everything that had happened was Mum's mistake and not mine. So the question was: Who should I follow in a moment like this? Mum or Gwen?

I crept out of bed and clicked the lock on the door, heart in my throat. When a few seconds passed and neither of the boys came knocking, I pulled the old book out from under the bed. Here went nothing. I started flipping through the pages. Maybe half were in English or Welsh, and even then, more than a few of the English pages used Old English words like "Ebba" and "Monajjfyllen." The shadeling helped where it could, translating the Welsh that I couldn't remember, but even it couldn't translate much. Not that it needed to. I was just looking. I wasn't foolish enough to pretend it wasn't a risk. This was where everything had gone wrong . . . but I knew that. I could be more cautious.

"Do you know what any of this means?" I asked.

"Not for me to know, Missy," it explained, swinging its legs hard enough that it bounced on the mattress next to me. "It's an old dialect. Not one we shadelings speak."

"Right." I grabbed my half-used book of math notes and

started scribbling what looked useful. Spells I could under-stand, patterns, theories on some of the other stuff that didn't make any sense to me. And the more I read, the more I was drawn to the same three pages, their titles sticking out to me like bright neon lights: *Gwella, Gwybodaeth, Freuddwyth.*

I shifted, resting my elbows on my knees. Dreaming. That couldn't be so bad. That one was just something that would take me back to the dreams with Mum, right? Maybe, if I could control it, I could ask her more.

"Hey." I gestured to the shadeling. "I want to try out this one. Can you help me?"

The shadeling shifted, tugging anxiously on its large, batty ear. "Are you sure, Missy?"

I nodded. "Just this one. I want to try it out."

"These are dangerous," it squeaked.

"Just this once." I clutched the book tighter. "What if it shows me exactly what I need to repel them? Or the name of the monarch we're up against? We need information. This could help everyone."

The shadeling stared at me for a few long seconds before nodding and scampering forward. "You gotta read it straight from the book, Missy. Won't work if you read it off anything else. It's not for humans."

"Why not? A spell's a spell."

The shadeling shook its head. "Not like this. This is our magic, Missy. It's not human. It's not just the words, it's the paper and the ink and the hand that wrote it. Your brains don't work like ours."

Right. I thumbed to the page I was looking for. Gwybo-daeth.

"So do I need anything special?"

"No, Missy. Just the words."

I took a deep breath and ran my fingers along the page, sounding out the unfamiliar Welsh words, starting over every time I stumbled and the shadeling corrected me. The weird part was every time I started, it was like I was reading the words for the first time all over again. None of them stuck in my head, no matter how many times I'd read them. On the third try, my heart began to flutter like a bird in a cage. On the fifth, my hand started shaking. This was insane. This wasn't just lighting a candle or writing out some old Welsh ogham letters. I was actually practicing fairy magic.

An odd feeling of calm washed over me. Maybe it was all in my head, but I swear I could almost feel something shifting in the back of my mind, shimmering like a mirage in the heat.

"Missy, you have to say what you want to dream and learn about now," the shadeling advised, but its squeaky voice sounded like a muffled call from the other side of a very thick wall.

What did I want to learn about? My mind flicked through everything like a slideshow. Mum. The woman in the gray dress. Even spying on them . . . but none of those felt quite right. It was like, even in my thoughts, I ran into a brick wall.

I licked my lips and let it come to me. "Show me what they want."

The soft whirr of stringed instruments filled the dark around me. I stepped forward. Leaves crunched under my bare feet, pricking at my unprotected soles. No steel-toed boots. I wiggled my toes and glanced around as the skeletal outlines of unfamiliar trees materialized from the shadows. The spice of burnt honey and something too sharp washed over me, enough to make me gag. I forced myself to take another step. This wasn't real. This was just a dream.

A huge table swam into view before me, spread with exactly what I'd expect at a fall feast. Candied fruits, sweet potatoes, pumpkins, apples, great bowls of honey and milk, fresh bread, bottle after bottle of wine, and, in the center of it all, a perfectly roasted suckling pig. Fae of every kind milled about, their actions mimicking a casual conversation, but every pair of large, luminous eyes was fixed on me. And there, in a clearing lit by moonlight, stood a tiny woman dressed in splendid robes of sapphire and violet studded with dewdrops, her magnificent crown perched atop her great mane of dark hair.

My stomach growled. I bit my cheek. Just a dream. That food wasn't real.

The tiny queen swept in front of the table and extended her arms, her little lips pulling into a perfect half-moon smile.

"Come, child," she cooed. "Come and warm yourself. Fill your empty stomach. Rest your weary body."

She waved her hands. Instantly, flames burst around the clearing in a tidy, contained ring. Behind the table, a trio of hags picked up their instruments again. One played an odd flute that seemed to be made of horns. Another snapped her gnarled fingers against some form of drum while the last one sawed away at a mix between a fiddle and a mousetrap. The music pierced my ears, and for a second, I couldn't think of anything else. But only for a second.

With a shuddering breath, I began to pick my way across the clearing, my eyes fixed on the little queen. "This is nice and all, but I was hoping we could talk one-on-one." I clenched my fists. "You've sent a drone and a bendith after me. So here I am. What do you want?"

Her eyes flashed with danger or amusement—I didn't know

which. I didn't want to know. She strutted behind the table, her eyes on me.

"First, allow me to repay you for your pains. Come. Eat. Warm yourself. In this clearing, you will know only my hospitality."

My stomach rumbled, and in spite of myself, my eyes flicked to the bread. The sweet, rich smells of everything on that table tickled my nostrils and made my mouth water. Not real. Not real. I swallowed. "You must think I'm some kind of stupid."

"Young," she hummed. "Inexperienced. But far from stupid. Not many humans could do what you have done. I must commend you." She tilted her head to the side, and from the folds of her dress, she pulled out the book. My heart jumped into my throat. I had to catch my breath as she set it on the table, nestled right between the pomegranates and round, perfect pumpkins. No. Mum's book was safely back on my bed, where I really was.

The queen's dark eyes darted up to me, her lips twisting into a smile, more wicked than clever, as she flipped it open. "I once gave your mother a book very like this one. A pity she cursed it against our kind. Very ungrateful of her."

I wanted to heave a sigh of relief. I wanted to recoil in horror. Without realizing I was doing it, my lips parted and my traitor voice whispered: "How do you know my mother?"

"Oh, my dear," she tutted, running her fingers over the cover of the book, and for just a moment, she looked softer. Almost maternal in the warm light of the fire. "Your mother was mine."

"A human can't belong to anyone."

Her eyes flicked up to me. "You should study your history, child. Do you think me so evil for claiming her when all of human history is marred by slavery? War? Poverty? Humans have used other humans as things as long as humans have existed. At least I cared for her."

She stepped closer, her robes trailing along the leaves and grasses. Fae and fairies stumbled back to give her way. She reached out, brushing her small fingers against my hair. I started back, my hand going to my chest, but I clutched only fabric. My nail was gone!

She gave me a pitying look. "Or perhaps you know the evils of your own species. That's why you think so ill of me. But she was no slave to me. She was my pupil. My handmaiden. Angareth was like a daughter to me."

My heart started to pound again. I had to take a few deep breaths to stop my voice from trembling. "My mother's name was Karen."

"So she said." The little queen cocked her head, folding her hands in front of her. "I think today you would call it witness protection?"

"And . . ." I swallowed, my gut squirming. "And what exactly did she witness?"

"Ha!" She threw her head back so far, it was a miracle that huge crown of hers didn't topple right off. "Perhaps I used the wrong word. She was simply hiding from me. The fool fell in love. Pitiful." She shook her head. "Centuries of searching for the descendants promised to me, and the only one I could track down was a little deserter."

I bristled, but at least I had the presence of mind not to rise to the bait. Not totally, anyway. "Descendants of whom, exactly?"

"Oh, just a hapless human who didn't think about consequences." The queen sighed and positively glided over to the table, leaning against it, but it didn't come across quite right. It was like a hungry tiger lounging in front of a rabbit. So that was it. Mum had been her prisoner. Her servant. Her . . . her child, it sounded like.

But Mum met Dad. Did he know what she'd risked to be with him? I wasn't totally sure what I ought to feel toward her . . . but it wasn't quite anger. Not anymore. It felt like a punch to the gut. I wanted to gag. I had to hold it in. I'd never really known my mum.

No. Of course not. I'd just been a kid! It hadn't been her fault she hadn't told me everything. It was this bitch who'd taken Mum's happy life from her. From all of us. I clenched my jaw and turned back to face her.

"So you get to ruin all our lives because some asshole years ago promised you, what, us?"

The queen's lips stretched across her pale face, her canines uncommonly sharp behind that wicked smile. "Understand, this isn't personal. Think of this as your birthright. You and your brothers were promised the power and privilege I can offer centuries before your birth. And I always keep my promises. Whatever the cost."

I glanced out at the woods. No hawthorn. No rowan. And certainly no iron or salt at the table. Nothing here would defend me if I tried to run. I stepped carefully, my hands tucked behind my back, as the heat from the burning ring of underbrush rolled over me. And that's when it hit me. Of course. I bit my cheek, worrying my blistered palm with my thumb until it stabbed with pain. "I knew you wanted the boys. Twins are said to be magically potent."

"Not just said to be," the queen scoffed, pushing herself off the table. "Your ill education betrays you, child."

"Whatever." I licked my dry lips and forced myself to take a step forward. "I'm not my mum. My name is Bryn Johnson, and you don't own me or my brothers."

The queen bit her lip, her eyes glittering. She offered me her hand. "I know. You must call me Mab. Queen of dreams and ruler of the Unseelie court."

Mab. I blinked.

"You mean . . . Romeo and Juliet? The fairy midwife."

Mab's perfect half-moon smile reversed direction. Her eyes grew frosty. "Suffice to say, that is not the way I intended to be remem-

162

bered. I was a midwife, but the bendith took over those duties after I took the throne."

A Shakespearean fairy. A Shakespearean fairy who wasn't even in the play about the fairies. She was the tiny bug lady from a monologue in Romeo and Juliet. That's who was responsible for everything. A giggle threatened to burst out of me. I barely managed to push it back down.

Mab folded her hands in front of her and, like a switch, all the humor inside of me dried up.

"I propose an exchange," Mab said tartly. "I could let you see her again. I know how you've longed for your mother, Bryn. Trade the burden of your brothers for a mother's love."

That was how they thought, wasn't it? Trading people like things. My heart throbbed, but I wouldn't go there. I wouldn't think of Mum right now. I clenched my fists until my nails dug into my palm, stinging as they broke the skin. It was all I could do not to wince.

"No deal," I spat.

"You need your mother's guidance," Mab crooned. "You've had to play the part of the mother in your family for far too long."

This actual bitch.

"Shut the hell up." I took another step forward, and what the hell? It was worth a shot. I took a deep breath and hurled myself at her. The bogles and Fae gathered around the table jerked toward me, their arms extended, but not before I shoved my iron-blooded hand against Mab's perfect, snowy cheek.

A clap like thunder slammed into me and pain burst through my head. My back hit the earth, leaves crunching beneath me as my breath hissed out. Mab lunged forward. Her dainty hand closed around my throat. In the disconnected way of someone about to die, all I could think was that, somehow, she was even lovelier in her fury, like a venomous snake.

Her tiny fingers pressed against my jugular, her dark eyes burning like coals. Then the world shifted around me, all the colors melting into dull gray, then sharp silver. The leaves under my back gave way to cool glass. The Unseelie courtiers faded away into nothing, leaving only the two of us as everything in the world hardened into a never-ending wood of mirrors. Oh God. We were in a dream. How in God's good name was I going to make it out of this? I needed to wake up. I needed to wake up!

Mab's fingers tightened around my throat. I choked, black spots dancing before my eyes.

"That was bold," Mab snarled. "But I'm afraid you'll have to do better."

She flung me through the air. I sucked in what breath I could a second before I crashed into the glassy world surrounding us. I tried to push myself up . . . but something caught my eye.

A dark-haired girl in a dirty dress, her skin as pale as snow. Sickly blue blood seeped from her ruined palm. And there, crouching on the ground under a tall, gnarled tree, was the beautiful Fae prince.

"No!" I shrieked, pushing myself to my feet.

Mab paced across the mirror wood like a lioness stalking its prey, her dewdrops shimmering, her figure reflected in a thousand trees stretching out in every direction.

"I own this place," Mab crowed, puffing out her chest. "I own your dreams. You think your life has been a matter of coincidence?"

"You cannot control me!" I shouted, clenching my fist, focusing on the red blood that trickled between my fingers. "These are my dreams. This is my life. You can't own it!"

"Can I not?" Mab flipped her hands. The woods rippled around us so violently I almost lost my footing. And . . . oh God. My heart nearly stopped. There he was, slumped against a tree, blue blood seeping through his ribs, pooling around him. Mab swept up to the prince's side, resting a hand on his shoulder. He gazed up at her, his handsome lips pulling into a smile. "Where do you think his wound came from?"

My breath caught in my throat. "He almost died . . ."

"And how lucky I knew to trust in the charity of a child." Mab smiled and pressed a kiss to the prince's temple. His grin widened and he rose, towering over her. The flow of blood from his wound stopped, as though it had never been. My hands flew to my mouth. It hadn't been random. It hadn't been just my stupidity. All of this, every second of it, had been her wretched plan.

The prince took one step forward, poised as a ballet dancer, and something inside of me snapped. I leapt forward and slapped my bloody hand across his perfect, alabaster cheek. A horrible, inhuman cry filled the wood as the prince staggered back. His skin popped and sizzled, awful purplish welts raising on his cheek.

"Bitch!" he spat, swiping out with one arm. I ducked, scrambling just out of his reach.

"Look who's talking," I snapped. "So, you're just her pet?"

The prince's face contorted with rage, but Mab rested one tiny hand on his shoulder, her brow raised.

"Such violence against one of my most delicate creatures," she remarked. "Perhaps I ought to have surrounded myself by redcaps. Iron doesn't bother them. They like blood."

"Pity you've only got him."

"Not only him, child. But he is my favorite with humans." Mab sighed and patted the prince's shoulder. "He does appeal to little humans. He told me you were a peaceful child once."

"Before you cursed my father." The words trembled as they tumbled out. My vision went blurry. I blinked, sending tears streaming down my cheeks. "Before you stole my mother!"

Mab's cool gaze turned icy. "Must I justify my every action to you?"

I squeezed my eyes shut and struggled to breathe. This was just a dream. Just a dream. I needed to figure out how to wake up. I needed to get home. Mab didn't have the boys. If I managed to get out of here, I could find them. I could keep them safe.

"Oh, Bryn," Mab sighed, that maternal tone sinking back into her voice. It made me want to puke. "You really don't understand what's been happening."

"I understand you invaded my head," I ground out. "And I'm gonna make you regret it."

Her small fingers brushed against mine. In that instant, I did all I knew I could do. I thought of one place she wouldn't be able to stand.

Sixteen

How it happened, I wasn't sure. But it felt right. For all her power, this was still my head. My dream. And I'd be damned if she was just going to take that from me.

The mirror wood shimmered and shifted around me. Glass strained to maintain its shape, but I concentrated, shoving my will against it. Spider-web cracks crunched across the glossy surface, distorting my face until, with a screech, it shattered around us. The silvery blackness of the mirror wood gave way to the sharp grays and glowing golds of an active steel mill. For just a moment, I stood alone, the new surroundings rippling around me until they solidified. Augustine Steel Mill, courtesy of my memories from a ninth grade field trip. My blood wasn't enough. Probably a nail wouldn't be enough either. But this? She'd feel this.

As soon as the world manifested, I sprinted for cover, crouching behind a low set of stairs, hidden in the shadows. It took everything I had to summon enough composure to glance around the corner of the stairs. Mab paced through the dark, dirty factory, every muscle in her body tense as a live wire, her eyes burning wide. The burning crucible behind her almost matched her fury.

"You think this will do anything?" Mab shouted.

A rebuke welled up inside me, but I had to swallow it back down. She was disoriented. It wouldn't last long. Time to look for a weapon. Something long-distance. Maybe I could dream something up. A gun? Did bullets have steel casings? Crap, that was something I should have known! A crossbow, for sure, with iron-tipped arrows. That should do the trick, right?

I closed my eyes and took a deep breath, imagining a loaded crossbow in front of me.

Tap. Tap. Tap.

Footsteps echoed through the empty mill, the reverberations pounding louder and louder. I leapt away from the stairs, scrambling over old tools as Mab crept down the steps, her fingers dancing just centimeters above the toxic iron railing. Her large eyes drifted back and forth. She didn't have to search for me. Not really. In her territory, she'd track me down sooner or later.

I clutched the crossbow tighter in my hands, willing it to solidify as she inched nearer. My breath caught in my throat. I forced myself to raise shaking hands, train the crossbow on Mab's chest.

She turned to face me, her lovely face cast in shadow and the molten light of steel.

"Now, Bryn. Is this necessary?"

My finger twitched a second too early. With a fwing the arrow flew, not quite at her heart, but it tore through the gauzy layers of her sleeve. Mab jerked back with a screech, one hand flying to her shoulder as royal blood seeped out like spilled ink. Good Lord. I'd actually hit her. I'd actually hurt her.

Mab straightened, her lips curled into a sneer. The crossbow flickered out of existence. Something in my brain switched on, cutting through the noise with a single, overpowering command.

Run!

I darted farther into the mill, my bare feet slapping against the hot, dirty ground. Doors appeared in the walls, shaking as snarls and hisses erupted from behind them. Pale hands banged at thick plastic windows, their palms leaving behind smears of purple blood. Shit!

Crash!

Glass exploded outward as the first bone-white hand burst through the window in the door, fingers splayed as it reached for me.

"This is not a game you can win, girl." Mab's words echoed around the mill, laced with venom.

The mill shivered around me. A ladder appeared just meters away. I caught my breath and ran, all but leaping for the first wooden rung as the door burst open. Drones spilled out in a flood of hissing, heaving inhumanity. My bare feet slipped on the rungs as splinters nipped at my soles. The ladder shook beneath me, wood groaning as the first of the Unseelie began to climb.

My chest ached. I struggled to suck in breath after agonizing breath as I charged upward, leaving a bloody stain on each of the rungs beneath me. My pursuer screeched below.

Three feet away. Two feet. Almost there.

Claws tickled my ankle.

I leapt for the second floor, ignoring the way the railing slammed into my arms. Blindly, I kicked back at the ladder. A slick, blistered hand wrapped around my ankle.

The ladder fell. And with it, the drone.

My stomach dropped as I plunged feetfirst over the side. Instinct kicked in and I managed to grab on to the railing.

"Augh!"

Lightning shot through my arm, but I didn't let go. Not when it felt like my shoulder was ready to pop right then and there. Not when that thing's claws dug into my leg, threatening to rip it free.

"Get off!" I screeched, slamming my bare foot into its face.

Bone and cartilage crunched under my heel. The claws dug into my legs, but I couldn't feel it anymore. My bloody fingers began to loosen. I kicked again. Teeth scraped against my foot. The drone slipped, its claws pulling down my leg.

"GET OFF!" I howled, and with one final kick, I sent it flying back down, crashing among its fellow abominations in a heap.

My arms shook as I heaved myself up. The drones snarled below, clambering against toxic walls they could not climb.

I sucked in a lungful of air and clambered to my feet. Machinery stretched out around me, a wealth of hiding places. This probably wasn't even remotely where all of this would be in a real steel mill. But it was what I needed. This was my dream.

I staggered forward as gingerly as I could, minding the blood-slick floor beneath my injured leg.

"You're doing very well, Bryn. Though I hate to see you put yourself through such unnecessary pain."

No!

I knew better. I knew she was trying to slow me down. But I whirled around, and came nose to nose with Mab. The rip in her dress had already been repaired. Like I'd never managed to hit her at all.

"I do hate to do this by force," Mab said tartly, grabbing my wrists with hands like shackles.

The mill faded, like a transparency sheet set over a picture of a forest. The distant sounds and smells of the feast crept in, pushing back against the reek of burning iron and the hisses of the drones below us.

No! No, this was my dream. I squeezed my eyes shut and, with everything I had, I pushed back against the woods. Against the

Unseelie. Against every horrible second of my life this heartless bitch had ever controlled.

"You can't control me!" I shouted, and the smell of the feast faded. "This is mine!"

The world shuddered around me. The ground lurched. I crashed back against the control panel.

My eyes flew open. Mab lay in a heap on the ground, staring at me with mixed surprise and horror. The steel mill rearranged itself underneath us, iron pipes writhing like snakes as the great, glowing crucible floated expectantly toward us. Drones scurried like ants.

"Bryn," Mab breathed, her large eyes locking with mine.

I rose slowly, reaching for the controls. This was a dream, so it probably didn't even matter what I hit. It was the intent that mattered.

Mab wrapped her arms around her middle, her huge mane of hair shifting as she cocked her head, her lips curling into a smirk as she extended her arm for the second time.

Mab pushed herself to her feet and took a small step forward, like a hunter trying not to startle a deer.

"Child," she breathed.

I slapped my hand blindly against the control board.

The floor let out an ear-splitting screech as it ripped open beneath her. Awareness sparked in Mab's eyes a split second before she plunged down into the molten iron. There wasn't even a scream. Just a horrible hiss and plumes of steam billowing out from the pool of glowing metal that had been the queen.

My hand dropped from the control panel. Sweat beaded on my skin, chilling it in the evening air as I gasped for breath. I'd finally done it. Mab was gone. The glowing mound of iron began to cool to a steely gray . . . and Mab was trapped inside of it. Poisoned or burned, whichever got her first.

I sagged into the control panel. I didn't know what to think or feel. There was too much to process. Too much she'd slung at me at once. I felt like a computer program with a flood of operations running at once, forcing me to freeze. Maybe that had been her intention. Overload me with information until I couldn't move.

But it was over. I just had to wake up and I could go home. A hysterical thought entered my mind. Did this make me the Unseelie queen? I'd killed Mab. Did that mean I'd overthrown her by their logic? A manic, whimpering laugh slipped out, and I clenched my fists, squeezing my eyes until tears leaked out. God, that would be the stupidest thing ever, wouldn't it?

The world rippled around me. I hugged my arms to my chest, my breath coming in short gasps.

The distant strains of a halting hymn penetrated the dark haze. Choir practice nearby. Somebody was off-key. The intermingled smells of must and old stone pulled me away from the filth and reek of the mill.

I took a deep breath, then another. My head ached. Soft fabric pressed into my cheek.

Seventeen

I jerked awake. The dull, stone room swam around me. Every muscle in my body ached. My heart pounded. Hot sweat cooled against my skin until, at last, the truth of it began to settle in. I had defeated Mab. In her own territory, with iron.

I blinked through the dark, but nothing felt real. The haziness of the dream still clung to me like smoke after a bonfire, but I was awake.

I scrambled out of the bed, and that's when the pain hit. Tiny stabs at the soles of my feet. Bigger ones at my legs. And something ripping at my shoulder. I bit down on my knuckle and waited for the pain to fade away. After a minute, it softened enough for me to look at it. My feet were filled with tiny rips. Splinters from an old ladder, only there was no actual wood to cause the wounds. Thick scratches wound like veins down my legs, already scabbed over where the drones had grabbed me.

The damage was real. They'd really hurt me. For just a moment, the thought wrapped around my chest like a python, but it loosened with the realization that it was *real*. They'd hurt me. That meant I'd hurt them, too. It meant Mab was dead.

I stumbled to my feet, not even bothering to pull on socks before I shoved my feet into my boots and pulled on my jacket. The shadeling stirred in the shadows by my bed, but I didn't wake it. It deserved to sleep peacefully.

Hard to say what it meant that I could slip out at God-even-knows what hour of the night without triggering a single alarm, and maybe I should have been a little more concerned about living there, but for the moment, it suited me.

The night air nipped at my exposed skin, but it was a peripheral feeling, like a growling stomach when you weren't really hungry. I hobbled into the woods on burning, stinging legs. Everything blurred around me. If anything lurked between the trees, I had no reason to fear it. On a night like this, I was invincible.

"Gwen," I called, squelching my way into the shallows of the pond. The cloudy night offered no glimpse of the village under the surface. Water seeped into my boots and bit at my feet. I splashed farther. "Gwen! I need you. It's important!"

Under all my splashing came the soft sound of pouring water, like a little brook somehow making itself known above a waterfall. Gwen rose from the pond, hands clasped together, her face pinched as the water ran down her face in thin rivulets. It was the first time she'd ever been anything less than perfectly composed. I must have just woken her.

"It's very late," she reminded me crisply. "Shouldn't you be in bed?"

"It was Mab," I gasped. "She came to me in a dream. She was the one behind all of it, but I stopped her."

Gwen's eyes widened, her hands flying to her shift to grip it tightly.

"Come, sit on the bank, this water is too cold for you," she instructed, gliding over to the muddy grass. I trudged behind her, my boots squelching with every step. I plopped down on the grass beside her, my wet nightgown sticking to my shins, and for the life of me I didn't know if the little shivers that ran down my back were from the cold or the excitement.

"My mum's been reaching out to me in dreams. It wasn't the gray lady, it was Mum. And she kept saying the same things over and over in Welsh and I looked in the book and they were spells—"

"Bryn!" It was the closest Gwen had ever come to a biting word. "I told you not to try it."

"It's okay. My mum—"

"Your Welsh is poor. You don't know enough to speak those spells. You don't know the cost."

"But I did it!" I flexed my palms, fighting off the chill that tried so hard to settle into the bones. "And I saw Mab. But I won! I tricked her into a steel mill. I trapped her under molten iron. No Fae can survive that. Especially not one who lives in dreams like she said she does."

Gwen pursed her lips and glanced away. "I believe you may have wounded her," she murmured. "But I cannot imagine her being so swiftly defeated. That is a fool's fantasy."

"I buried her in iron, Gwen." I grabbed her hand and brought it to my scratched legs. "She did this to me. What happened in that dream was real, and I buried her!"

Gwen's eyes darted toward me, bright and fearful in the night. The cool feeling of water washed over my legs. I caught my breath as my skin knitted itself back together, leaving behind only faint, red lines to suggest anything had been wrong at all. When it was done, Gwen nestled her hands in the folds of her shift and gazed over the water.

I scooted closer to her. "Tell me that, even in a dream, that wouldn't be enough to kill anything. Especially a Fae."

"It should," she mused. "But was it not also a dream that told you what spell to use?"

"I . . ." My stomach clenched. I didn't want to think too much about it, but there was that other bit of information Mab had given. But if she was gone, maybe I wouldn't have to think too hard about the implications. "I think my mum knew how to reach out through dreams. That's why I can believe it was her. Mab said that she belonged to her and learned from her. Like a changeling, only Mab seems to think she owns our bloodline or something."

Gwen went still. Pale as she was, for just a moment, she looked like Lot's wife. A lovely, silent pillar of salt. A stronger shiver ran down my spine. I pulled my knees up to my chest, not daring to speak.

After what felt like forever, Gwen lifted her chin to the cloudy sky. "The woman in gray stood before a red banner with a gold dragon."

I frowned. "Yeah. Wait. Do you think she's the one who promised us to Mab? Maybe her bloodline didn't die out after all. Maybe . . . maybe it's us."

"It doesn't matter. Her power is nothing now. And you have bigger concerns." Gwen turned to face me. "Samhain is still coming. I cannot believe Mab is gone, but even if she is, whatever plans she put into place may still come. The Seelie court will not help you here. Be cautious."

She leaned forward, pressing her cool lips to my forehead. Something like ice washed over me in waves, flooding from the burning spot where her lips touched my skin. My teeth began to chatter.

"W-what was that?" I gasped, finally giving in and wrapping my arms around myself.

"Protection," Gwen murmured, but her words came out stiff and unsteady. "Keep your head down, Bryn. But for now. Go home. Be warm. And do not do this again. I will have to speak to my sisters."

I stumbled to my feet as Gwen crept back into the water. The last I saw of her was her frown before the pond closed up over her head. Uncertainty curled in my gut. I think that was Gwen's equivalent of being pissed at someone . . . but she'd get over it. She'd felt my legs. She'd seen the damage. She couldn't ignore it.

I staggered back through the woods, my skin a ripple of gooseflesh in the crisp air. The cold dragged at me like an anchor and very nearly stole my breath. Gwen might have been nice enough to give me some sort of magical blessing that felt like hot cocoa or fuzzy blankets.

Back in the convent, I couldn't bundle up quickly enough. My wet, muddy things were banished to the corner where all of my dirty clothes had been slowly accumulating while I changed into a pair of threadbare long johns complete with faded pictures of reindeer stamped all over them and some truly garish and deeply comfortable wool socks. Warmth began to creep back into my bones, but I couldn't get comfortable just yet. A buzzing energy kept me on my feet. Somehow, the shadeling still slept soundly at the foot of the bed. The whole world might have changed tonight, and nobody even knew.

I slipped into the hall and padded as silently as I could from room to room. Dad lay sprawled across his bed. A to-do list was taped to the wall next to him, half the items scribbled out in blue pen. Maybe, with Mab gone, the next order of business would be to force the Unseelies to back off completely and take his curse with them. It'd be nice to lighten his load.

In his room, Jake was bundled up and sleeping with headphones on. I could faintly detect some movement on his phone as the song changed. Jake stirred for a moment, but didn't wake.

As I pushed Ash's door, however, I was met with a flurry of movement. A history book flew to the ground as a light was shoved under a pillow. I wasn't sure how clever he thought he was being, but I couldn't bring myself to be annoyed by it at that moment.

"If you need help with homework, just tell me," I said. "You don't need to stay up all night."

"I don't know what you're talking about, I'm asleep" came the muffled voice from under the covers.

I smiled and closed the door.

Eighteen

The familiar, tattered chairs in the library felt like plush, fraying thrones. I curled up in one, plucking at the little bits of foam sticking out from the ancient tweed. Jasika sat on a matching chair. Dom lounged in a beanbag—the school's admittedly feeble attempt at feeling relevant and relaxed. When I was sure that nobody was watching, not even the hawkish librarians, I told them everything. About Gooding and the book, about Mab and the steel mill. And Gwen's warning.

Dom rubbed his hands together with a frown.

"Gwen's done well by us this far," he pointed out. "Maybe she knows what she's talking about. Maybe we can practice some more spells. I've been trying to get a spell for good luck working. I think I've almost got it."

Jasika remained notably quiet, drumming her fingers on the chair's armrest and sending little bits of frayed tweed dust floating up in the air, but there was just a shadow of a smile tugging at the edges of her lips.

"What about the wild Fae?" Dom pressed. "And the courtiers. Sooner or later there'll be some other ruler and all the trouble will start over."

Jasika's smile faded. My heart thumped, and I shifted in my seat. "You remember when I told you about them taking my mum?" I took a breath. "Mab said that she owned us. Some ancestor made a deal with her."

Dom struggled with the beanbag a moment to sit up, his eyes wide. "Did she say who?"

The woman in the gray dress. The mystery banners that led to a lot of Medieval Times logos. My gut clenched. Someone had so much lasting impact on my whole life and I didn't even know who she was. But now that Mab was gone, maybe that snake in my dreams would go away, too.

"All Gwen would tell me is that she was probably powerful and untrustworthy," I muttered. "She wasn't exactly eager to draw pictures of the family tree if she knows for sure. But maybe we can figure it out and see if there's any other threat we didn't know about."

"You know me. Big research guy." Dom spread out the side of his brown paper lunch bag and pulled a pen from his backpack. "Shoot."

"Whoever it is, she's pale with dark hair."

Dom scribbled "Looks like Bryn" on the side of the bag. Well, he wasn't wrong.

I cleared my throat. "But I think the key's in the banners. She keeps showing up with red flags that have golden dragons on them."

"Red flag with a golden dragon," Dom mused, his pen *tap-tap-tapp*ing against the table. "That sounds kind of familiar."

"Still, it sounds like the primary threat is gone," Jasika

180

pointed out. "All we need to do is keep things stable until after Samhain."

"But we still don't know what caused all of this to pick up," Dom insisted. "Why did Mab strike now? I think there's more that we aren't seeing." He jabbed his pen at the notes on the sack. "If you could kill Mab in your dream like that, don't you think she'd have taken precautions?"

"Maybe." I picked at a bit of fluff and frowned. "But even if she did survive, she'll be weaker from last night, probably for a while. We've got a chance to start putting the whole puzzle together."

"So, even if she is still out there, she's been weakened enough that she can't get to us for a bit," Jasika pressed. "You think she won't notice anything we do."

"We should go talk to Gwen about all of this," Dom said, pushing himself to his feet.

"I already did."

"And?" He arched a brow.

I picked at the chair fluff a bit more. And she absolutely wouldn't approve of us going and looking into the mystery woman. "And I think we should only talk to her once we have a little more information of our own."

The bell rang to mark the end of lunch. Dom hesitated, then shrugged. "All right. If you say so." He grabbed his back-pack and made his way out.

Jasika hadn't moved. She just stared forward at the reference section like it had insulted her GPA or something. The second the door closed behind Dom, she sat straight up and turned to face me, her dark eyes wide and bright.

"So, using the spell from the book, you were able to pull together enough power to knock her down."

"Um . . ." I hesitated, glancing at the clock and back at her. "I think so. I mean, yeah. Pretty sure."

My stomach clenched, though I wasn't totally sure why. Because this was Jasika. She was going to suggest I help her tutor or that we should volunteer at cleaning up the church or whatever it was that Type-A choir girls did.

"I need you to help me with something." Jasika grabbed my wrist and squeezed it like a lifesaver. "A spell."

"I . . . You're better at that sort of thing than I am," I said uncertainly.

"Not one of my spells. One of yours." Jasika picked at the hem of her blouse. "My cousin. William. He's always been sick but this summer he just . . . He slipped into a coma. The doctors don't know what's wrong with him."

My heart skipped, and in an unintentional burst of sympathy, I couldn't help imagining Dad or Ash or Jake in a hospital bed.

"Wait. Is that why you started volunteering at the hospital this summer? Why didn't you say something sooner?"

Jasika snatched back her hand. "I didn't want people to feel sorry for me like . . . like some kind of charity case." The words fell like a hammer between us. Jasika's eyes widened. "Wait. I didn't mean it like that."

"It's fine," I sighed. Of course, even Jasika saw me that way. I grabbed my bag and rose. "I don't know. I could have gotten killed last night."

"But you didn't. You stood up to Mab and you survived. And you were alone. Imagine the two of us working it together.

Mab can go on the back burner for one night. You just proved that!"

"Why not invite Dom, too?"

Jasika crossed her arms, glancing away. "Come on. Don't make me say it."

"That's something people tend to say before they say something assholish. And I thought there was only room for one asshole in this group."

Jasika's expression hardened. "Because he'd tell us to listen to Gwen and not do it. And because he doesn't have the knack for it. This isn't some good luck spell. This is my cousin's life."

Something buzzed in my veins. I couldn't quite push the rush of the memory aside, sinking into the dream. The overwhelming surge of victory when Mab disappeared. I could still taste the iron on my tongue if I thought hard enough about it.

"We have magic at our fingertips," Jasika insisted. "What good is it if we can't help anyone?"

I thought of Dad, brows furrowed, the days when it took everything he had to focus. I thought of the pill bottles and the days he'd had to miss dinner for some late-night appointment. How much better would his life be if I could ease this burden for him?

It was Mum's book. What would she have wanted for him?

"Just this once," I allowed. "But next time, I need more forewarning. And we bring Dom and Gwen into it."

Jasika brightened like a star and nodded. "Of course. I'll pick you up around seven."

Nineteen

Jasika's family car was pretty clean aside from the granola bars crammed into just about every available space. I tugged one out from the glove box and gave the wrapper a once-over. Chocolate cherry. Not a bad choice.

Jasika squirmed in her seat, her eyes darting between me and the road. "Mom likes to make sure we always have enough. Especially when we've got extracurriculars," she explained. "Help yourself."

Well, if I had permission. I peeled open the wrapper and took a bite. Jasika drummed her fingers against the steering wheel. I held the granola bar out to her.

"No thanks. Seriously, I've had enough of those for a lifetime." Jasika took a deep breath and shifted in her seat. "So. How deep is the crap this'll put you in with Gwen?"

I swallowed my bite of chocolate cherry. "Pretty deep, probably. But as long as I don't show up with a broken leg, she never really gets too upset. I think it's in their DNA to be pretty chill."

A little smile tugged at the corners of Jasika's lips. "How do you even meet a water fairy in the first place?"

I shrugged. "I was out in the woods and stumbled on her pond. I'd just started learning to see past glamours, and I think she was as curious as I was."

"So you just stumbled on them. Your very own ladies of the lake." Jasika snorted and smiled. "Only you."

I waited for her to say something more, but nothing came. The silence stretched between us again, cut through only by the faint sounds of traffic as we wove through the wealthier side of town. Finally, Jasika flipped the stereo to a classic rock station.

I alternated between nibbling at the granola bar, staring out the window, and just watching her. I'd never been alone with Jasika Witters this long. Up close, she had one of those perfect jawlines, like the bust of Nefertiti, and a soft dusting of eye shadow so subtle I would have assumed she wasn't wearing any if she weren't this close. And her scent. She smelled like sage and her floral body lotion. Safe, but strong. Jasika's eyes darted to me, and I looked away, my face burning.

Jasika cleared her throat. "So, is this just your life?" she asked. "Fairies and kid brothers? Don't you have any hobbies?"

I frowned. Did I have a life outside of all of this? I used to. Probably. "I like to knit, I guess. Can't really afford to go out and buy Christmas gifts or anything. But all of my yarn was in the fire, so . . . I guess, right now, this is it. Fairies and family." Maybe that would change in college. I didn't even know what I was going to major in. Just that I was going to get out of here soon, get whatever degree a person needed to get a nice, safe job. Given how I'd basically kept the house running for years, I'd probably make a decent office manager. I shifted, stretching my legs out as much as I could, and tucked my head between the window and the seat, watching her out of the corner of my eye. "What about you?"

"Me?" Jasika laughed. "I've done everything. Choir. Art. I was in soccer back in junior high, but it was too much to keep up with when I got to high school. You know, it was actually gardening that got me into playing with all this magic stuff in the first place."

"Really?" I grinned. "What, did you accidentally grow some anti-fairy weeds?"

Jasika shook her head. "No. I was, like, thirteen? Yeah. I think thirteen. Anyway, I had this little herb garden. I think I had like ten plants. And I had this gut feeling that I ought to name each individual plant after a member of the family. I sort of forgot about it until one of the basil sprouts wasn't doing so well. And there was absolutely no reason for it. Well, it was the one I named after Jade, and I don't know why, but it got in my head that something was up with my sister. So I went and talked to her. Turned out there was this whole thing at school. She was getting bullied, the teachers had no idea . . ." Jasika shrugged. "When Jade felt better, the plant did, too."

"Really?"

Jasika grinned at me. "Oh yeah. I was playing with this stuff long before the redcaps got into our bathroom. You and Father Gooding just lit a fire under my butt."

"Me, Father Gooding, and William."

Jasika's smile faltered, like a shade thrown over a lamp. "Yeah. All the magic in the world and I haven't found a thing to help."

"Do you have a plant for him?"

"Yeah." The smile disappeared completely. "It's not doing so great."

"Does your family know you do this?" I couldn't imagine her parents being thrilled that she was playing with magic, especially not now that they'd all met some of the nastier types of fairies out there. Plus, they were pretty Catholic.

Jasika snorted. "Oh yeah. The boys think it's a hoot. Jason got me a crystal ball for Christmas. Well. He said it was crystal." She shook her head. "We've all got our things. And, hey, they like it. They think I'm some sort of super-witch here to protect them all. Sometimes Jade picks up sticks and waves them like magic wands whenever the boys are bugging her. Tells them I taught her."

Little Jade Witters was probably the cutest thing ever to wear pigtails. And the spunkiest. She would do that, wouldn't she?

Jasika sobered. "But, truth be told, sometimes I wish I didn't have this . . . thing. Whatever you call it. A knack or a cunning or a witch-sense."

"You seem awfully into it not to want to have it."

Jasika gave a little half shrug. "Yeah. I mean, I like it. But it sucks when there's nobody else to talk about it with. It's not that anyone in the family didn't believe me. They just . . . didn't understand. I thought I was alone until you and Father Gooding showed up with those redcaps."

I'd never really thought of it that way. For all that I tried to do things alone, there'd always been someone else in it with me. Mum or Gooding or the shadelings. What would it have felt like to be in it alone?

Jasika glanced at me. "What about you? What do the twins think of all of this?"

"They don't know," I muttered. "I mean, they know the Fae are real, but they don't know what I'm doing about it. Dad does. Well. He found out. But we all think it's better that the boys don't get involved." And how would they respond if they found out? Would they think it was cool? Stupid? Dangerous? Would they be scared of losing me or expect me to do it because I was their big sister and protecting them was my job? How different might things be if they knew? Not that it felt like I had much of a relationship with them lately. They were so caught up with being angry at each other it was like walking through a hurricane to try and talk to them.

Just thinking about it made my heart ache. The whole world had gone topsy-turvy since the fire.

Jasika's fingers *thrum-thrumm*ed against the wheel as the street signs whizzed past.

"That's too bad."

"Yeah." I sighed and stuffed my hands in the pockets of my ugly windbreaker. "I was thinking of waiting until I left for college to tell them. For now, it's better to keep them safe."

Jasika snorted. "You're pretty obsessed with keeping everyone else safe. Especially for someone who throws herself into danger all the time."

"You've got siblings." I glanced sidelong at her. "And parents. And a cousin. You know how it is."

"Not really, no. Look, when I first started playing with all this stuff, I was scared of getting caught. Thought they'd call me Devil Worshipper or something. So I told Will first, and you know what he said?" Her lip curled into a half smile. "He said there's lots of ways of doing the same thing. And if I was doing it to try and help people, it was fine by him. But he also told me I had to be safe about it. He said you can't save someone when you're drowning."

"That sounds like you're trying to teach me a lesson here."

"Maybe. Pretty sure he got that from a fortune cookie. But I think it's a pretty good philosophy, anyway."

I glanced down at my backpack on the floorboard. Mum's book was nestled inside of it, safe for the moment. I wanted to shoot back some sort of clever retort, but none came. The car came to a stop. I glanced up to see the hospital, lit from underneath like a scary story around a campfire.

Jasika flipped off the ignition, and for a moment, we didn't move. Maybe she was having second thoughts about this. Fae magic. What the hell were we thinking?

A warm hand rested on mine, heavy like an anchor and light like that first breath coming out of the swimming pool. I swallowed. My heart tightened in my chest, but I didn't look over at her. If I did, I'd have to pull away. Right now, we both probably needed a little reassurance. I moved my fingers, lacing them through hers for just a few long heartbeats as we stared together at the hospital.

In the end, it was Jasika who pulled away.

"Come on," she said, pushing her door open. "Visiting hours are almost over."

THE HOSPITAL INTERIOR looked sort of like a hotel, all green-and-gold walls and soothing paintings of people hugging one another. It didn't even smell like antiseptic. Jasika headed straight for the reception desk and spoke softly with the woman at the computer before returning with a pair of sticky name tags.

"We've got one hour," she said. "Let's make it count."

William lay in a smallish room, made smaller by all the flowers and cards on his bedside table and the pervading *whoosh* and *click* of the ventilator protruding from between his lips. Jasika sighed and gathered a bundle of wilted daisies from the vase, chucking them in the trash.

"Useless," she muttered before turning back, arms crossed. "Guess I can cross those off as something helpful to coma victims." She gnawed on her thumbnail, eyes fixed on William's still form.

"I've tried everything," she murmured. "Spells, oils, candles, talking to him, playing music. The doctors say that's supposed to help but it doesn't."

"I can't promise this will work," I pointed out. "I mean, there's only one healing spell in the book that I can read, but I have no idea what it's capable of."

Jasika stared down at him with enough love to light a city. "I don't care."

She said that now. If I screwed this up, there was no way she'd be so forgiving. I pulled the book out, running my fingers over the smooth leather surface. Just holding it, being this close to using it, lit me on fire. "It might not work out the way you want it to. I don't think this magic wants to cooperate for humans."

"I don't care."

"It could kill him."

Jasika swallowed, and I caught a faint glimmer in the corners of her eyes. "Aunt Allie's thinking about pulling the plug. Medicine won't help him anymore."

My heart hammered. Last shot, then. No pressure on us to get it right or anything. Just a person's life hanging in the balance.

I opened the book and flipped to the healing spell. It looked like old Welsh, but only Mum's scribbled title made any actual sense to me.

Jasika straightened, rubbing her eye with the heel of her palm. "Right. Let me just get us started."

She started pulling things out of her bag. A compass. A bottle of water. A candle. A lighter. A rock. A knife. Clearly, Jasika wasn't one to improvise ingredients like I was. I watched as she carefully arranged everything in its cardinal direction and lit the candle.

"You don't have anything for air," I pointed out.

"I usually just breathe out for that one," she said, positioning herself behind the rock. She licked her lips and raised the knife, drawing a half circle behind herself. As it came close, I took the knife from her fingers, neatly closing the circle behind me. It felt oddly nice to do it the human way. Grounding, even. We were about to play with Fae magic. It felt right that we should start ourselves off doing things the human way.

We joined hands, and a warm thrum of energy crashed like waves over me. Jasika Witters was a lantern of a person, brighter and clearer than humans ought to be. I felt weirdly on edge just doing this with her. Like she was ten shots of espresso all at once.

"I'll take earth and air if you'll invoke fire and water," she said, closing her eyes.

"What? Oh. Yeah."

She called to the elements with the practiced ease of a priestess. I fumbled through mine, unable to shake the feeling of energy surging all around me. When it was over, Jasika spread the elemental bits far enough apart for me to lay the book in the center and flip to the appropriate spell.

Jasika squirmed. "Do we need, I dunno, an offering or something?"

I shook my head. "I just have to say it out loud, I think."

"Fae magic," Jasika muttered. "It feels too easy."

"To be honest, I don't think a little prayer for luck would hurt our chances here." I bit my lip. Hard to say what was worse. If it worked and something went wrong or if nothing happened. Either way she'd never forgive me. I wiped my sweaty palm on my jeans and took a deep breath. No turning back now.

I ran my fingers down the page, practicing the unfamiliar words in my head. But they didn't stick. No matter how many times I read through the page, the second my eyes left a line, the words left my mind.

I took a deep breath, and I read, carefully sounding each word out before moving on to the next. There was a life on the line.

The text wavered on the page in front of me. I blinked and caught my breath, almost tripping over one of the lines. The world went blurry at the edges. My cheeks flooded with heat as the page shimmered in front of me. The words pushed forward, flooding through me like water through a pipeline. Faster and faster, ringing in my ears until my own words were lost in the torrent. The words faded to a murmur. Then a whisper. Then a wheeze.

A hand caught mine. My heart lurched in my chest, my vision sharpening.

"I'm with you," Jasika said. "Keep going."

I swallowed and blinked. The words came out stronger. Jasika made them stronger. I almost stopped to look at her, to try and understand *how* she could do this, but the flood only intensified. It was in control now, not me. This spell performed itself through me . . . no. Through us. Jasika's voice joined in mine, identical in tone, in speed.

The steady beep of the heart monitor picked up. My own heart fluttered against my chest as a throb started to build right between my temples, pounding like a gong inside my skull. The peculiar reek of burned honey washed over me. The other voice broke off.

"Bryn!" Jasika's voice sounded muffled and distant.

I couldn't tear my eyes away from the page. I tried to back away, jump to my feet, but my limbs locked into place, immovable as stone. Electric pinpricks traveled up and down my arms, my chest, my whole body, first pressing, then stabbing into me as the ringing in my ears built up to a roar.

I gasped, tears pricking at my eyes. The words came out in wheezes, but they came out all the same. Oh God, what was happening? This was different. This was wrong. It felt like I was—

"Bryn!"

The world went dark.

Twenty

An oak table in the woods.

Mum sat on one side, her dark hair strung with cobwebs and flowers, palms down on either side of the book.

FREUDDWYTH sat on the open page, the black ink stark against the old vellum. Dreaming. Why was she showing me this again?

I sat across from her, twisting my fingers in my jacket, heart pounding. I needed to get out of here. Something about this place wasn't safe. I needed to go home and check on the boys. But they were with Dad, weren't they? Surely that meant they were safe. And more than anything, I just wanted to reach across that table and hug her, but something in my gut told me it wasn't allowed.

"Mum, why am I here?" I asked.

Mum flipped her hands palm up. The book fluttered, pages flipping, sending a musty cloud of dust into the air between us.

DIRGELWCH.

Secret.

"Because we are valuable to them. You need to be strong, cariad." She reached out, her fingers hovering an inch from my cheek, but she didn't touch.

Cariad. The little Welsh endearment I hadn't heard in so long made my heart pound. I took a deep breath and shifted to rest my cheek against her hand. Like a rabbit fleeing, she snatched her hand back before we touched, but her expression remained unchanged. Cool and blank. Distant. Like a recording. Something knotted up in my chest. All I wanted in the world was to crawl over that table and hug her close, but that wasn't allowed here.

The pages flipped again.

GWIRIONEDD.

Truth.

"We are so much more than we seem, Bryn," she breathed. "For generations before you were born, she wanted our bloodline. She can unlock a power in us that you couldn't imagine."

"I stopped her, didn't I?" I demanded, pushing myself up from my seat, but Mum didn't seem to hear me. She raised her hands slowly, like she was moving through water, and pressed her fingers to the pages.

"We're probably the only humans in the world who can use this book. You and your brothers alike."

"It doesn't matter. They'll never have to." I blinked. The dappled light filtering through the branches dimmed. The earthy scent of an imminent storm washed over us as the trees began to shake. I glanced over my shoulder. I needed to get home soon. They would be waiting for me. They would be scared.

"You cannot deny Asher and Jacob their birthrights, Bryn. They are just as powerful as you."

"I'm protecting them." I turned back to her, my brows furrowed. "If you really think we should use it, why did you never show us this book when we were kids? Why didn't you teach us then if you knew they were after us?"

Mum stood up, and leaves fluttered down from her hair, crumbling to dust even as they fell to the ground at her feet.

"You need to teach the boys, cariad."

"No!" I shouted. I balled my hands into fists. "If you knew we were in danger, why didn't you tell us anything? You should have taught me this yourself!"

"Bryn."

She gave me a small, sad smile, and closed her eyes.

There was a crunch of leaves underfoot. In the space between two blinks, Mum disappeared. The air filled with the thickness of impending rain. I turned, and . . . no.

There was the prince, blue blood dripping from his side.

I scrambled back, reaching for my iron nail, but my neck was bare. Pain exploded across my jaw as his knuckles slammed into my face, sending stars dancing in front of my eyes. I stumbled, my back slamming into the side of the wooden table. The breath rushed out of me. I wheezed and kicked out, but it was a bare foot that met his chest.

The Fae leered at me, wrapping his thin fingers around my ankle. The world slowed down as he yanked me up, hurling me away. My head collided with the earth and the world spun. But the Fae was coming back. I had to run. I had to get away from him. I forced myself to my feet, but everything was off. The table and the Fae loomed over me. My dark clothes had been replaced with my little sundress, my small, scabby knees poking out from the hem.

"Little one," the Fae positively cooed, reaching down for me. "Where will you go?"

No! I had to get home. I had to protect Mum and Dad and the twins. I turned and tried to run, but the grass curled up around my ankles, holding me in place. My knees hit the ground first, followed *by the rest of me. Claws dug into my shoulders. Chills ran down my spine, pooling and flooding and covering me in ice. The grass tightened. The claws dug deeper until, first with a crack, then a mighty thunder, the icy feeling shattered. All that remained was heat stabbing into my shoulder.*

"Stop!" I screamed, my cheeks burning. "Get away!"

The nails ripped down my back, trailing fire in their wake. I screamed until my throat went raw. I was going to die here. And the prince would go home and take the boys. I pressed my forehead into the grass, tears streaming down my cheeks as I prepared for the end of it.

"Bryn!" a distant voice called. I blinked through the tears. Red banners with gold dragons tumbled down from outstretched branches. The woman in the dove-gray gown flickered between the trees. Her skirts billowed around her as she ran, legs charging against the ground, but she never drew any closer. Instinctively, I pulled away.

"What do you want from me?" I called, but my voice came out in a wheezy whisper. "You already sold us!"

The woman stretched out both arms and, in a rumble of flapping fabric, she transformed into a withered crone. Then again, into a delicate white doe.

"Who are you?" I cried.

A hand touched my shoulder. I flinched, my breath hitching in my throat.

"Come back," a familiar voice cried from the distance. "Come on, Bryn. You're not ditching me like this."

It wasn't him. He was gone. It wasn't him. I was safe now. Cold washed over me in waves until, like a rubber band breaking, it stopped. I turned, staring up. Through the blur of the tears and pain, I saw Jasika staring down at me.

Twenty-One

The steady *whoosh* and *click* hissed in time with every throb between my temples. At once I was too cold and too hot, my skin burning in an icy room.

"Shit, shit," Jasika hissed, her callused hands pressing against my face. I leaned into the touch, right until those callused fingers pinched my cheek.

I winced and jerked away, peeling my eyes open. The room spun above me before it settled into white walls. Jasika knelt next to me, her eyes wide. She looked like she was going to throw up.

"Oh my God," she breathed. "Bryn, we need to get you a doctor."

"I'm fine," I insisted, pushing myself up. Fire ran down my back, and I almost collapsed onto the floor. The taste of blood filled my mouth. What the hell? I touched my cheek, right where the Fae had hit me. The tender skin ached.

I turned and stared down at the floor. Blood smeared the white tile right where my back had been.

"Little one. Where will you go?"

They could still get to me. Through my dreams. I hadn't

even used the dream spell. And, like a stab to my chest, it really hit home. They could get into my dreams, and Mum hadn't been able to stop them. My ears rang as it all pressed in too close, too tight, too loud. The whole world crashed into me like the deepening ocean, pressure building and building. A scream bubbled up inside of me that I couldn't vocalize. I wanted my mum. I needed her. She wasn't here to protect me. Nobody could.

I wrapped my arms around my middle and squeezed my eyes shut. I had to breathe. I had to think. Dammit, I'd been so stupid! Why did I think playing with the book would be a good idea? I'd all but invited them in, hadn't I? Gwen was right. I hadn't stopped Mab. Not if they could still find me anytime I closed my eyes.

"Bryn, what hurts?" Jasika demanded, dragging me back before the panic could send me spiraling out.

I blinked at her.

"What?"

"I need you to tell me what hurts. I need to make up an excuse to tell the doctors."

"No doctors." I pushed myself to my feet and wobbled back and forth for a moment. Jasika leapt to her feet, ready to catch me, but I waved her off. "I'm fine. I . . . I will be. Grab some paper towels. We need to clean up the blood."

Jasika didn't move, so I stumbled forward, trying to ignore how and why my ankle ached as I searched for something to destroy the evidence that I'd even been here. One step at a time. One problem at a time. Clean the room. Get out. Get help.

I found a handful of antiseptic-wipe packets in a bowl next

to the door. When I managed to shuffle back to the spot, Jasika was already at work, tucking the book back in my backpack.

"Bryn, we can't hide this," she insisted.

My hands shook as I tried to rip the packet open, and that just made my heart pound and my eyes sting and *oh God, oh God, they could find me in my dreams* . . .

Jasika took the packet from my fingers and ripped it open, but she didn't hand it over right away. Instead she made to press it to my back. I stiffened and caught her hand.

"We can deal with me later, we need to clean all this up."

Jasika twisted her hand in mine, giving me a little squeeze. "Okay. But Bryn, you're hurt. You're scared. I need you to tell me what's happening."

"I . . ." My heart leapt into my throat. "I think I just messed up."

"How?"

Out of the corner of my eye, I saw it. The faintest twitch of a hand on the stiff sheets.

Shit!

I glanced over at the heart monitor. It was speeding up. Somewhere in this building, some doctor was getting an alert about William. If they saw us here, if word got back to Dad . . .

"We need to go," I insisted. "I promise, I'll explain everything in the car."

Jasika hesitated, her eyes flicking back to her cousin. I could see how much she wanted to stay with him. She must have been so worried about him for so long. The thought that he could wake up and she could somehow miss it must have been agony. I was ready to take off on my own, call a cab if I had to, but she took a deep breath and nodded.

"Okay." She handed me the wet wipe. I lowered myself down to the ground, grinding my teeth together as my back burned, and started wiping up the bloody smear. In a second, Jasika was on her knees next to me, and between us, we managed to clean it all up. She snatched the filthy wipes and tossed them in the garbage next to William's bed. Then, after a moment's hesitation, she scooped up the trash bag and tied it to her belt loop. There would be no trace we'd been here.

"Come on," she said, grabbing a spare blanket from the edge of the bed. "Where are we going? I assume not to the church."

I pushed myself up slowly and swallowed as the room spun again.

"The woods."

"To Gwen?" Jasika looked at me like I had a concussion. Maybe I did. I just felt bad for making it her problem.

"Trust me," I pleaded.

"Trust you." Jasika shook her head, but her eyes drifted back to William. He was still motionless, but the heart monitor didn't lie. "Sure. Yeah. Let's go in the fairy-infested woods after dark."

I reached up to touch my throat. The nail necklace was there.

"Do you have iron?"

"Of course."

Jasika shook her head but held out her arm. Maybe something was wrong with my head because it took me a few seconds to realize why. I grabbed my backpack and stumbled forward, leaning against her. She secured the arm around my middle, and I wish I hadn't yelped when she did, but there was no helping that. She threw the blanket over my back and half led, half dragged me out of the hospital room and down a different corridor than the one we'd come through. Apparently Jasika really knew her way around this place. We didn't run into a single person on the way out. I leaned against her, my head pounding as my feet tripped over each other, but she caught my every stumble.

JASIKA SPREAD THE pilfered hospital blanket across the back seat of the car and helped me crawl up onto it. I settled onto my stomach and spent the whole drive trying not to breathe too deeply or fall asleep. Jasika flipped through radio stations like she had some sort of compulsion. I watched her punch the buttons every few seconds. At every light, she took a break to check her cell phone. Nobody ever called, though.

I didn't notice when we reached Postoak, but the door flew open, and her hands were on me, helping me out of the back seat. Huh. Time flies when you're bleeding on someone's back seat.

I stumbled out and wrapped one arm around her shoulders, head lolling onto her sternum as I tugged my nail free.

Jasika pulled an iron crucifix from her pocket and held it out. Her heart pounded so hard I could feel it against my cheek. I took a deep breath and let the steady *ba-dum ba-dum* beat through me.

We crept through the trees, shoes crushing leaves and twigs as the sweet pine smell settled over me like a shroud. I struggled to keep my eyes open. Dark shapes danced between the trees, but after everything that had just happened, no wild Fae could possibly scare me now. Maybe it was the shadelings. I'd lost their loyalty but I couldn't imagine they'd let anything happen to us.

"What do you think Dom will say if he finds out we practiced magic without him?" Jasika whispered.

"Betrayal. He'll probably disown us."

Jasika let out a weak laugh, and swung her crucifix in an arc, like some sort of warning to whatever invisible threat might be out there. "He'll never let us out of his sight again."

I had to fight not to laugh. Right now, any motion was a bad idea. "Maybe we should get him a crystal as an apology."

"Or his own magic succulent terrarium?"

"Maybe a—"

I froze. A pair of orange eyes shone out from the dark, wide and familiar. I sagged a little more against Jasika and held out my hand.

"It's okay. It's only—"

The eyes blinked out, leaving behind only the darkness. Oh hell, I'd held out the hand with the nail in it.

"Bryn, what was that?" Jasika hissed.

"A . . . a friend," I murmured, tightening my grip on the nail. "I think I just offended it."

"Is it hostile?"

"Never." My heart sank. Every time I had ever seen a shadeling, they had been excited to see me. This one didn't even speak to me. The little purple one who'd braved the convent really was the only one left who gave a damn about me.

Jasika huffed and continued forward. I shuffled along, my whole body a single throbbing ache. A fluke. It had been scared off by Jasika or the nail; that was all. After all, I had told them to stay away from humans. I'd deal with it later.

Gwen waited by the edge of the pool when Jasika and I staggered through the tree line. Somehow, the water wives probably knew we were coming.

Gwen rushed forward, grasping my arms and tugging me from Jasika's grasp.

"Oh, Bryn, what have you been doing?" she gasped, leading me to the edge of the water.

"We were trying to help her cousin," I muttered, gesturing toward Jasika. "Something went wrong. I ended up in a dream and the Fae attacked me."

Gwen fixed me with a stern look. "You used the book."

"I had to."

She hissed under her breath. Of course, Gwen wouldn't believe that. She wasn't stupid. Still, she helped me to sink down onto my stomach next to the pool. A second later, water sprinkled onto my back through my shirt. I bit back a yelp and pressed my forehead into the grass. Gwen laid her hands on my skin. I waited for the familiar warmth and the spread of relief . . . but they never came.

Gwen snatched her hands away. "Why isn't it working?" she murmured.

I started to push myself up, but before I could, there was a loud *rrrriiiiip* and cold air on my back.

Jasika swore.

"What is it?" I gasped, craning my neck, but I couldn't see whatever it was.

"Bryn, give me your nail." Gwen's voice shook as she spoke.

"It'll burn you," I protested.

The grass crunched as Jasika knelt on my left. "I'll do it."

"Do what?"

Jasika pulled the nail from my hand. "I'm sorry, I'm so sorry, geez I hope you got a tetanus shot."

"What's hap—" I choked back my words as the nail's sharp tip dug into my already aching back, dragging across my sore skin. Something hot bubbled up. I kicked out, knocking her to the ground in a struggle as I jumped to my feet. "The hell do you think you're doing?"

Jasika stared up at me with wide eyes. Her hand holding the nail shook. "I think I'm saving your life, Bryn."

"There was an eye carved into your back," Gwen murmured. "The queen is trying to watch you. To find out where the boys are. It broke through my protections like nothing. Bryn, I told you not to attempt anything you didn't understand!"

"What?" I reached back, pressing my fingers to my stinging skin.

Gwen let out a huff and brushed her fingers against my cheek. "Was it a court Fae that attacked you?"

My jaw throbbed under her touch. My stomach sank. How could she still be so kind to the person who dumped her? Maybe it was the pain, but I felt my eyes stinging with tears because, really, I didn't deserve someone like Gwen in my life. I swallowed and nodded.

"Yeah. The same one from Wales."

"The queen sent him to mark you. It's a great fortune you chose to come here. Jasika just broke the pattern of the eye. You're hidden again."

The implication nearly made my heart stop. If the Fae had hurt me any less, if I had decided to go back to the church, they'd have been able to see the boys through me. Maybe they'd have even figured out how to get in. My knees felt like jelly. I sank back down onto the ground.

"Oh . . . thank you."

"Yeah, uh . . . don't mention it." Jasika grimaced and held the nail back out to me. "Sorry, it's kind of bloody now. Guess that's just what happens." She smiled weakly. I took the nail, wiping it on my shirt. The shirt was pretty much ruined now anyway.

Gwen took a deep breath and gazed down at the water. "She'll have seen us now. We need to build up our defenses. At least we know now just how crafty she is."

"I'll build up my defenses, then," I insisted. "I'll reach out to Mum. I can . . ."

Gwen gazed back at me, a thin sheen of tears swimming in her lily-pad eyes. Water wives. So sensitive. They could feel another person's pain before that person even knew it was there. Dread settled in my stomach like thick, burning coal.

"I'm sorry, Bryn. But if it were truly your mother in your dreams, Mab would never have been able to break my protection and mark you. You cannot trust anything you see there."

My heart skipped a beat. It made sense, of course. It made more sense than my mum suddenly reaching out after all these years to find me. But my brain pushed back against it, like a dog refusing a pill. I didn't want it to be true. I didn't want to smother that little spark of hope. Not yet. I wasn't ready to let go of it. My breath caught in my throat. I struggled to breathe as my eyes and cheeks began to burn.

I must have looked pretty freaked out because Gwen pulled me into her arms. Tears seeped out of my eyes. I swallowed and buried my head in Gwen's shoulder, breathing in the earth and algae scent. Stupid. She'd been watching me all this time, like a ghost at the edge of my dreams, and I hadn't even put it together. For crying out loud, Mab had told me herself that she could do this!

"My poor human," Gwen sighed. "I wish we could do more to fight this evil for you."

I huffed and shook my head. "No. No, I need to do this. She's threatening my brothers."

"She's threatening *humans*," Jasika cut in. "Don't worry. Humans'll be enough to stop her."

Gwen pressed her lips to the top of my head before she let go. It was hard to miss the strange way she considered Jasika. For just a second, I wasn't sure whether it was good or bad.

"Yes. I do believe you will," she murmured. "And I must say, I quite like the humans Bryn has brought to me. It makes me sorry we did not meet sooner." She reached out, taking one of Jasika's hands in hers. "You're quick on your feet, Jasika. Thank you for saving Bryn tonight."

"It . . ." Jasika shifted nervously, but she didn't pull her hand away. "It was my fault we were in danger in the first place. I just wanted to help my cousin."

I heaved an inward sigh of relief as I straightened.

Gwen nodded. "Love is often the birthplace of haste. It is unfortunate, but difficult to condemn." She dropped her hand and turned back to me. "I cannot heal you and undo their magic, but perhaps my sisters can do some small thing to help."

"I'd be grateful for it."

Gwen crept back into the water, and in an instant, she

was gone. Jasika rushed forward, staring at the dark, rippled surface.

"I'll never get over the way she can just disappear like that," she breathed.

"They're sneaky. It's nice to have them on your side," I agreed, staring down at the dirt. It felt like I was sitting at the center of an implosion, everything flying in toward me at once. The dreams. The eye. The book. The queen. If I focused too hard on anything, I'd get hit, and that would take me down.

Jasika settled on the ground next to me, wrapping her arms around her knees. For a long time, the only sound was the insects chirping in the trees and the water lapping against the stones at the water's edge.

"I'm sorry," Jasika murmured. "I guess I got cocky. I really thought we could pull this off."

"So did I." Really, I was the one who ought to be apologizing to her. I was the one who'd honestly thought I knew better than Gwen. But try as I might, I couldn't seem to force my mouth to form the words to apologize.

"Maybe Gwen was right. Maybe we shouldn't have even tried to mess with that stuff." She swallowed. "You think we'll ever be able to leave all this crazy behind?"

I shrugged. "I dunno. I just know I'm . . . getting tired of all of it."

"That makes sense. When this is over, you deserve a vacation."

My lip twitched. "I'll be satisfied with taking off for college."

Jasika opened her mouth to say something when the telltale buzz of a phone cut her off. She whipped it out of her pocket, her thumb jabbing at the screen like a woodpecker. In the harsh blue light of the little device, she looked positively ashen. Then, after a few long seconds, her face split into a wide grin.

"He's awake." She turned to me, tears shimmering in her eyes. "Oh my God, he's . . . We did it!"

And before I could congratulate her, her lips were on mine, soft as rose petals but strong. My heart began to skip all over the place like someone had just zapped it. My brain just sort of shorted out. All I could think was that she must have had a serious caffeine fix before we left because I was sure I could taste something sweet on her lips. Maybe I ought to grab her or kiss her back or do something, but mostly I was trying to wrap my head around the notion that Jasika Witters wasn't straight and she must have read me like a freaking book and why were her lips so soft?

It seemed to last forever, and nothing else mattered. No pain, no fear, no anything . . . and then she pulled away, her eyes still shining. Part of me wanted to reach forward and drag her back into another kiss. She looked so beautiful, cross-lit by the moon and the phone, grinning from ear to ear like joy herself . . . and holy crap.

Fabric swished against grass, and just like that, the moment was over. All the pain and fear and worry slammed into me like a freight truck. I glanced back at the pond to see Gwen setting a bowl of what looked like goopy seaweed on the ground, her face hidden in her sheets of ash-blond hair.

Oh, God, no.

"Gwen," I grunted, pushing myself to my feet.

Gwen rose, her hands folded in front of her. "You should have your friend rub this on your wounds. It will help with the healing."

"Gwen, wait!"

But she didn't. Of course she didn't. She turned, darting into the water like she was rushing down a flight of stairs. I caught one last glimpse of ash-blond hair floating in the water until all that was left of her was a ripple in the dark. The bowl left behind, half in, half out of the water, soiled by the thick mud. I stared at the water, and it felt like a lump of clay had settled in my chest.

Somehow, without trying, I managed to keep hurting her.

Twenty-Two

We didn't talk on the way back, and I couldn't quite decide what made me feel queasier: the memory of Gwen's expression or Jasika's silence. I knew I ought to say something. Anything, really, to fight off the gnawing guilt as she helped me back through the woods and into her car. The radio blared during the short drive back to the church, but for the life of me, I couldn't pinpoint exactly what was playing.

When we reached the church, I wrapped the hospital blanket around my shoulders. Jasika watched me from the driver's seat, her face a blank mask.

"You sure you don't want a little help?"

Of course I did. But if I even gave a hint at that, I'd lose my resolve. I shook my head. "I don't want to raise suspicions."

"I think the big bruise on your cheek might do that."

I touched it and winced. It was still nothing compared to the mess on my back. "I'll figure something out. Thank you for driving me back."

My whole body screamed with every little movement, but

I forced myself to grab the backpack and shuffle toward the church.

"Bryn," Jasika called. I turned back, my stomach wriggling, but she glanced away after a second. "I'm so sorry. I didn't think it would be like that."

"She played us both," I murmured.

"But it was my idea."

"And I went along with it." I took a deep breath. "We're fine, if that's what you're worried about. I'll see you tomorrow, okay?" I turned and began the shuffle to the church.

I didn't hear the car pull away until I reached the door. Clearly, Jasika had decided to watch and make sure I made it in. I crept across the hall, and froze when I heard my father's voice. Oh no. If he knew where I'd been . . .

". . . yes, of course. But I assure you the children were in school when the fire started. The only damage was to the property . . . Yes, I understand. There was an investigation, I'm sure the police can tell you the cause of . . ."

Insurance company, probably. Tension seeped out of my shoulders. He probably didn't even know I was awake. Lucky me.

I gripped the backpack a little tighter and hobbled toward my room. Music blared from behind Ash's and Jake's doors, the dueling songs discordant and unrecognizable against each other.

As soon as I closed the door to my room behind me, the shadeling popped up from the bed, momentarily cheered by my arrival. Until it got a good look at me. Its spindly hands flew to its mouth.

"Missy, what happened?"

I stared at it for a few seconds, feeling the world wobbling around me like a water bed. Of course. The shadeling would want to know what happened.

"Mab." I swallowed and shuffled forward. "I just . . . I want to take a hot bath, that's all."

The little imp shifted from foot to foot, its head bobbing as it wrestled with what to say. An instant later, it hopped into a shadow and was gone. I gathered up my towel, underwear, and some pajamas before I turned and inched my way toward the communal bathroom.

The steady *whoosh* of running water was a welcome sound. I pushed my way in to see the shadeling sprinkling the water with dried lavender buds. Probably stole them from Gooding. I ought to rebuke it for stealing, but the familiar smell tickled my nose, and I couldn't help relaxing just a little bit.

I waited until the shadeling turned around before I stripped down and sank into the warm water. I had to bite back a yelp of pain as the water lit my back on fire again, but a small whimper still got through. In seconds, the sweet-smelling water was already tinged with an unpleasant shade of pink.

Usually, this was the point when the shadelings left me alone, but this little purple one didn't seem interested in doing that. It curled up on the ground next to the tub, toying with the mess of bloody clothes I'd dropped onto the floor. "She got you?"

I took a deep breath and nodded, running my fingers through the water. "Yeah. That's what Gwen said."

Its large, batlike ears drooped. "Mab . . . Mab doesn't like shadelings, Missy."

"Why not?"

The shadeling pulled its little knees to its chest and rested its chin on them. "We're not like other fairies. We weren't born. We were made."

"By whom?" But I already had a good idea.

"Mistress made us."

I closed my eyes. Of course she did. There were so many things Mum had done that she'd never told us about. Of course she'd have the kind of power to manufacture a new kind of fairy.

"How?"

The poor thing's ears twitched. "We were brownies, Missy. We were hurt. Mistress mixed us with the shadows and saved us. But . . . the nasty Unseelies didn't like that she did that. Their nasty queen wanted to kill us." It stooped its shoulders. "Thought she'd be gone by now."

My gut squirmed. No wonder they'd been so loyal to us for so long.

"Do you know why she made you?"

The shadeling shrugged. "Dunno. Can only guess . . . I think it's cause . . . maybe Mistress was a little bit lonely." It shifted, glancing up at me. "I think . . . sometimes Missy is lonely, too."

I stared down at the pink water that swirled around my knees. At the moment, I felt a little cramped. Gwen. Jasika. Dom. I wasn't sure what exactly each of them wanted from me, or how to make any of them happy without upsetting one of the others. I leaned against the edge of the tub, staring down at the little creature. Those bright eyes in the woods had just blinked out like they didn't even care that I was there. Every day I was surrounded by people and creatures who needed something from me, and yet I felt as though I lived in a glass casket, unable to reach any of them.

"The other shadelings aren't coming back, are they?"

It tugged at its ear and stared up at me with such wide, shining eyes that I already knew the answer. "They don't feel safe anymore, Missy."

It was like a punch to the gut. My pains in the ass. My pets. My . . . my friends. I gripped the side of the tub and took a deep breath before the tears could come. "Why are you here, then?"

The shadeling's wide, thin lips twitched into a smile. "I like it with you. And being with humans. Living in your houses and eating your food."

I huffed, pressing my forehead to the side of the tub, but I couldn't help smiling. At least it had a real reason. One that wasn't going to dissolve anytime soon. "And you don't want to go live with the others?" I asked, raising my eyes.

It shook its head until its ears slapped its cheeks. "I'm my own shadeling."

Something warm bloomed in my chest. I reached down to rest my fingers on its head. "I'm not allowed to thank you or give you gifts," I murmured. "But there's gotta be something you want from me. You know we humans like to show our gratitude."

The shadeling pursed its lips, reaching up to rest its hands on mine. After a few seconds, it gave me a sheepish smile. "I want a name, Missy."

"A name?" I blinked, but nodded. "Okay. What sort of name do you want?"

The shadeling frowned for a few seconds before it finally

spoke. "What're those things Missy puts in the cocoa? They're soft and squishy and sweet."

"You mean marshmallows?"

The shadeling's smile could have outshone the sun. It nodded so vigorously I had to pull my hand back. "Yes. Marshmallow. I wanna be Marshmallow."

Marshmallow. Marsh. I grinned, biting the inside of my cheek, then winced at the sudden ache. "All right. Marshmallow it is."

"Marshmallow!" It squeaked, hopping around in glee. Then, it whirled around so quickly it fell to the floor, but it picked itself up again. "Is Missy a boy or a girl?"

"What? A girl," I laughed.

"A girl!" The shadeling . . . Marshmallow tittered. "A girl. I wanna be a girl, too. Can I be a girl?"

"You can be whatever you want, Marsh," I assured her.

Marshmallow looked so excited she didn't know what to do with herself, so she settled with throwing her arms around her torso and rocking back and forth in unbridled joy. My little shadeling. The only one I had left.

At least until the doorknob jiggled. The shadeling yelped and disappeared into the shadows, but I didn't have the same escape. *Shit!* I thought I'd locked it. Before I could think of what to do, the door swung open and Jake walked in, a towel draped over his arm. All I could think to do was cover my chest.

His face drained of color as he stared at me, and I didn't even have to guess what he was looking at. I could still feel the angry stinging on my back.

"Don't tell anyone," I hissed.

His eyes flicked to my face, and for a moment, it looked like he might start to cry. I shifted, shimmying down deeper into the water, though it wasn't going to change the clearly pink tone.

"Bryn, what have you done?"

My heart hammered in my chest. *"Please,"* I begged. "Don't tell anyone, Jake."

He fidgeted, and he looked like he might say something more, but he didn't say anything aloud. He just nodded and tiptoed back out of the bathroom, shutting the door behind him.

I pushed myself out of the tub as quickly as I could with my back throbbing as it did. As I reached for my nightgown, Marshmallow reappeared, holding up a first aid kit. I gritted my teeth.

By the time we finished, a lot of that wonderful warmth from the tub had already seeped out of me. I rose, stiff as an old tin man, and changed into my nightgown.

As I pushed myself to my feet, I saw that Marshmallow had gathered my ruined clothes into a pile.

"What should I do with these?" she asked.

"Just toss them," I said, shuffling to the door. "And I'll see if we have any marshmallows in the kitchen later."

The shadeling shook its head, ears flapping. "No, Missy. You should go straight to sleep."

"Not yet. I need to talk to my brother."

Twenty-Three

I knocked twice and pushed the door open. Jake sat on his bed, his shoulders slumped, feet tapping against the stone floor. In that moment, he looked six years old again, devastated that he didn't have anyone to bring with him to Muffins for Mom Day at school.

I sighed and shuffled into the room, kicking aside the flotsam and jetsam of used clothes until I sank down onto the bed next to him. "It's weird. Usually Ash is with you."

"Ash is still being an idiot." Jake looked up, shoulders hunched. "And you know what? So are you."

So, we weren't going to take our time with this, were we? I cleared my throat. "About what you saw—"

"You're killing yourself."

That might not have hurt if it had been a little further off the mark. This was the part where I should have argued that I knew what I was doing, that it was fine . . . but I couldn't scrape together enough energy for the lie. "I never meant for it to turn out this way."

"But it did!" Jake turned to me, his eyes wide and red

rimmed. "It's them, right? The fairies? The ones who took Mom and hurt Dad?"

At this point, it was going to be pretty useless to try to hide it from him. I counted to ten, fingers curling into fists. "Jake, I'm just trying to keep everyone safe."

"Right," he snorted, clenching his jaw and shaking his head. "Like that matters. The second they show up, it's just you trying to keep everything from us like everyone does."

That stung more than it should have.

"Jake—"

"Doesn't it bother you that Ash and I don't have any memories of Mom? Not one." Tears shone in his eyes, threatening to spill over the edge and onto his burning cheeks. "It's like you and Dad have one reality and Ash and I have another. And you don't even care that we're left out of it because you're still so focused on that place and those things!"

He sucked in a shuddering breath and scrubbed his face with one hand, smearing the tears over his face. I reached out and wrapped my arm around his shoulders. He felt like stone under a soft layer of threadbare cotton. It took a few tugs before, at last, he relented enough to let me pull him to my side. He didn't fit the way he had a few years ago. Too tall. Too strong. Everything was changing and I didn't know how to fix it.

Jake sniffled. "You can't go, too," he whispered.

I rested my chin against his head and squeezed his arm. "I'm not going anywhere, Jake."

"You're going to college," he bit out. "You're just going to ditch us as soon as you can. And then I'm going to be alone."

"No," I insisted. "You've got Ash, remember?"

"Ash barely talks to me anymore."

Right. I barely even managed to greet him in the hall these days. How much harder did that have to be for Jake?

"What's going on with him?"

Jake clenched his jaw. "So, you suddenly care."

"Jake, I *do* care."

"Just not enough to tell me anything." He sniffed. "We were working on a project together. It didn't go the way he wanted. So he decided to keep doing it on his own. Then the house was gone. He's pissed. About everything. And you know what? So am I."

I thought back to the lost kid curled up in the hall, holding a box of ruined belongings. No. Not just a lost kid. These days, Ash was like a wounded animal who'd bite you even if you tried to help.

"I'm sorry this has happened. Can I ask what the project was?"

"No." Jake ground his teeth, glaring at the wall.

"Is he getting into fights?"

"I dunno." He paused. "He let me bring him some ointment, though, so I guess it's getting better."

I gave him a weak smile. Maybe it wasn't too late to start bridging this gap. "You know, when I was just a kid and got scared, Mum would sing this song—"

"Don't you think it's a little late to start talking to me about her?" Jake snapped, and it was like a slap to the face. My breath caught in my throat. This wasn't my Jake. He was the quiet one. He was the sensible one.

What was happening to my family?

"I . . ." I didn't know what to say. Maybe he was right. Maybe it was too late. But I had to try. "Look, Jake, even when I leave, things are going to be better. Safer. I'll make sure of it."

"Unless you do something stupid," he snapped. "We know you've been doing this for years, Bryn. We just never told because . . . because we felt safer knowing you were out there. But now we're going to lose you just like Mom. We just want all of this to end already!"

It was like whiplash. Jake was upset about me going to college, about Ash, about the danger, about Mum, and God even knew what else. My head spun just trying to keep up with it.

I took a deep breath. "I can't promise it's not going to get scary. These Fae . . . They're dangerous. I don't want you or Ash going anywhere near them. But I'm going to stop them from coming for us again. And then Ash is going to pull his head out of his butt, and everything's going to be good, okay?"

Jake bit his lip, but he nodded as he pressed his wet face to my shoulder. I wrapped my other arm around him.

"I know Ash is being a butt right now, but we're all going through some stuff. And I'm still here." I paused. There was a niggling itch in the back of my brain. I was going to be gone this time next year. Dad would never let the boys work with Gooding. Not now.

We sat like that for what felt like ages until, at last, Jake pulled away and curled up against his pillow. My cue to leave.

When all this was over, I'd find a way to make it up to him. I'd teach them everything they needed to know.

* * *

SLEEPING THAT NIGHT wasn't easy. A couple of months ago, my life had been so much easier. Now Ash was angry with everyone. Jake was terrified. Gwen was hurt. And I had Dom and Jasika to muddy the waters even more.

My thoughts circled around to that over and over and every time, all I could do was bury my face in my pillow and try not to groan too loudly. I hadn't known Jasika even liked girls. Was she a lesbian? Bi? Pan? Did it even matter? It was just a kiss. A stupid kiss, and she'd only done it because she got good news and I happened to be there.

And yet, all I could feel were butterflies and the echo of her warmth on my skin. I really, really wanted to love that kiss, but all I could feel was guilt. There was no unseeing Gwen's face in that moment.

I sucked in a deep breath and grabbed my glass of water.

"Gwen," I whispered into the water, willing her to hear me. Willing it to work. The seconds ticked by, and there wasn't so much as a ripple, no matter how much I wanted one. I scrambled through my backpack, dropping an Altoid and a hardened butterscotch candy in. Still, even as they dissolved, nothing.

Tiny claws scratched against the stone floor.

"M-Missy," Marshmallow said in a small voice. "The water wives will be hiding, Missy. I think the nasty queen saw them before your friend broke the mark on your back."

"And they have to protect themselves," I murmured. I wrapped my arms around my middle and squeezed my eyes shut, but it didn't stop the feeling of glass tearing up my insides. I wouldn't have the chance to explain. Gwen was never going to forgive me.

Tiny arms hugged me with a strength that defied their small size. But all that did was squeeze the tears out of me.

"It's okay, Missy," Marshmallow whispered. "Miss Gwen will come back. You'll see."

But what if she didn't? Had I finally managed to break her heart after all this time? My oldest friend in this country, and she probably thought I'd gone and dragged some girlfriend to the lake to make out in front of her. Oh God. Oh God, I was going to be . . .

The bin appeared almost instantly below my mouth, and just in time. I felt the cool touch of spindly fingers on my forehead and the base of my neck. Made it all a little bit more bearable. But not by much.

Twenty-Four

The next morning, I stuffed the backpack with a water bottle and Advil. Marshmallow watched me with wide, glowing eyes. "Missy should be resting," she warned.

Right. Lazing around the church agonizing about what had happened was about as helpful as a neon light blazing HEY DAD! FATHER GOODING! GUESS WHAT I'VE BEEN UP TO! Sounded about as appealing as sitting in a stiff plastic chair for seven hours with my back throbbing away.

"Yeah, well, not much of an option," I huffed. "I'll be back when school hours are over."

The shadeling wrung her thin fingers, but she didn't make any move to stop me. She did, however, follow me to the kitchen as I raided the fridge for some milk and a can of spinach, helping herself to the crusty jar of marmalade that had probably been sitting in the door for years. Did shadelings stress-eat? Something to wonder later.

When I stepped out of the room, however, it was into an occupied hallway. Ash shuffled toward his room, a blanket pulled around his shoulders, a bowl of oatmeal in his hand. He looked awful. Dark bags hung under his eyes, made sharper by his pale face. I doubted I looked much better.

For a moment, we stared at each other. It was pretty clear we were both skipping school that day. Neither of us could snitch on the other without outing ourselves. Nothing to say. Nothing to discuss. He'd made it pretty clear he didn't want anything to do with any of us. But he was still my brother. I had to try.

I almost remarked on his appearance. He was clearly sick. Was it a cold? The flu? Or was he just not sleeping well? That felt like exactly the thing he'd ignore and storm into his room over.

Then again, that was true of basically everything, wasn't it?

"Jake misses you," I settled on instead. "You should talk to him. And Gooding keeps vitamin C tablets in his office if you need to ask for any."

Ash stared at me for a long moment before he slipped into his room and closed the door behind him. I really wasn't sure what else I'd expected. I swallowed my disappointment and continued on outside.

The air nipped at my cheeks as I trudged toward the woods. It was hard not to focus on the painful tug of the bandages on my stinging back. Harder still to ignore my surroundings. The whole forest blazed with leaves reddening and browning as autumn stripped them of their vitality. Everything went up in flames, these days.

Gwen's pond appeared to be as deserted as Marshmallow had said it would be. Even after I prepared the milk and greens, there was nothing. No ripple, no blond head. No Gwen. I leaned out over the water, my heart in my throat as I whispered. "Gwen. Please, I need to talk to you."

Nothing. My stomach turned as I curled into my side on the grass. I wasn't going to be able to make it up to her until all of this was over. Freaking perfect. I swallowed and choked out what I should have said last night.

"I'm sorry, Gwen."

A thousand horrible scenarios itched in the back of my brain. Situations where things with Gwen, things with Jasika, all this chaos didn't resolve itself. It was Mab's fault. It was Mum's fault . . . but mostly it was my fault. If it wasn't for me and the damn book, I wouldn't be stuck in this situation.

The itching in the back of my brain worsened, an urge I could only ignore for so long until, at last, I couldn't stop myself. I pulled the book out again and tried reading it, knowing full and well that nothing was going to stick in my mind . . . until something did. When I came to the knowledge spell I'd used and the healing spell Jasika and I had cast on William, the words just . . . stayed. They were still nonsense, but they didn't slide like oil back out of my brain. Was that how it worked? I needed to cast a spell in order to remember it? Was this how it had worked for Mum?

"Even now, you continue to invite harm to yourself."

Gwen! I scrambled to my feet. Gwen stood in the pond, her shift floating out behind her. I wanted to run to her, grab her hands, apologize for everything, but something deep inside told me that I wasn't allowed to do that. Not today.

"I'm sorry." I licked my lips and fumbled for the right words. "I forgot to bring you bread."

Gwen folded her hands in front of her. "We both know that isn't important now."

"What I mean to say, um . . ." I ran my hands through

my hair. God, why did I suck so much? "I didn't know Jasika would kiss me. It caught me off guard, too."

"Bryn."

"I know it looks bad, okay? I break up with you because I said I didn't want to date anyone my last year in town and suddenly you see me kissing her right in front of your pond. I swear, I didn't want to hurt you. I would never want to—"

Gwen held up a hand. Maybe there was some magic because, like a cork in a wine bottle, the words stopped right there. Gwen took a deep breath.

"I am not human," she murmured. "I understand this."

"That's not what I meant."

Gwen stared down at the water, her pale hair falling forward, half shielding her face.

"My sisters have retreated from the threat. I will do what I must to protect them."

It felt like a snake had curled around my lungs, tightening and tightening until I could barely breathe. I stumbled forward until my boots began to sink into the mud.

"What does that mean?"

Gwen sucked in a shuddering breath. This close, I could see the faint red that lined her lily-pad eyes. She pressed trembling fingers against my cheek.

"It means goodbye, Bryn." She brushed a lock of hair behind my cheek, like a dashing romance movie hero. "If all goes well, we might not see each other for some time. Trust in your humans. They have good hearts. And extend my apologies to them as well."

"Please don't go," I choked. My vision swam. I couldn't have possibly fucked this up worse, could I?

Gwen shook her head. "You're giving your heart to someone else. This should be easier for you."

"I don't want you to leave."

Her lips twitched. And, as she had in the summer days we used to spend together, she drew closer, her lips barely touching mine in a kiss as gentle as the small current of her pond.

"I also have a family to look after, Bryn," she murmured. "Be careful."

My eyes slid shut as she pressed closer, nibbling softly at my lip. And then she was gone. I was alone, shivering and standing in a pond in October.

Numbly, I stumbled back to the shore and lay against the grass. Tears came and went and came again.

Somewhere around noon, the texts came. All from Dom.

> **Dom:** Bryn, are you not in school today?
> **Dom:** Jasika said you got hurt last night. Are you okay?
> **Dom:** Bryn, text me back.
> **Dom:** I'm going to swing by the church after school.
> **Dom:** If you don't reply I'm going to assume you're
> dying and I'm going to react accordingly.

It took way more energy than it should have to shoot back a reply.

> **Bryn:** Alive. Not at church.

A few seconds passed. I almost turned back to the book before my phone buzzed again.

> **Dom:** Ok so Jasika caught me up. We're coming over
> tonight. I've got research to share.

I sighed. Looked like it was time to face them.

Twenty-Five

I wanted to forget. I wanted to pretend the last twenty-four hours hadn't happened, but every time I saw a puddle of water or a slice of bread, it slammed back into me. Gwen was gone because of my stupidity. For just a little while longer, I refused to dwell on it at all. Beyond just putting it out of my mind. I was determined to stop thinking about it altogether. I'd need to set alarms to wake me before I could fall into too deep a sleep and risk entering Mab's realm again. Add to the mix the old bottle of caffeine pills tucked into the medicine cabinet in the kitchen and I could stay awake during the day, at least. In a few days, it would all be over.

Jasika showed up at the convent with her laptop, a two-liter bottle of strawberry soda, and a bag of that pre-popped popcorn they sold in the gas station. Ash and Jake gawked at her, as if I'd never had a friend over before . . . which, to be fair, I hadn't.

"I brought you something for your back," she said, pulling a Tupperware container with some sort of thick, grayish goop out of her backpack. "Put it on after you've showered tonight. Make sure the skin's dry or it won't stick."

"Thanks."

I set the Tupperware on the floor by the bed. She set the laptop on the little bedside table and crawled onto the flat mattress. I sat beside her, and it was like sitting next to a space heater. I couldn't help but feel horribly, painfully aware of her presence. How close she was. She smelled like jasmine body lotion with the herby undertones of sage and echinacea. Probably what was in the poultice.

She took a deep breath and smoothed her hands over her jeans. "About yesterday, I wanted to say sorry. I wasn't really thinking about boundaries and, um . . . I didn't mean to make you feel . . ."

"It's fine." I picked at the old sheets and tried not to look directly at her. "I was just surprised is all."

"Yeah, but most people ask someone on a date. They don't just grab someone and go for it. It's not really, you know, classy or . . . um . . ."

I blinked and forced myself to glance up. Yeah. Still looked like Jasika. No glamour that I could detect. Which meant this was real. She was really sitting here in my room saying that. My insides hummed to life like someone had just let a bunch of butterflies loose inside.

"You want to date me?"

Jasika let out a little puff of breath and tucked her hair behind her ears. "I mean, yeah? I just figured you weren't interested. You seemed pretty hung up on Gwen."

I thought back to Gwen, and guilt stung at my gut. I'd broken things off with her because I didn't want to be tied down while I was getting ready for college. And now here came Jasika. It was hypocritical how much I liked the idea of it. Just going to a coffee shop or a movie with her. A normal, human thing.

I licked my lips. The words danced just on the edge of my tongue. Last chance to back down.

"I really screwed things up with Gwen. And I might screw things up with you, too. But . . . I'm interested."

Jasika's smile lit up the whole room. "Okay," she said, nodding. "How about after Halloween? When everything's over and we know for sure the town is safe, let's go see a movie together. Just the two of us."

"Okay." And I couldn't help returning her smile. It was so stupid. We had bigger things to deal with, but it all felt so far away. "So, I guess we can just put things on hold and pick up then."

"If you want to be all business about it, sure," Jasika said.

Still, within an hour or so, I'd curled up on the bed close enough that my shoulder was actually touching Jasika's while some Korean drama played on the screen. Sitting close enough to smell her jasmine body lotion brought the butterflies back to life, but the vipers in my belly kept fighting them. It took more effort than it should have to focus on the show when my mind wanted to pick apart this new problem. What did Jasika want? Did she want grand, romantic gestures, bouquets of roses delivered on horseback, declarations of love in public, wearing ball gowns? Or was this, right here, right now, eating junk food and watching TV together what she wanted?

Did I even know how to be a normal human girlfriend? Or was this something everyone struggled with?

I watched her out of the corner of my eye. The sight of her made it a little easier to push the fear and doubt out of the way. Something about her. The way she bit her lip to hold back a laugh when the heroine did something embarrassing. The way she kept reaching up to toy with one of her dark coils of hair. I just sort of wanted to grab her and kiss her again. Was this the time? She'd initiated before. Were we at a point where I could do it, too, whenever I wanted? Or was the situation still not right? Would I ever be able to tell the difference?

When the second episode went to credits, there came a distant knock, echoing faintly from the end of the hall. I sat up a little straighter. The hell? Had one of the boys invited someone over?

Before I could say or do anything about it, Marshmallow popped up onto the edge of the bed in typical shadeling fashion. And in typical human fashion, Jasika shrieked, one hand clapping over her mouth to muffle the sound while the other dug in her pocket for her cross.

"No no no!" I cried, pulling it out of her hand to toss it on the bed. "This is Marshmallow. She's friendly."

"She—what?" Jasika stared at me like I'd just started speaking in tongues.

Marsh hung by the foot of the bed, toying with her ear as she glanced between the two of us. I sighed and held out a hand to her. She kept one eye on Jasika but scampered forward, tucking herself into my side.

"She's a friend," I repeated, trying not to be obvious as I rubbed my palm. "This is one of the shadelings. Marsh used to be a brownie. She's been with my family for about a decade."

Jasika jabbed a finger at Marshmallow. "Wait . . . you're telling me you have one of them living with you, and you still go out hunting fairies in the woods?"

"Only the nasties," Marshmallow insisted. And I was

going to add to that when I heard voices, muffled but drawing closer. *Shit.*

"Hide!" I hissed.

"But Missy, it's only—"

"Hide!"

And, to her credit, she did. With a bit of a pout, Marshmallow jumped right into a shadow. Jasika jumped, eyes wide.

Knock knock knock!

I scrambled off the bed and pulled the door open to see . . . oh. Dom stood in the hall, holding a paper grocery bag in one arm. With, of course, both the boys hovering behind him. Both boys. Together. I couldn't help smiling at that.

Ash scowled, arms crossed. It might have actually looked serious if he didn't still look sleep-deprived and only half-recovered from his cold. "Bryn, is this your boyfriend?"

"No, and go away," I snapped.

Ash rolled his eyes and skulked off. Jake smirked. Typical little punk.

Dom cleared his throat and stepped into the room. Right. He'd said Jasika had told him everything. Apparently, that also included the private stuff.

Jasika rose and stepped forward, pulling Dom into a hug. "Hey, I'm glad you made it," she said, then shot me a side look. "I think we can all agree we need a night to just chill out. As a team."

Dom returned the hug with one arm. I bit my cheek and stuffed my hands into my pockets. Had to get it over with quick like ripping off a Band-Aid.

"Hey, um . . . I'm sorry about us not telling you about

what we were doing at the hospital," I managed. "And I know Jasika probably already told you, but Mab is still around."

Dom looked me up and down, his expression carefully blank before he stepped forward, wrapped an arm around my shoulders, and gave a tight squeeze. "Okay. Quick download. I'll tell you what I found, and then tonight we're taking a break from all the fairy stuff. Call it a mental-health break."

He set down his bag and pulled out a half-empty bag of pretzels and a bottle of clear vodka. Jasika's eyes bugged open.

"Dom, you can't bring that in here. This is a church."

"This is a convent," he pointed out. "Besides. They keep wine in the church." He helped himself to a plastic cup and poured himself a little cocktail of vodka and strawberry soda before offering it to me. Jasika shot me a "don't you dare" look, and I almost didn't drink it . . . but hey. It's just days, now, until Samhain. Smoke 'em if you got 'em. I took the glass and sipped. It went down like strawberry-flavored lighter fluid. I coughed but went back for a second sip.

Jasika primly turned down the offer for a cup of her own, very pointedly sticking to her strawberry soda.

Dom sprawled out next to us, one arm propped up on the bed.

"So I was right. I had read about that banner somewhere. The night after the fire." He leveled a finger at me. "It represented the Pendragon family."

I snorted. "I think you wound up on the Medieval Times website."

"No, it's real. I triple-checked it."

I took another sip from my drink, cringed, and took a deep breath. "Okay. But if what you're saying is true, then apparently I'm descended from King Arthur. Who wasn't real."

"I dunno. Lot of folks think he was based on real people."

"He didn't have any kids when he died."

"Actually, he did," Jasika cut in with a frown. "According to the story, King Arthur died at the hand of his bastard son Mordred."

My head felt suddenly light and swimmy. And it wasn't just from the vodka. I licked my lips. "Well, that's well and good, but I'm pretty sure Mordred died, too. And I'm not seeing him. I'm seeing a woman."

"Come on, you've got to know the story," Dom pressed.

I did. And I didn't want to think about it. Because if I thought about it, it would make way too much sense. Too much sense if Mordred went around and had a couple of bastard children of his own that none of the storytellers knew about. But Mab could find them, if she really wanted to.

Jasika fixed me with a level stare and shifted to face me fully. "Mordred's mother was Arthur's half-sister. The witch Morgan le Fay. Or Morgause. A Mor-sister, anyway. But if it was Morgan, well, you don't get a name like 'le Fay' if you don't deal with the Fae."

I closed my eyes and took a deep breath. Right. Well. I'd asked for it. I wished Mum was here. I wished I could just walk down the hall and ask her if all of this was true because it sounded absurd.

"Bryn, if that's true, you have the potential to have incredible power," Jasika said softly. "Think about it. The firstborn, that's always a big deal especially in the really old traditions—"

"I'll look into it, okay?" I ran my fingers through my hair.

If my ancestor was Morgan le Fay, then she was one of the most famous witches in mythology. How was I going to get us out of a bargain struck by someone as powerful as that? I took a big gulp of my drink, gagged a little on the aftertaste, and shook my head. "Thanks, Dom. Let's just . . . let's just have a normal night. I'll deal with all of that in the morning."

Dom and Jasika exchanged a glance. We relocated the laptop to the floor and started the next episode, all the while Jasika explained to Dom under her breath what he'd missed in the first two. I kept sipping at the soda and vodka, watching the actors wander on and off the screen as the sting on my palm faded slowly away.

Eventually, the subtitles went fuzzy. I glanced over at Jasika and Dom, both perfectly content as they munched on popcorn and pretzels, their eyes glued to the drama unfolding on the little screen. At some point, Marshmallow had crawled out of a shadow and into Dom's lap, her ears perked as she watched the screen, too. The room smelled like strawberries and popcorn and jasmine, and everything was . . . absolutely perfect. As perfect as it had ever been or would ever be. And it was the sort of thing that filled me up with that warm, fuzzy feeling a person could spend their whole life chasing. Which was probably why I had the guts to close my eyes and just rest my head on Jasika's shoulder.

The dark fog of sleep began to form at the edge of my mind. Without meaning to, I slid into that gray place between sleeping and waking, where I could still hear the hum of the show even as I felt myself slipping deeper into sleep.

Into *her* realm.

And that was all it took for me to kick myself back out of

it. I started with a gasp, and the world jerked into focus like a lens being flipped on a projector. Jasika's arm wound around me, holding me firm. I was safe there. Just for a little while I could let myself be safe.

I sighed, relaxing against her again, when Dom spoke up. "Hey, are you and Bryn . . ."

Jasika's arm tightened around my middle. "We're trying it out."

"So . . . are you lesbians?"

I couldn't help the loud snort that slipped out. Muzzily, I pushed myself up and stared at him. He looked a little embarrassed to have asked. Sweet lamb.

"Not all girls who like girls are lesbians," I pointed out. "I mean . . . I like guys, too. At least, I have no problem being attracted to them. I just haven't dated any."

Dom arched a brow. "So you're bi."

"Last I checked." I gave him a little smirk and sipped my strawberry vodka. "Or maybe pan? I dunno. Depends on who you talk to, I guess."

"Is there a thing as Fae-sexual?" Dom asked.

"Oh, shut up!" I leaned against the bed and gave him a shove with my foot.

Dom grinned and turned to Jasika. "So where do you land here, hm?"

"I'm still figuring it out." Jasika raised her glass in a mock toast. "But hey, here's to having this conversation on hallowed ground."

"Some old nun's rolling in her grave. Probably been doing it since Bryn moved in." He waggled his brows at me.

I grabbed a piece of popcorn and turned, pegging Dom with it. "Okay, what about you?"

"What about me what?"

"Come on," Jasika said, nudging him. "We both basically came out to you in, like, the space of two minutes. Your turn. And remember, we're in a church, so no lying."

"Adjacent to a church." Dom knocked back the last of his drink. "And you've probably never heard of it."

"Should I just call out hetero and kill the anticipation?" Jasika laughed.

"You could." Dom grinned. "But you wouldn't exactly be right. I mean, I like the ladies, sure, but I'm ace."

Jasika's brows furrowed. I tried to wrack my brain for what the hell that was. Somehow, I doubted he meant he was an ace fighter pilot. I'd heard the phrase somewhere before. "Ace as in . . ."

"Asexual." Dom prepared himself another drink, his eyes focused entirely on his cup. He moved a little too fluidly. Probably a good idea to cut him off soon. "I just don't really get attracted to anyone. Not like that, anyway."

"Wait, like . . . like anyone?" Jasika stammered. "Are you sure?"

"Pretty sure, cause Lord knows I've tried." Dom shrugged and leaned against the wall, sipping from his cup.

"But you flirted with me," I pointed out.

"I flirt with everyone." Dom winked and shrugged.

"Are you sure? I mean, have you tried with, um . . . anyone?" Jasika asked.

Dom looked like he might bust into giggles. "Oh yeah. And I'm willing to bet I'm the only non-virgin in this room." He glanced between us, and it felt as though he was waiting for one of us to challenge that. Of course, we didn't. He nodded. "Thought so."

"Wait . . . why have sex, then, if you weren't even attracted to your partner?"

Dom took a deep breath, swirling the pink drink in his cup thoughtfully. "I dunno. Why do you eat a breakfast taco when you're not really hungry? It's still good. You still like it. Even if you weren't craving it. Wow," Dom laughed. "Definitely not the conversation I was expecting to have tonight. Guess we're lucky nobody walked in on us right then."

"So sex is like a taco to you." Jasika smirked at him.

"I never pretended to be good at metaphors. Why do you think I have a B in English?" Dom took one last swig of his drink and plopped the cup lip-down on the floor. "Anyway, if everything goes to hell, at least I can say I didn't die a virgin."

Well, that was a real mood killer. Nothing like thinking about our impending deaths to suck the fun out of a party. So if we died, what could I say about myself? I did a good job keeping the boys fed? I could knit? Apparently I was descended from a king and a witch who were related, so . . . gross. Not exactly something for the tombstone.

I glanced at the screen and sighed. "Is it just me, or does it feel like the mood for Korean TV has passed?"

"Well, since we're all here . . ." Jasika pulled her knees up to her chest. "I guess we could always talk about Halloween. The bendith said Samhain. Same night, this year. So that confirms it, right?"

Samhain. Right. I cleared my throat. "There's more than that, though. The water wives are gone. They retreated to protect themselves."

Dom and Jasika sat silently for a long moment, each of them staring down at the floor.

"This is my fault." Jasika scrubbed a hand over her face.

"No." I clenched my jaw. "She's got to do her own thing and we've got to respect that."

"But with Samhain so close—" Dom began.

"If she thought they could really help, she'd have stayed."

Unease settled like smog around us. Gwen had taught us all these spells, all these ways to fight back. But now she wasn't here to fight with us.

"Well, obviously we need to figure out where the Unseelie plan to attack," Jasika muttered, one hand reaching out to me. I breathed a deep sigh and took it. Hell of a way to end an evening. "And then figure out how to keep everyone in there safe. Just in case. Bryn, maybe you should look into . . . you know. The witch stuff."

"Even if it turns out to be true, it's not like I can suddenly become some master spell-caster overnight," I said. "Look, my specialty is just knowing what to throw at them to make them go away."

"Maybe we can get some of the local wild fairies to help," Dom suggested. "I mean, this is their home, too. A lot of them won't be cool with the Unseelie."

"You can try." I rubbed the back of my neck. "I'd rather not count on the cavalry showing up here."

"Then I guess we should coordinate our costumes now," Dom said. "I'm calling one of those giant cards. Ace of spades."

I forced myself to smile, but it felt like more of a grimace. Time to say a eulogy for that warm, cozy feeling. We wouldn't be getting that again until everything was over.

Twenty-Six

It took longer than it should have to settle down that night. Somehow, in spite of Mab and the Unseelies, it was Gwen keeping me up. That and the happy butterflies-on-acid feeling I got in my gut when Jasika smiled at me. It felt wrong, being excited about something like that right now. Especially when it hurt someone else.

Of course, maybe it was the lingering vodka spinning around in my head that kept me up.

After I'd showered and had my helping of the night's casserole (some ungodly combination of tuna, chipotle, and spaghetti), I sat in the room, my nightgown pulled up to my shoulders, while Marshmallow smeared Jasika's goopy poultice on my back. It hardly even stung anymore.

"Missy's going to have an awful scar," the shadeling muttered.

"Guess that's no more string bikinis for me." I checked my phone, confirmed no new messages, and drummed my fingers against the stiff mattress. Marshmallow set the now-empty Tupperware on the bed and expertly bandaged my back again. She was becoming quite the little nurse.

As I rolled my nightgown back down, my mind wandered to Samhain. It was so close, but we didn't know Mab's plan. We didn't know how to stop her. There was too much that depended on us succeeding here. If we could stop her, the boys could feel safe. Gwen could come home. Maybe Dad would even get better.

My better judgment told me to leave it be, but I was rapidly running out of options. I hauled my backpack up onto the bed and pulled out Mum's book.

"You shouldn't do this," Marshmallow insisted, scuttling back and forth across the floor.

I flexed my fingers and grabbed my nail, drawing an invisible circle around myself in the air. After all the group spells, it felt strange to draw a circle alone. I probably needed Jasika or Gwen's skill to guide me, but at the moment, I was alone. And whatever happened, I didn't want Fae magic getting out of this room.

"I know who she is now, Marsh, and I know what she can do. I can protect myself."

"That's fighting her in her territory!" the shadeling insisted. "That's what she likes. She likes to put people where it's easy for her to win."

"As it is, I think she may win anyway. And my friends . . ." My heart tightened. "I've got more people to protect now."

"But we shadelings know her. We fear her. Better to stay safe. Stay hidden!"

"That hasn't worked!" I took a deep breath and lowered my voice. "Samhain is almost here and look how close she was able to get! Our home is gone. The water wives are in hiding."

Marshmallow shifted from foot to foot, tugging at her ear. I turned back to the book, Mum's words ringing in my ears. Gwella. Gwybodaeth. Freuddwyth. I wanted so badly to cling to the threadbare hope that it had been Mum reaching out to me. My hands shook as I turned the pages.

Dreaming. Healing. Those had led to stumbling around in her territory and a life saved. Now it was time for knowledge. And if I ran into Mab again, well, I was ready.

I paused at the page for *Gwybodaeth. Knowledge.* My heart fluttered in my chest. Marshmallow scrambled onto the bed next to me, taking my sleeve.

"Missy. If you see the dark queen, you mustn't let yourself fall into her traps," the shadeling warned. "It's the same rules as for the Faelands. Eat nothing. Drink nothing. And if they invite you to dance, you must run away. She tricked you once before."

I rested my hand on the shadeling's back.

"It'll be fine. I promise." I gave her a tight smile. "And I'll feel better knowing you're looking out for me. If it looks like I'm in trouble, wake me up."

Marshmallow nodded and took a few small steps back, wringing her long fingers. I took a deep breath and leaned forward, staring down at the pages. The words came more easily this time. I almost didn't even have to think or focus. It felt like they were just using me, blurting out entirely on their own . . .

And then I wasn't in my room anymore.

These weren't the Welsh woods. They had a distinctly American smell about them. Different trees. Different plants.

"Bryn." An unfamiliar voice floated on the air.

I turned, leaves crunching under my feet. Dove-gray silk floated between the trees as a willowy form swam into view, her dark hair dancing behind her. My heart leapt into my throat.

"Gwen said I shouldn't trust you," I announced, clenching my fists. "But it's time we talk."

The figure raised one arm, her pale fingers stretching out between the dark trees. "You will lose," she said, but her words came like a distant shout. I started back, heart in my throat.

"I can't. I have people to protect. Tell me now. Are you Morgan le Fay? Or Morgause? Did you promise our family to Mab?"

Her lips moved, but the words seemed to come from the faint hiss of the breeze.

"I am Morgana, child, called Morgan. And I hate that trickster woman as much as anyone. I did not know what I'd done until it was too late. I wanted a throne for my children. Not chains."

It was impossible. But something about the hatred in her voice cemented it as surreal truth in my mind. The sister of King Arthur. Her son, Mordred, who'd killed him and changed the fate of the entire kingdom, maybe the world. My head swam with questions. Did that make us royalty, or just a line of illegitimate bastards spawned from killers? Had Mum known? Had Dad? Whatever the what-ifs, the reality of what this meant settled in front of me like a puzzle piece finally fitting into place. King Arthur and Morgan le Fay were real.

I was their descendant.

And Morgan had royally screwed us all.

I balled my hands into fists. "If that's true, help me now. How can I protect our family from her?"

In the creak of the tree branches in the wind, I heard her response.

"Hide."

"No. I have people to protect."

The figure dipped her head until dark hair fanned over her face, hiding it from view.

"Then you will have to salvage victory from loss. You could be more powerful than any of them."

"Because I'm the firstborn?"

"What else do fairies want?"

My heart pounded and, in the dreamscape, it seemed to thrum all around me. That was how fairy tales went. Rumpelstiltskin. Rapunzel. It was always the firstborn lost in the bargain. That had to be at least as powerful as twins, if not the very thing Mab had been after all along.

"She was after me all along."

The fire. The changelings. All of it was because of me. But why? Couldn't she have just kidnapped me with a drone? Why the game?

"Mab likes things just so. You didn't suit her purposes before."

I caught my breath. "So what? If I make sure I'm not what she wants, she leaves us alone?"

"She will mold you. It's what she did to my son."

Right. Mordred. One of the great villains of British mythology. Just thinking that I was descended from that particular figure made my skin crawl. But I was nothing like him . . . was I?

I swallowed. "So does this mean a firstborn is more valuable to her than twins? She might leave the boys alone?"

Morgan raised her head again and moved her lips, but nothing came out. Then, like a light flickering, the figure disappeared.

"Come back!" I spun around, my hand going to my throat. No nail. In Mab's territory. And with my own ancestor basically guaranteeing Mab would win. Not a great start.

I took a deep breath and forced myself to wander into the ancient forest. Each tree towered over me, marred by that strange, scribbled symbol carved into their trunks. And each one burned for it. There were no flames, but I could feel the heat and energy and power radiating from them. I took a deep breath, brushing my fingers against the torn bark. Something like an electric pulse shot through my fingers. I yelped and jumped back, heart hammering.

"Dangerous to touch that, sweetheart," Mum breathed.

I whirled around, holding my burned hand to my chest. Mum smiled at me and tilted her head. Leaves tumbled from her dark waves of hair, fluttering to the ground. My heart skipped a beat. Mum. Maybe she could help.

"What does it mean?" I asked.

Mum frowned, reaching over my shoulder. For a moment, I thought for sure she was going to touch the symbol, too, and I almost grabbed her hand, but she stopped just shy of the bark and tutted softly.

"It's quite a curious mark, this one," she murmured. "Did you know that not everyone can see it?" She pressed her fingers to the bark and traced the outside of the symbol, never quite touching the spot where the wood had been sliced.

"Why not?" I asked, unable to tear my eyes away. Where was she going with this? "We need to go. I've got questions but it isn't safe here."

"Not just yet." Mum smiled. "It's a Fae mark. Not at all intended for humans. It can create doorways when a human carves it in their own world, but by a Fae hand, it has quite a different effect. Think of it as creating a doorway in yourself. For Fae, of course."

"Yeah but . . . but humans can see the writing in the book. And that's Fae magic."

"Did they really?" Mum turned to face me, her pale lips pulled into a coy smile. In the dark space of a blink, the wood was gone. The sickly smell of antiseptic washed around us.

I opened my eyes. We were in William's hospital room, but his bed was empty. The monitors shut off. Mum rested on the bed, one hand on her hip as she watched me. Something felt off. There was something I was supposed to remember. Something we'd figured out about Mum.

"There was a girl with you when you read in here, wasn't there? Tell me, when was she truly able to help you?"

"Well it was . . . after she touched my shoulder." I frowned and blinked, turning around just to make sure. And there was a transparent, ghostly version of me, reciting the spell. But it didn't sound like me. Unintelligible words hissed and spit out of my lips. I sounded like I was possessed. Jasika watched me with wide eyes, and she looked like she'd be sick. Then she took two deep breaths, knelt down, and took my hand. Just like that, the horrible, hissing words were coming out of her, too.

"She is powerful, but her gift is human magic," Mum explained patiently. "Humans can't use Fae magics so easily."

"I did." I blinked. "Is that because of Morgan?"

Mum gave me a sad smile. Then, without any explanation, she sat up and started drawing right on the milky white sheets, big, bold strokes with delicate little embellishments at the corners. It took me a few seconds to realize she was drawing the symbol from the trees.

I rushed forward, just as she was about to press her palm right onto the symbol.

"No, Mum, it'll burn you!" I cried, just as my fingers closed around her wrist.

Dark, cold eyes locked onto mine, dark and deep as the sky on a moonless night. Eyes that were too big for her delicate, impish face. No. This wasn't Mum.

I jerked back and tried to run, but my foot slid against something slick. I slammed to the floor, and for just a second, all I could see was red streaked across the tiles. My blood. My back! Not again, not . . . no. This had happened before. It wouldn't happen again. Not the same way. Gwen had been right.

Mab rose from the bed as nimble as the air itself. She was tiny, maybe four feet tall, and delicate, but somehow, she managed to look more threatening than a tiger.

"Bryn," Mab said, and her voice was so saccharine sweet that I wanted to gag. In spite of everything she'd done, everyone she'd hurt, she managed to shove enough warmth and gentleness into her voice that my blood curdled.

I swallowed and forced myself to stand, blood dripping from my clothes.

"Where's my mum?"

Mab's perfect, heart-shaped lips twitched as she folded her hands in front of her. "Are you asking if she's alive?" she purred. "Don't worry about her. She's quite comfortable. I'd say we should be more concerned about our other interloper, but I suppose she's already come and gone with no harm done."

My heart skipped a beat. Mum was alive out there, somewhere. She had to be. Fae couldn't lie. I knew it. I'd always known it deep down. Mum was alive, which meant that somehow, someday, I could find her. The hospital room flickered to our old house, then the woods back in Wales, then back again, like a frenzied slideshow around me. Mab glanced about her, looking bored.

"My dear, you really must learn to control that," she mused.

"You do wear your heart on your sleeve. I'm growing weary of the blood you spill in your anger."

Blood? I glanced down, and the red blood on my clothes had turned to blue. Bendith blue. I winced and sucked in a deep breath.

"She threatened my town."

"After you attacked her. For simply doing her job as I instructed her to do."

"Well, I couldn't very well get to you." I glanced around, searching for something. Marshmallow had said that the Fae rules applied in dreams. Maybe if I could find something iron . . . but then what? What could take her down when molten steel had failed? Maybe I needed to be simpler. More direct. A blade between vertebrae.

Mab strode around the hospital room, her long skirts swishing against the tile floor. She looked like an unearthly specter, prowling the edge of the room like that.

"Very soon, my dear, you will see that what I do is for the best. You don't belong in this place."

For just a second, her back was to me. I reached under the pillow and by the magic of dreams, my fingers curled around the cool hilt of a scalpel. I slid it up my jacket sleeve before she turned, facing me again.

"I told you before and I'll tell you again. We don't. Belong. To you."

Mab heaved a heavy sigh. "Your tedious bloodline. I hope your generation will be more compliant, in time. Moreso, at least, than the witch. Or, heaven forbid, your mother."

My mother. My heart throbbed. "You took my mum." I shifted, keeping the sleeve with the scalpel on the other side of my body, away from her.

"She abandoned me," Mab heaved an exasperated sigh,

completing her circle of the room. "And she's made it a real effort to collect the rest of what is mine." She ran her fingers over the splotchy, black mark on the sheet. "It was luck, really, to see the boy. Human medicines are advancing. Our magic is hard to disguise, but elf-shot can be so easily mistaken for a blood clot. I never imagined he would baffle his doctors."

I froze, the scalpel still nestled in my sleeve. "You . . . you put William Witters in a coma."

"Not me directly. My court is cunning in ways that impress even me." Mab let out a laugh like a tinkling of bells. "But you and your human did very well for him. Congratulations."

Cold realization washed over me. "You wanted me to use the book."

Mab smiled puckishly at me. "I'm surprised it took you this long, dear. I needed to prepare my future pupil."

Her future pupil. Soot filled my mouth. Morgan was right. Mab was trying to mold me. She had nearly killed William Witters so she could. Everyone in this town was a pawn for her . . . which meant it wasn't going to stop. Not until she got what she wanted.

I whipped the scalpel out and plunged it into her hand, pinning her to the bed. Mab's lovely face contorted with horror, and she shrieked as purple blood spurted from between her knuckles. The hospital room wavered around us, black spots dancing against the immaterial walls like the vision behind closed lids after staring too long at the sun.

"We don't belong to you," I snarled.

The darkness enveloped everything in the room except the bed I'd pinned her hand to. For a shadow of an instant, we were surrounded by dark trees curling over us, threatening. Fae skulked between the trunks, watching us with bright eyes. And in the distance was a dark-haired woman. My heart jumped into my throat. Mum!

"You will suffer," Mab hissed. "You think you know agony, child. But you are as ignorant as you are young."

"What are you planning?" I shouted, twisting the scalpel in her hand.

Mab screamed like a thousand crystal glasses shattering, and just like that, we stood in the middle of the high school gym. The largest venue in town. And there in the center of the crowd, clutching identical masks in their hands, were the boys.

Somewhere in the distance, a clock chimed eight.

Darkness fell over the gymnasium. Screams rose in the air, first from surprise, then from horror. And the sounds. Shattering glass and something liquid hitting the ground. Sobs and shrieks and feet pounding in chaos.

The lights returned . . . to carnage. Bodies littered the floor, human and Fae alike, their blood pooling against the basketball court. Glassy eyes stared up at me, their mouths hanging open . . . but the boys weren't among them.

The scene rippled again, the blood-streaked gymnasium shuddering between the carnage and the hospital. Mab had regained control.

"I will do whatever it takes to claim what is mine," Mab crooned in my ear. "If not you, I will take your brothers. They are of the same bloodline."

No!

I wasn't even sure when the bed had disappeared, but the scalpel was no longer in my hand and she was behind me, and oh God, she was going to slaughter the entire gym and I didn't know what to do I couldn't stop it they were already dead oh God oh God this was all my fault and I couldn't even think. My body moved on its own.

I whirled around, fist raised in the air. But before it could connect with her cheek, Mab raised one hand and caught it effortlessly.

"It's best not to fight this, child," Mab crooned.

She gave my wrist a squeeze and forced it down onto the symbol on the bed. My fingers, still stinging from the burn from the tree, lit into a blaze. My already pale skin began to lighten even more, as though bleach were being poured down my fingers until my entire hand was bone white. Fae-drone white.

"Time to open the doorway within yourself," Mab hummed, pressing her lips to my fingers. "Sweet dreams, child."

I JERKED AWAKE, my scream muffled by a pair of slender hands pressed to my lips and oh God they were here. They already had me. I almost swung at my assailant before I smelled the telltale odor of moldy cheese. I never thought I'd actually be relieved to smell it.

I sagged against my pillow, tears burning in my eyes. I started shaking, and once I started, I couldn't stop. I curled onto my side, squeezing my eyes shut and giving in. Just for a minute.

"I'm sorry, Missy. I'm sorry. You were making noise, see, and I knew you didn't want to be disturbed so I had to keep you quiet."

It took a few tries before I managed to choke out: "It's fine. It's fine. You did good. You did wonderfully . . ." I swallowed, then took a few deep breaths. Just a dream. I'd known it might get bad. But I was alive. I was still alive.

I rubbed my face into the pillowcase, smearing away most of the tears before I pushed myself up.

"Marsh, can . . . can you hand me my nail?" I whispered. "Be careful. Just touch the cord, okay?"

The shadeling scrambled off the bed. There was a clatter

as she went through my things. I shivered, gooseflesh rippling up my arms. Just as I pulled the blanket up around my shoulders, she hopped back onto the bed. The nail dangled from her hand, swinging on its cord. She stared at it as though it might bite. Well, for her, it very well might.

"Th—" I caught myself and smiled. "Good job."

I grabbed my nail . . . and jerked back. It felt like a wasp had stung me on the palm, right where the iron touched my skin.

Twenty-Seven

I stared down at the angry, red rash that spread out from the little welt on my palm, where the iron had stung me like a jolt of electricity. My own iron.

No. Iron was my ally. It always had been. It always would be. This was another one of her tricks.

I sucked in a sharp breath and blinked back the tears as I tore through the book, my hands trembling. I searched for the English and Welsh spells for doorway, but all I found were little ways to keep hinges from needing oil or discouraging unwanted visitors. None of them had the strange squiggly symbol Mab had forced on me. The one she'd been trying to force on me all along.

"Missy, breathe!" Marshmallow squeaked, bouncing from foot to foot as she reached out, hands hovering just inches from my arm.

"I . . ." I scrubbed a hand over my face and shook my head. "Mab did something. I don't know . . . Have you seen those symbols in the woods? I scratch them out whenever I see one."

"It's hard even for a shadeling to get in and out of here,

Missy." Marsh tugged on one of her ears. "What did the nasty queen do?"

What did Mab do? I didn't know. Because what it felt like wasn't possible. I swallowed, showing her my burned hand.

Marshmallow recoiled.

"Missy, that looks . . ."

"I can't stay here." I swung my legs over the side of the bed and shoved my feet into my boots. "I'm going to find Gwen."

"I thought—"

"I'm going to try." I pulled on my jacket and grabbed the book, but I couldn't quite bring myself to go. Suddenly, the thought of being alone right now was more horrifying than anything. I held out my hand. "Will you come with me?"

Marshmallow nodded and scrambled onto my shoulder. She felt like a weird, hairless cat and smelled like mildew. It was more comforting than anything else in the world at that moment.

I didn't even bother trying to be quiet. Everyone was asleep. And I needed to go. I needed to move. Marshmallow clung to my hair, tensing as we passed over the boundary of the church grounds. The faint sprinkle of a drizzle before a storm pricked at my cheeks until I plunged into the woods. Twigs and leaves snapped and crunched as I plowed through. Sharp *yip*s of wild fairies or foxes pierced through the air as many fled.

"Missy should be careful!" Marshmallow gasped.

My heart hammered as thoughts struggled to worm their way into the front of my mind. Exactly where they couldn't be right now. My eyes stung. But it would be fine. I just needed to find Gwen. Gwen would know what to do.

The trees gave way to open air. I shivered and dropped to my knees at the water's edge. Mud soaked my knees and nightgown.

"Gwen!" I called. "Gwen, please! I need you!"

Marshmallow tugged at her ears and let out a soft keen before she leapt off my shoulder. Cold seeped into my bones. I hugged the book tighter.

"G-Gwen, I . . ." I took a shaky breath. "I think I messed up. And I need you to tell me how to fix this."

The first drops of rain fell to the pond, rippling into the surface. And that was all. No glimpse of an underwater village or a head of golden hair.

Gwen was gone. Just like the shadelings. Just like Mum.

I wasn't sure how long I sat there. The drizzle gave way to fat, pelting droplets smacking against me like even the weather knew what I'd done. I shivered for a while, until I couldn't feel the cold anymore.

And then Marshmallow was back, tugging at my jacket sleeve.

"Missy. Is this what you saw?"

I glanced down at her. In the dark, I could just make out a lump of bark in her hand with a strange squiggly symbol carved into it. I swallowed, willing the words to come before I nodded.

"Yeah." The words came out like a frog's croak. I cleared my throat. "Y-yeah. Do you know what it means?"

Marshmallow set it on the ground and scrambled up to my side, her bright eyes wide in the dark.

"It opens things, Missy. It can make the veil thin, or it can open you up to things you don't like."

I clenched my jaw and flexed my hand. Of course. That was how all the Fae had been getting in. All she had to do was get a drone or a wild fairy who answered to her to start carving on this side and *boom!* Just like that, she could walk a whole army through if she wanted.

And, apparently, she needed me to touch it, too.

"What do you think Mab just opened me up to?"

"Don't know, Missy. It's not shadeling magic."

Unseelie magic, more likely. Making me weak to the same thing they were. Making me, what? Faeish? She'd wanted me to use the book to prepare me for whatever came on Samhain. Was this her way of claiming me forever?

There had to be a way to undo it.

Numbly, I opened the book. The rain splashed against the vellum pages, smearing the ink in places. Page after page, I saw all the same, familiar spells. There were the unfamiliar languages and runes, but not once did the doorway appear.

When I got to the end, I went back again, and that was when I saw it. A couple of pages cut out so neatly and so close to the spine I hadn't noticed it until now.

I pressed my fingers to the cut edges. Nobody'd had access to this book without me since I found it. If there had ever been information about the spell in here, it had been removed before I even knew it existed.

I'd never stood a chance.

I STUMBLED BACK to the church as the rain fell in sheets. Everyone was asleep, which was just as well. My heart hammered as I knelt down on the ground, the smell of petrichor and grass rising up amidst the downpour. Marshmallow stood next to me, but made no move to act before I did. I took a deep breath and shoved my fingers into the wet earth. Roots snapped as I dragged the first handful of dirt away.

Every pull of the earth felt like a betrayal to Mum. Even if she had hidden it, even if she hadn't told me about any of it . . . this book was still part of her. Which was about the only reason I bothered wrapping the damned thing in my jacket first. Whatever came next, I was done playing with fire. Mab wasn't going to use me again. Whatever Mab had done or tried to do to me, she wasn't going to get the chance to finish it. I was a human.

Thunder rumbled overhead. Marsh joined in, digging as the rain turned to a flood. It felt like we were pulling more water than earth. The jacket did nothing to protect the book. Who cared? I dug. I dug my hole deeper and deeper, wider and wider, every pull of the earth a penance for the colossal idiot I'd been.

Who did I think I was, pulling the same crap Mum had? What was I, now that I'd screwed up?

Mud dripped from my fingers into the hole. God. What was I now? I couldn't touch iron. What would come next? If I read again would my eyes grow? Would all the pigment drain from my skin until I was the same bone-white monstrosity as the drone?

Had that happened to Mum?

I sucked in the too-thick, too-wet air, my breaths dissolving into hiccups. What had I done? Hot tears ran down my cheeks, almost a comfort against the chilly rain. Oh God. What had I done? With shaking hands, I plunged into the muddy grave, slinging the earth everywhere until the hole was as deep as my elbow. I could dig down to the center of the earth and it wouldn't be deep enough.

I shoved the book in and covered it up, staining my second-hand nightgown. But even as I filled the hole, I could feel it down there. Mum's book. My mistake. Buried in an unmarked grave.

When it was all done, Marshmallow crawled into my lap and clung to the front of my nightgown. I hugged her close and carried her into the church.

Twenty-Eight

In the morning, I made myself text Jasika and Dom about the dream. The confirmation from Morgan. Where Mab planned to strike. What we needed to do about it. The dangerous carvings in the woods. It was as close as I could come to keeping my promise to be honest with them. But for the rest of it, whatever curse Mab had laid on me, I couldn't bring myself to tell them. It wouldn't be forever. If we could just get through Samhain, then I'd have the whole winter to figure out how to reverse it with Gooding, maybe even Gwen if the water wives returned. In a few days, I'd be able to put all of this behind me.

And if I couldn't? Well. At least the boys would be safe.

The replies popped up a few minutes later. Dom would look for any unusual carvings to scratch out after school. Jasika would check possible entry points in the gym if Dom and I could look over the rest of the school. We only had until tomorrow. No time to waste, at this point.

On my way out, I started making a mental checklist of all the places to double-check both in the school and the woods. It might not be a bad idea to put additional protections around the houses on Postoak, though Dom and Jasika could probably pull that off more covertly than I could.

Just as I pulled on my boots, someone knocked at the door. I checked my phone. We weren't supposed to leave for another twenty minutes, and the boys were never keen to get going.

"Just a minute," I called.

"Meet us in the kitchen. Quick family meeting before school," Dad replied. By the time I opened the door, he was gone. I grabbed my backpack and hurried toward the church kitchen.

Ash and Jake sat at the table on either side of dad, the empty chair between them. Jake poked at the pliable edges of a granola bar. Ash scratched at one of the nicks in the table, looking like he might slump over any moment. And there sat Dad, looking tired and drawn between them. Nothing about this screamed "fun." I had to force myself to take a seat.

Dad cleared his throat.

"Kids, I know things have been tough lately. And tensions are high. But I wanted to let you know we may be able to get into a new home soon."

Ash glanced up at that. "How soon?"

"That'll depend." Dad took a deep breath. "You never really know with insurance companies. But we did have a decent policy. Maybe enough to get us into a home on Postoak."

"The haunted street," Jake scoffed.

"None of that." Dad leveled a sharp look at him. "None of us are too good for a safe, dry place to live. Keep in mind, the Gosling house wasn't exactly a mansion."

"So, what's the catch?" I cut in. "You wouldn't have gathered all of us like this if there wasn't something you needed us to do."

"Yeah." Dad grunted and rubbed the back of his neck. "I need the three of you to behave. I'm going out of town for a couple of days. Apparently, the insurance company saw some evidence that the fire wasn't just an electrical failure. On the one hand, that means it wasn't caused by neglect on my part. On the other . . ." He rubbed his brow. "They want a fresh psych eval for me."

"That's bullshit!" I smacked my hand on the table. "You were at work. We're as likely to have caused the fire as you."

"I know, Bryn."

"She's right." Jake glowered at him. "This is just discrimination."

"Use whatever word you like. But at the end of the day, they've got the money we need to buy a new house. And, unless we dip into your college funds, we need that money. I'm willing to play their game and see however many doctors they ask."

"You didn't do it, Dad," Ash cut in. "We should be focused on stopping the people who did."

Dad took a deep breath. "At this point, we have to accept that the police aren't going to find any new leads. This isn't a discussion. I didn't ask you in here to talk about how fair it is or isn't. I've called you three in here because the doctor they want me to see is in Harrisburg. After my shift tonight, I'm going to drive straight over. It'll probably be a full day before I can finish up all their tests, so I'll end up staying there another night. I won't be back until the first at the earliest. So you three need to listen to Father Gooding while I'm gone. Is that understood?"

He was going to be gone for Samhain. It felt almost like a stroke of luck had finally fallen. Maybe it was unfair, but at least he would be hours away and safe.

"We don't need a babysitter," Ash objected.

"Then tell me the last time you did your homework without someone reminding you." Dad folded his hands in front of him. "This is not open for discussion. I'm going to be gone the next couple of nights. Listen to Gooding. I'll know if you don't."

I straightened and nodded at him. "Yes, sir."

Dad arched a brow, but gave no other sign of surprise as he gestured to me. "See, boys? Maturity."

"Spineless," Ash muttered. "Can we go, now?"

Dad sighed and nodded. "Fine. Ash, no going outside. You'll catch a chill. Again. Jake, I want to see the floor next time I see your room." The boys shot up out of their chairs and darted through the doors like a couple of hormone-driven tornadoes. Dad managed to look even more exhausted now than he had before.

I rose and pressed a quick peck to his forehead.

"Let us know how it goes."

"Don't you worry." He smiled and patted my shoulder. "I'm already planning out the garden in our new place."

THE SCHOOL DAY blurred by in a haze of lectures, quiz reviews, and sneaking around between classes to count how many different ways the Fae could feasibly infiltrate the school. Lunch saw us meeting in the library to plan. And the whole time, Jasika kept giving me the side-eye and asking if I felt okay before, finally, declaring that I looked tired and that I should leave the bark-scraping to her and Dom.

I didn't even bother to object. I could always double-check after dark in case Mab was right and they couldn't see all of them. But they were right. At the moment, my mind simply wasn't with them. It was with my dad, a city away. If things went well, he'd come home to a safer Easterton. If things didn't, then I didn't even know what I'd say to him.

When I returned to the convent, Dad was already gone. I couldn't help checking his room just in case. And yeah. His work boots were gone, along with his keys and charger. It felt silly to want him here so badly. Late nights were nothing new with his job. I could just pretend that's all this was. Just another late night, and I would definitely see him again in a couple of days.

I made my way into the church proper. I'd probably walked through these familiar rooms a thousand times, even if I hadn't actually attended a service in the last year. There were the pews where the boys and I would organize the hymnals. If we did a good job, Father Gooding sometimes rewarded each of us with a crisp dollar. Absolute wealth if you were young enough. There was the door to the room where the knitting groups met, and next to it the choir room. The confession booths where the boys used to pretend they were jumping in and out of time machines until Gooding shooed them off. It had all seemed so grand when I was younger. Now I could see the discolored spots on the cushions in the pews and the chips in the wood.

I took a deep breath and turned down the hallway, knocking twice before I slipped into Gooding's office.

The office was pretty much unchanged. Still cozy. Still packed with books on theology, philosophy, psychology, and mythology. And yet it felt different. This was where I'd received my first lessons from him. Years ago. There'd been fewer lines on his forehead. He'd caught me going through his books.

"The thing to remember, Bryn, is that the creatures you call the Fae aren't native to these shores. They can be like an invasive species, the way a yellow jacket invades a beehive. We favor the ones who live in peace, but try to push back against the yellow jackets."

Gooding glanced up from behind his desk, frowning at me. "Is everything all right, Bryn? It feels like I haven't seen you in ages."

I sank down into one of the chairs. "I need your help."

"That takes me back." Gooding laced his fingers together. "But, Bryn, your father forbade me to continue—"

"I know who took my mum." I balled my hands into fists. And I told him everything I dared. "Dom, Jasika, and I have been working with one of the water wives to try and protect the town. And we know that the Unseelie are behind all of it. The fires, the fairies on Postoak, my mum." I swallowed. "More than that. We know who their queen is, and we know she's planning to attack the gym tomorrow."

"That . . ." Gooding pinched the bridge of his nose. For a long moment, he looked as though he had a brain freeze before he straightened. "That is very forthcoming of you, Bryn. I take it you didn't tell your father about this."

I arched a brow.

Gooding's jaw tightened. "And what, exactly, is your plan for tomorrow?"

"We're going to ward up and protect the school. And be there with iron if any of them manage to get in. We have better odds than all the other people at the party."

"So, you decide to tell me only when there are lives on the line and I can't possibly say no."

"It's the best plan of attack." I leaned forward onto his desk. "You'll be here at the church social and you can keep an eye on anything coming out of the woods. Anything that gets past you and into the gym, we can stop."

"And I expect you want me to keep the boys here, of all years, the first time they're old enough to actually go to the Halloween Haunt."

"It's like you're reading my mind."

"Or I know the magical significance of twins. Tom and I never did think it was a coincidence that the Fae arrived after the boys were born." He nodded to himself and crossed his arms.

My insides wriggled, but I schooled my face into a neutral expression. Better for him to think that. It wasn't like the boys weren't Mab's backup plan, after all. And if he knew the whole truth, he'd never let me out of the convent.

"I expect you'll need supplies for tomorrow," Gooding said.

"Couldn't hurt."

"All right, then. You'll have it. But when your father returns, you will tell him everything."

Maybe everything would include a promise that we would never have to deal with the Fae again. Dad could ground me until graduation, and it would be worth it.

"I promise."

"Then God bless you and keep you safe, Bryn." Gooding leaned forward, resting a hand on mine. "After tomorrow, you'll no longer be an apprentice."

I glanced around his office. Every folklore book tucked cleverly out of easy view, every herb and tool hidden behind the cabinets, I'd already practiced with for years. I had killed a bendith and healed a man near death. Win or lose, I'd already fought the Unseelie queen. I hadn't been an apprentice for a while now.

For some reason, the thought tugged like a fishing line at my heart. It felt like I was fighting against it as I rose and offered him a tight smile.

"Well. Wish me luck."

Gooding smiled. "If you need it, you'll have it."

Twenty-Nine

I slipped into my candy corn costume. Well, it wasn't so much a costume as a stained seersucker dress the church ladies had let me dye using their supplies. I had never been more festive. Just as I reached for my nail on the nightstand, I felt a thin hand slap onto mine.

"This hurts you now," Marshmallow insisted.

"Not as much as it hurts Unseelies," I said, pulling the nail out and slipping the lanyard it now hung on around my neck, careful to keep the iron on top of the dress, well away from my skin. It definitely ruined the whole cute candy corn aesthetic, but my iron-toed boots probably didn't help, either.

I didn't fit in here, anymore, not like I was supposed to. Was I becoming a yellow jacket myself? And if I was, could I find my way back? Or did I just have to move forward until I found a beehive to ruin?

I hesitated, perched on the edge of my bed. When I left this room, everything would change. Had I been wrong in all of this?

"Marsh. You said you and the shadelings know Mab." I hadn't dared speak about the dream since that night. Even

Jasika and Dom didn't know. It had all felt like a big jinx, like Bloody Mary in the mirror. Say it aloud, and it would come. But she was coming tonight, whether I liked it or not. "Morgan promised us to Mab. Do you know anything about the deal she made?" Or, more specifically, how to find a loophole."

"Lots of Fae lay claim to human bloodlines," Marsh murmured. "But Mistress was the first of yours we met."

I sighed, running my fingers through my hair.

"What was it like for her there? With the Unseelie."

"She was lonely, Missy." Marshmallow pulled her spindly knees to her chest. "And trouble. Always trouble for the nasties. Too human to fit with them."

Too human. I rubbed my fingers together. I had always been pale, but I didn't look like Mab or the prince or, God forbid, one of the drones. I was human. And a human belonged in a Fae court like a yellow jacket in a beehive.

"Right." I rose, shaking out my skirt. "Lie low. Take it easy. Stay in the church tonight, okay?"

"Missy . . ." Thin fingers tugged at my skirt. "Please be careful. Come back."

"Of course." I turned back, rubbing my hand over her purple head. "And you be safe, too. Stay here. Watch after the boys. Gooding's got every corner of this place protected. You'll be okay."

Marshmallow nodded and wrapped her spindly arms around my leg. I smiled and knelt down, pulling her to my chest. I hoped she felt the "thank you" I wasn't allowed to say out loud.

I left her safely in my room as I slipped out to find Gooding. The golden light of early dusk washed over everything, and parents escorted their princesses and angels and space aliens in, chattering in eager anticipation of a night of good, clean fun. Not a single one of the children was over the age of eight. Father Gooding greeted each of them at the door, complimenting every costume. I could see how pointedly he was ignoring the two killer clowns sitting in the back row of pews, sulking their hearts out. Looks like Ash and Jake couldn't get any friends to come over. I almost went over to talk to them, but thought better of it. Right now, I'd probably only make things worse.

I just hoped, when the night was over, they understood what had happened.

I adjusted the strap of Gooding's duffel on my shoulder and took a deep breath. Gooding gave me a little nod on my way out, but said nothing. He had the church, tonight. I had the fight.

The whole school had transformed into a near-manic testament to Halloween, alive with the promise of taboo, even if it was well-behaved taboo. The lockers were papered over with tasteful Halloween greetings like HAPPY HAUNTINGS and HAVE A PHAN-TASTIC TIME! Volunteers patrolled the halls dressed as zombies, armed with markers to scribble out any less-than-tasteful Halloween greetings anyone tried to add. Lining the hall, all manner of fake or real psychics offered to read your palm, your tarot, your runes, or your tea leaves. A table was stuffed with every jack-o'-lantern imaginable for judging. Another with scary cakes. And another inviting everyone to sign up for the spooky costume contest that would take place at nine. And overhead, "Werewolves of London" played, the soundtrack to a perfect Halloween.

I checked my phone.

> **Jasika:** Finished securing all entrances. Extra
> protection at cardinal points.
>
> **Dom:** Laid rowan and salt along all unopen doors just
> in case.

I shot back a quick text.

> **Bryn:** Halls secure. Spread Saint John's wort and salt
> around classrooms.

Hopefully the janitors wouldn't arrive until well after the festivities were over. Though I could only imagine what they would think.

I pocketed my phone and clutched the duffel bag. I'd probably have to stash it. Sooner or later I was going to run into someone who knew I wasn't a volunteer, and they were bound to ask why I had a bag filled with random herbs and bottles of holy water. Somehow, I doubted "The priest gave it to me" was going to keep me out of trouble.

I hung by the gym entrance trying not to look too suspicious. When I was sure nobody was watching, I pulled the bare necessities from the duffel, folded them under my arms, and slid the full bag under the raffle table. Thankfully, the shimmery black-and-purple tablecloth hid it beautifully. Then I leaned against the wall, arms crossed as I tried not to make eye contact with the partygoers.

Before nine, the gym was filled mostly with the junior-high-school kids chugging down diabetes-in-a-can off-brand soda, but a few of my own peers made early appearances, all with pretty much everything that Easterton's one-rack Halloween store had to offer. Slutty nurse, slutty firefighter, werewolf, slutty cop, superhero, slutty lumberjack . . . Wow, Dennis Holtzmann was really stepping up his game this year. I sort of expected to see Brooke Tanneman following the crowd in a slutty anything, sauntering in late as the tweenies headed home, but here she was, bright and early, dressed as a hot dog. Much as I hated to admit it, it was impressive. She'd even glued on what looked like homemade foam sesame seeds. I crossed my arms and glanced away, waiting until her bun-covered bum slipped into the gym before I turned back to the hall.

Dom found me, half a dozen socks bouncing from where they'd been pinned to his shirt.

"All right. We should stick close to the gym windows. That's how they'll try to get into the—what?" He glanced down at himself.

I bit my lip and forced myself not to smile. "That's, um . . . an interesting costume. Are you where the missing socks go when they get lost in the dryer?"

"Static cling." He tugged at one of the socks. "But I guess that works, too. And what are you, the looming horror of cavities?"

"Har-dee-har. Anyway, here." I held out the necessities for him—a little vial of rowan ash, a flask of holy water, and Gwen's fairy stone. "I can see through glamours all right. But you need to be able to look after yourself."

Dom reached out, but hesitated, eyes darting up to mine. "Are you sure? This thing's pretty useful."

"I've got years of experience seeing past glamours. You're still a beginner. You need it more than I do."

Dom's lip twitched, but he plucked the stone from my fingers, sliding it into his pocket.

"Well, thanks. I guess now I can definitely see them. And I can throw stuff at them. Keep the ash; I wouldn't know how to use it. Too bad our lady in the lake didn't have a sword to give you, too. I feel like I'd rock Excalibur."

I smiled, my chest tightening as I tucked the packet into my boot. "I doubt Gwen would think of her pond as a lake."

"All right, I think we should be set," Jasika called as she pranced up to us, all done up with delicate deer makeup and a flower crown. The illusion was only slightly marred by the oversize, green tote that bounced on her hip, but even that had been pinned with silk flowers and leaves. I grinned at her, but before I could offer a slightly more genuine compliment, Dom groaned and rolled his eyes.

"Get a room, you two!"

"Sure." Jasika planted one hand on her hip and arched a brow. "I've got three siblings and Bryn lives in a church. So obviously we should just take yours."

"Real cu—" Dom broke off, going stone-still as he stared down the hall. "Did you see that?"

"What?" I turned, but all I saw were the quasi-fortune-tellers and the throng of eager tweenies and bored teens probably waiting until midnight to go smoke in the graveyard.

Dom narrowed his eyes. "Something just went down the hall . . ."

I caught my breath and checked my watch. 7:32. Twenty-eight minutes until my dream said the Fae would attack . . . but what if a couple of them had already gotten into the school? We could stop them before the bloodbath.

"One of them might have snuck in early," I murmured.

"They went down the science hallway."

Right. I took off first, and by the thump of their shoes against the tile, Jasika and Dom followed close behind. The science hall had been marked off with novelty plastic tape that read CAUTION: ZOMBIE BIOHAZARD. I ducked underneath it and darted off into the darkness. Right up until the light from the main hall no longer offered any help. I skidded to a stop.

In seconds, Jasika and Dom slowed next to me.

"Shit," Dom hissed. "Which way did it go?"

Jasika turned and rummaged through her tote bag. "Here," she said. "That nail's not gonna do much."

Without looking, I reached out. And yelped as the wasp sting shot an electric current straight up my arm. I started back as something clanged loudly on the floor.

"What the hell, Bryn?" Dom snapped, scooping up a . . . frying pan. An actual frying pan with a rubber handle and what looked like the charred remains of breakfast caked into it. Jasika had literally stuffed an iron frying pan into her tote bag and lugged it around for this very purpose.

"Sorry." I rubbed my aching hand against my arm and winced. It still felt hot and not as smooth as it had been a second ago. A sour taste filled my mouth, but I swallowed it back down. Later. There would be time to deal with this later. "Caught me off guard. Don't worry about it. I'm fine with my nail."

Jasika watched me out of the corner of her eye as she pulled an iron pipe out of her bag.

"I say we go right," she said. "Left and they'll just circle back to the main hall. This way we can cut them off outside the science rooms."

I nodded and followed her into the dark of the hall. There were no Halloween decorations here. Just bulletin boards packed with student work and Fun Facts About DNA, unreadable in the dark. I could only make out Jasika's form when it moved. My heart jumped into my throat, and not for the first time, I wished the other shadelings were here, that it wasn't so hard for Marshmallow to move in and out of the church, that . . .

That this hall didn't slam into a dead end.

Jasika froze. I slid behind her, painfully aware of that pipe in her hand. A dozen science fair trophies glinted behind a glass case, almost mocking in the dark.

"Guess we were wrong," Dom remarked, turning around. "We should just—"

Something scuttled in the dark. Black against black, its edges fluttering against the shadows like something deeper, eating away at the hall. And it was coming closer. My breath caught in my throat. My hand twitched and almost went to my nail, but I stopped myself. No. Too soon and I'd only hurt myself. It could be a distraction. I needed to be at the ready. Why hadn't I grabbed Gooding's duffel before running off into the hall? How stupid was I?

Dom scrambled with the fairy stone, holding it up to his eye.

"It's too dark, I can't see!" he whispered.

As the dark thing gathered close, everything went hazy at the edges, something new swam to the forefront of my mind. A spell I'd skimmed over a dozen times, looking for Knowledge or Healing or Dream, but I'd never said it aloud before.

Hurt.

I didn't know the words. Not consciously, but the first line gushed out from between my lips like a faucet turned on high. Somehow, it was coming out and I was just a mouthpiece. I couldn't stop it. Not until a hand slapped onto my wrist, startling me out of it. The edges of my vision sharpened back into reality and I heard the faint *hsssssssssss!*

Oh God, what fresh hell? Were these snake fairies or . . .

"Ash, we've got to go."

"I told you, you didn't have to come."

"You're vandalizing school property. You seriously don't see anything wrong with that?"

"I thought you wanted this to stop."

"I wanted *you* to stop. This is crazy! It's sucking the life out of you!"

Boys?

Ice and iron raced through my veins, freezing and burning all at once. I stepped forward, eyes wide. The dark thing split into two forms. Another step. Two forms a little shorter than me. Twin clowns, their costumes stained with red dye. One of the clowns held a can of spray paint in one hand, two crumpled vellum pages in the other. The missing pages from Mum's book.

"You're supposed to be at the church," I said.

Jake stiffened, eyes going wide in the dark. Ash turned to face me, his white-painted face set in a dark scowl.

"So are you."

"Bryn, this isn't what it looks like," Jake said, snatching the spray can from Ash's hand and staggering back a few steps. "We were just going back, I swear. We should *all* go back together."

This wasn't happening. This wasn't how this was supposed

to go. Every inch of my skin crawled as I forced myself to step forward, glancing from Ash to Jake and back again, heart hammering until, at last, I forced myself to look at the wall.

A scribble of bright yellow paint. Marked here and there by ogham and futhark runes. It looked an awful lot like the crude carvings Dom and Jasika had peeled off all the trees they could find.

Every step of the way I'd fought to learn who she was and how to push her away. Every cursed spell from that awful book, every scar on my back, the burn of the iron on my skin. All of it to protect them, and . . .

"You're trying to draw her out," I whispered.

The hall returned in an explosion of noise.

"It wasn't me, I tried to stop him!" Jake shouted.

While Ash screamed, "She's after our family!"

Jasika and Dom joined in.

"You have no idea how dangerous this is—"

"What were you thinking—?"

"Could get everyone killed—"

"Why didn't you come to someone—?"

My hands shook. The symbol shifted, runes shimmering against the painted concrete, tendrils of heat reaching out to me. I wasn't the first one to find the book. It was Ash. He'd torn the pages out. My own brother had been doing this to himself. To me.

"Go back home!"

The words escaped before I even knew I'd opened my mouth. Fire and ice burned around me. The hallway flickered, going blurry at the edges. Hot tears stung my eyes.

"You have no idea what you've done and you're still doing

it. These things took Mum and you're bringing them back into our lives!"

"It's no different than what you're doing," Ash pushed back, but his words came out muffled.

I swiped at my ears and grabbed the pages from his hand. "I'm not inviting them here. I've been trying to send them away."

"So, they can keep coming back again and again?" Ash jerked his chin up. "Don't you want to stop them for good?" In the dim light, I could make out how drawn he looked. How tired. He wasn't sick. He was paying a price for magic he didn't understand. How much longer until it killed him?

"Don't you dare. You have no idea." I clenched my stinging hand.

Jake edged closer to the wall and began swiping at the red paint with his sleeve. Dom joined him, sprinkling a bit of holy water onto the wall to loosen the paint up. After a moment, Jasika tugged a rag out of her bag and started helping, too.

"You think I don't? I know you've been running out to fight them for years. You think we're so ignorant. But we're not! The only difference is that I'm willing to go after the head."

"The head?" Shit. "Mab came to you in a dream, didn't she?"

"She said she'd make a deal with me."

"That's fairy-speak for kidnap you, dumbass!"

"I wasn't actually going to make a deal with her. I'm not stupid."

"Oh, really?" I gestured at the painted blob the others were eradicating on the wall. "That doesn't look smart to me."

Ash reached into one of the oversize pockets of his costume and pulled out what looked like a rusty old railroad spike.

For just a moment, the world blurred. Everything went muf-
fled and hazy, like I was underwater, then it snapped to again.
I blinked. It was like looking at myself a month ago. Arrogant.
Stupid. Itching for a fight he didn't know how to win.

And because that's where I'd been, I knew just as well
there wasn't a thing I could say to talk him out of this. He
wouldn't understand until I made him. My throat tightened.
I thought back to the book, still newly buried behind the
church. I'd have to teach him my own bitter lessons.

"We'll talk about this in the morning," I snapped. "This is
not the time—"

"What's wrong with your eyes?"

What?

My hands flew to my face, just touching the corners of my
eyes. For a fraction of a second, they felt too big, stretched
out on a face not designed for their size. But a blink later, they
were normal.

"Nothing's wrong with my eyes," I gasped.

"What are you talking about?" Ash bit.

"Bryn, nobody said anything."

I whirled around. Jasika's brows were furrowed. She
looked at me like someone might look at a rabid dog.

"What's wrong with your eyes?"

I turned back, my eyes darting to the boys.

"Which of you—"

And then I saw her, resplendent in her glittering gowns,
shining like a beacon in the dark.

"What's wrong with your eyes?" she purred.

Chime . . . Chime . . . Chime . . . Chime . . .

My heart leapt into my throat. There it was, the clock

chiming in the exact tone and timbre of the one in my dream. Oh God. This was it.

I yanked the nail from my neck, hissing as it burned my palm, but I didn't let go. Humans didn't mind a little iron on their skin. I could take it. I stared at the entrance, just in case.

Chime . . . Chime . . .

"Boys, get behind me," I commanded. "Whatever you do, don't talk to her." The burning in my palm grew worse. Tears pricked at the corners of my eyes.

"Talk to who?"

"Bryn, there's nobody there," Dom pressed.

"Use the fairy stone!"

"I have."

Chime . . .

I took a deep breath and straightened. Okay. Just me then. "When the clock chimes eight, you two get the boys out of here."

"Bryn, there's no clock." Jasika reached for my shoulder but I shrugged her off. I couldn't drag her into this.

"Then look at your phone. Just get them out of here!"

Mab smiled and took one dainty step toward me. Then another. I held my breath. The last, distant song from the gym faded, replaced in an instant by "I Put a Spell on You."

Whatever came next, it would be all right. The boys weren't here. Mab would fail. Something hot seeped between my fingers.

"Bryn, are you sure you—" Jake's voice hitched behind me. "Bryn, your hand!"

Chime . . .

Morgan shimmered to life in the hall, her dark hair blow-ing in an invisible breeze. She held her hand up, pointing into the distance, but when I turned, there was nothing there. Nothing but my brothers, their eyes wide in the dark.

"Bryn?" Dom rested a hand on my shoulder.

I turned back, but Morgan was gone. The moment had passed. The Fae weren't here. Mab must have been counting on Ash opening the door for her. Without that, she didn't dare enter a place as iron-filled as a public building. But I couldn't bring myself to believe for a second that she was going to give up.

A hand closed around my wrist. I jerked away, but not before Jake pried three of my fingers free from the nail. Blood dripped onto the linoleum. Ash swallowed.

"Why's your hand bleeding?"

My palm burned in the open air, and I could feel four pairs of eyes settling on me. The silence settled between us like heavy black rainclouds ready to burst. But tonight wasn't the time for it.

"My hand's bleeding for the same reason you're not doing well, either," I muttered.

"You promised!" Jake shoved at me. I stumbled back a step. My heart lurched in my chest.

Dom jumped between us, arms out. "Hey! The last thing we need is to start fighting each other."

"Look at her hand," Ash shouted. "The iron burned her. She's been screwing with the Fae, too!"

"Bryn." Jasika's voice was so full of something in that moment that I couldn't stand to think about it. Later. If we all made it out of tonight, I'd stop to consider whether it was love or fear or just plain old disappointment.

"Yeah. I have." I eased past Dom and stared down at Ash. He looked so furious. He looked so much like me it hurt. I swallowed and shoved the nail into his hand. "And I regret it more than you could possibly know." I turned to Jake. "I am stopping. I buried Mum's book because all it does is create a straight path from Mab to us. I'd rather fight this fight as a human and come home at the end of the day."

"You buried the book?" Jake's voice sounded a bit lighter.

I nodded. "Didn't you want me to be safe? Same as I want for you?"

Jake's lips twitched into a small smile rendered only a bit disturbing by his clown makeup. Ash's fingers curled around the nail.

"Yeah," he agreed. "But we should fix you up after we kill the queen."

"I agree, but I don't think she's coming." A queasy feeling rolled through my gut. Mab hadn't come to the school. Something was wrong.

"Then where will she be?" Jasika asked. The boys stared up at me expectantly. Dom crossed his arms. They all looked at me like I had all the answers. If they had any idea how desperate I was, they'd probably all collectively wet themselves.

I shook my head. "I don't know. But let's find out."

Thirty

We dodged between princesses and frogs, banshees and superheroes as the Halloween Haunt raged around us.

Not for the first time, I felt that old longing. I wanted to be out there in that circle. I wanted to know how to do that. I wanted to stay here all night and slow dance with Jasika. Maybe this December, at the Prancer Dance. Or, hell, even prom. Once Samhain passed, there wouldn't be another thinning of the veil until Beltane. That would give us more time to prepare. If we could just make it through the night, we could afford to breathe for a little while. But I doubted Mab would give up just because one door had closed.

It took me five minutes to discreetly retrieve Gooding's duffel bag from under the table in the hallway. Ash and Jake helped themselves to the candy strewn across the fortune-teller's table, stuffing whatever they could reach into their creepy clown pockets.

"You'll give yourself a stomachache," I warned, slinging the duffel over Jake's shoulder.

"Your face'll get a stomachache," Jake countered.

I turned back to Dom and Jasika. "Thanks. For all of this. But we need to get ready in case Mab tries something else."

Jasika arched a brow. "You think she'll try coming through the woods instead?"

"It would be the next best thing," Dom pointed out. "If she couldn't get at the three of you directly, all she has to do is send a weaker Fae through to open up a door for her. Then she might come looking. So what it's going to come down to is keeping you away from her without drawing her close to anyone."

Easier said than done. "All right. First stop, we get back to the church." I took Jake's hand first, then Ash's. My palm burned at the contact, but I gritted my teeth and pushed through as I led them out of the school. It was probably pretty telling that, for the first time since they were six, neither of them argued.

We stepped into the crisp outside air as one. The doors slammed behind us, muffling the music and the noise of the crowds. And that's when I heard the sirens.

An ambulance zoomed past us, red and blue lights punching through the dark as it sped toward the church.

"Oh my God," Jasika breathed.

Ash tried to dart forward, but I tightened my grip on his hand. My heart throbbed. Off in the distance, a glow lit up the old building in front of the woods.

"Bryn, come on!" Dom's voice sounded far away as he raced ahead of me.

Mab was one heinous bitch, and the night wasn't over. I steeled my nerves and forced one foot in front of the other, then again, then again until I ran with the boys toward another broken home.

The church blazed before us like a torch. The reek of smoke clogged my nostrils. The flames roared as they consumed the old brick and wood. The heat pounded against me like a hammer on an anvil. Oh God. The whole second floor had been packed with children and parents and volunteers. Had they made it out? Marshmallow. Father Gooding.

"It's them," Ash cried, skidding to a halt in front of the burning building. His face paint melted away from the heat, leaving only the terrified expression of a kid. For all that he wanted a fight, he'd never seen their work in person.

I grabbed his shoulders.

"Listen, I'll take care of this. We just make it through the night, okay? But tonight, she can get to us more than ever. You two need to get somewhere safe while I take care of this."

"No, we have to go after them together!" Ash jerked away, his chest heaving.

"I'm not going after them; I'm securing the church. In the morning this will be over."

"It won't be over!" Ash shouted. "It's never going to be over until we stop every single one of them."

"We can't!" I snapped.

"They'll keep coming." Jake's voice came out so small, I thought it might break my heart. He looked ready to crumble where he was, the duffel bag from the school so big around him it threatened to drag him down to the ground. He met my eyes, and he looked so young. "You promised me that you wouldn't let them get you."

I had, hadn't I? "They won't. Stay here," I said firmly, glancing between them. "I'm going to check the tree line. It'll be just a few minutes. If anyone tries to talk to you, use what's in that bag. Make sure they're human first. Make a circle of salt around you. Plug up your ears; there are earplugs in one of the pockets. The Fae may try something else tonight." I started to pull away, but a hand caught my skirt.

"You can't do this!" Ash grabbed my skirt, tears in his bloodshot eyes. "This is what happened to Mum. She split away from us."

He was scared. Of course he was scared. It meant he wasn't crazy. I bit my cheek and closed my hand around his fist still clutching the nail.

"I'm not Mum." I squeezed his hands, forcing them off my skirt. "I promise. I'm coming back. Just stay here. Keep this close. Stay safe." And Lord. I hoped with all my heart that I hadn't just lied to them.

I raced around the far end of the church. Parents gathered their children close, a safe distance from the oppressive flames, kissing their little heads and promising it would be all right.

One of the congregants, Mrs. Perez, stumbled around outside, looking stunned. I reached for her arm. "Did everyone make it outside?"

She started and nodded, taking a deep breath. "Y-yes. I think so."

Okay. Nobody was hurt. Probably the same move they'd pulled at the house, trying to flush everyone out. They couldn't have known, then, that the twins had gone to the school. But they had still gone after them, which meant Mab wasn't completely married to the whole firstborn idea. If tonight didn't work out, she'd still take the boys.

I pushed through the crowd, trying not to gag on the taste

of soot on my tongue or the horrible mix of hot and cold battling on my skin.

"Jasika!" I called out. "Dom!"

"Missy," a small voice squeaked. Marshmallow quivered on the ground, her long fingers wrapped around her thin shoulders as she crouched near the corner of the convent. I sprinted forward, gathering her into my arms. Wordlessly, she returned my embrace, her small body trembling. If anyone saw the small, dark figure in my arms, none of them said a word. They had bigger problems right now.

"Bryn!"

I glanced up to see Jasika kneeling next to a figure on the ground. How had I missed it? I scrambled to my feet, not daring to take my hands off Marshmallow as I stumbled over.

The front of Father Gooding's sweater was singed. His arms and a good portion of his cheeks and neck were covered in burns, bright and blistered pink against his tan skin. I stared in horror, cold sinking in deeper and deeper for a few seconds until I saw movement in his chest. He was still alive.

Jasika dug through her tote, pulling out another Tupperware container of her healing salve. "Help me get it on him."

"Okay. Marsh, I've got to put you down for a little bit. Stick close to me, okay?"

Marshmallow gave another little shiver, then nodded, reluctantly loosening her arms so I could lower her to the ground in front of my knees. Jasika popped the top off the Tupperware and I dug my fingers in, spreading the goop across Father Gooding's burns. And all the while the chorus played in my head.

My fault. My fault. All my fault . . .

"Evan!" a scream tore through the night.

I whirled around to see a small child flailing in her mother's arms, trying to pull away. His glassy blue eyes were fixed on the woods. No. Not just him. Every child from the church party strained against their parents, struggling toward the woods. One little girl sobbed, trying to hurl herself from her father, her arms outstretched toward the woods.

"Get her in the car," cried what looked like the girl's mother as she scooped up a toddler who whimpered, his eyes fixed on the distant trees.

And the longer I stared . . . the easier it was to hear the soft strains of an oddly familiar, lilting lullaby, soft and breezy as the wind rustling through the leaves. Clearly the Unseelie were fans of the Pied Piper.

Jasika dug through her bag and swore. "Bryn, have you got any Saint John's wort left?"

What? I took a deep breath and turned, my gooey fingers and bloody palm reaching for a bag that wasn't there.

"I gave it to the boys," I whispered. Then sucked in a sharp breath, reaching into my boot. "But I have some rowan ash."

"That'll work." Jasika snatched it from my hand and raced forward, something long and thin bouncing in her belt. She screwed the lid off the flask, dropping it on the ground as she dumped some of the ash into her hand before scrambling up to little Evan squirming in his mother's arms.

"Ssh," she hissed, pressing her wet palm to little Evan's head. "Don't hear them. Don't hear them."

Evan blinked up at her, stunned. Jasika nodded and turned to his mother. "Get him home now. Don't stop for anything until you're inside!"

The mother nodded and scrambled toward her car. Jasika jumped to the next child and the next. I reached for Father Gooding's throat and checked for a pulse. Still there. For now.

"Has someone called 911?" I shouted, but fresh sirens interrupted me, distant but drawing nearer. I squeezed Gooding's hand. "The paramedics are close. You're going to be all right."

He probably couldn't hear me, but Marshmallow sure as hell could. She latched on to the front of my dress again, babbling and shedding fat tears.

"Came right through the windows, Missy. She got flying nasties on her side. Threw them right with the ittie bitties. They got burned, Missy. She's angry. She's trying to get at you."

"Are you hurt?" I demanded.

Marshmallow shook her head, but she didn't stop sobbing, rubbing her sooty face into my dress, leaving behind awful black smudges. I wrapped the hand that wasn't in Gooding's around her.

"You will not have them!" Jasika shouted.

I whipped my head around, just in time to see her yank what looked like a carefully sanded wand with a little bit of quartz at the end. The kind used by people who knew how to play with energy and the like. Proper witches. She cast it in a wide circle around herself and shouted at the woods again. "Relent!"

Children screamed and lunged against their parents' arms. Jasika tightened her grip on the wand, squaring her shoulders as she held it aloft. "You will not have them. Relent!"

Wails rose up among the children. So many parents from

the better parts of town, who had never in their lives had to experience something like this, cried out, pleading with their children to calm down, to stay with them. The ones from Postoak went still as they stared at Jasika.

"Relent!"

I don't know what shifted, but Jasika stood there, and she *was* power. I could feel it deep in my bones, rattling from my teeth to my toes. The spell strained like a glass dam against a flood, but Jasika was the flood. She whipped her wand through the air again and the spell shattered. The children burst into wild sobs, shrieking in terror of what they weren't sure had just happened.

Jasika lowered her wand, wavering in place. Her eyes were wide. Her chest heaved as she turned back to me. I had to catch my breath as I took a step toward her. But before I could reach her, a voice called out.

"Miss, what happened?" I jumped and turned around to see several paramedics kneeling on the ground next to Father Gooding.

"I . . . He got burned," I stammered. "I wasn't here. I was at the school. I heard the sirens. I thought . . ." It didn't matter what I thought. It wasn't true. He would be fine.

The paramedics nodded and lowered a stretcher, helping Father Gooding onto it before rushing him to an ambulance. I watched, my heart in my throat. Still more paramedics rushed onto the scene, checking over the families. Somewhere in the throng, Dom appeared, his face ashen.

"Where are the boys?" I demanded.

Dom's mouth bobbed open and closed for a moment. Behind him, plumes of smoke belched up into the air as the firemen aimed their hoses at the chapel. I clutched Marsh a little tighter and moved back. My foot plunged into the dirt, and I stumbled onto the cold ground.

A hole.

Where I'd buried the book.

Oh God, oh God, someone had the book I thought it would be hidden I thought . . .

The cold settled on me, in spite of the heat from the church. I rose and turned back to the woods. Jasika was making her way steadily toward us, stopping here and there to make sure everyone was all right. More than a few parents looked like they needed reassurance that wasn't coming. And beyond them . . . the woods.

Everything fell into place in that moment. Ash had already been screwing around with magic for God only knew how long. He wanted vengeance. Jake wanted to keep me from charging into danger. I wasn't sure if they'd seen me that night or if they just saw the fresh plot of earth and guessed well. I had told them I'd buried it, after all.

But Mab's backup plans just took a book of Fae magic and charged right into the woods. Right where she'd want them.

Stupid, *stupid* boys.

"Ash!" I cried out, jumping to my feet.

"Wait, Bryn!"

"Where are you going?"

No. God, how had I been so naive? Ash knew Mab's symbol. Ash knew about the magic. Of course he'd try this. But Jake! He was usually so much more sensible.

I skidded to a stop. Gooding's duffel bag lay abandoned on the ground.

The ground rocked beneath me.

"I have to go after them."

Marshmallow wailed and clutched at my dress, and I didn't want to put her down. I didn't. But I had to. "Try and follow Father Gooding," I instructed. "The hospital's not guarded, but it's full of iron. You have to be careful. Don't touch any of it. There's plenty of food for you. I'll come back for both of you when this is over."

"When what is over?" Jasika demanded, grabbing my shoulder. I spun to face her. Some of her makeup had started to melt, creating a ghoulish effect in the flickering light from the fire.

"Bryn's brothers went into the woods," Dom explained. "I tried to get them back to Helen's house, but they got away from me."

"And my mum's book is missing," I bit out. "This is just the sort of boneheaded thing Ash would do. And Jake wouldn't let him go alone. They want to strike the Unseelies now. To stop them from coming after us ever again."

"This is insane!" Dom cried. "You said yourself the veil is thin. The Unseelie will be everywhere."

"Which is exactly why they think they can hit them hard," I snapped, setting Marshmallow down on the ground. "Go follow the ambulance. I'll find you there when this is over. Go!"

The shadeling stared up at me with wide yellow eyes. Then, ducking her head, she plunged into the shadows. She would be safe where she was going. Safer than we were about to be. I shouldered Gooding's duffel bag and rose, turning back to the others. "You two should stay here. This is officially my fight now."

"No way. We're part of this fight, too."

My stomach lurched, and I realized that I'd never told her what Mab had told me about him. The elf-shot. The aneurysm. It was only because of me and my family that her cousin had even ended up like that.

"Jasika—"

"Bryn." She grabbed my right hand and pulled it out, forcing my fingers open to reveal the blood that coated my still-stinging palm. It was only here, fully exposed and lit by the dying flames, that I could see the angry blisters, some swollen, some popped. Dom swore. Jasika fixed me with an even stare. "I don't know what you've done to yourself, but you need support. A little human muscle on your side."

Human. Did that mean she didn't think of me as a human anymore? Was I? My ears started to ring. Something tightened around my chest. No. No, not the time. I forced myself to take a deep breath. Later. When the boys and the town were safe, I'd deal with it. I jerked my hand back and stared at the woods.

"I am human, Jasika."

"You know that's not what I meant. I . . ." Jasika ran her fingers through her hair, ruining her perfect coif. "Shit. How could this happen?"

"Doesn't matter. You're not going in there alone, Bryn," Dom insisted. "It's suicide."

I turned back to them, my heart in my throat. I wanted to grab them both and pull them into a tight hug, but if I did that, my heart would burst open and I wouldn't have the strength to go on. So I nodded and took a deep breath, looking them over. "Dom, you still have that frying pan?"

"Yeah." Dom hefted the frying pan up in the air and pulled the little bottle of holy water out of his pocket.

I nodded to myself. "Good. If you use the water, be sure to run. It only irritates them, it doesn't really hurt them."

Jasika took a deep breath, both hands gripping the strap of her tote. And I politely pretended not to notice how they shook.

"Okay," I said, turning back to the trees. "Let's go."

Thirty-One

My heart pounded in my throat as I stepped beyond the tree line. I wished, suddenly, that I could still hold my nail. And glad as I was for their company, I wished Jasika and Dom were home and safe. I wished the boys were home and safe. *Oh God, the boys . . .*

The reality of the situation settled on me. Mab herself had orchestrated this attack, and it was going to play out. If she couldn't get at me in the school, she'd get at me anywhere she could find me. Anything could happen. It was well past the time of giving any craps. These were no-holds-barred, smoke-'em-if-you-got-'em, pull-out-everything-you've-got stakes. Because if we failed, this would be it. No more Postoak Road. No more boys.

I grabbed Jasika's arm, my bloody palm staining her lacy sleeve as I dragged her down, crushing my lips against hers. She tasted like candy corn. She smelled like jasmine and sage. Her soft lips against mine felt like hope. Somehow, some way, we were going to see morning, and I was going to have the chance to do that again.

Jasika yelped, but only for a second. Then she cupped the back of my neck and relaxed into the kiss for just a moment. Fireworks exploded inside me, sparks tickling right down to the tips of my toes. I wanted it to go on forever, but with a little nibble to my lower lip that made me see stars, she pulled away. Her eyes positively gleamed in the darkness. "That better not be a goodbye," she warned.

I swallowed and shook my head. "Just for luck."

Dom crept past us, his brows furrowed. I waited for some comment, or even a thumbs-up, but it didn't come. He wasn't even looking at us but at the woods beyond. I turned in the direction of his gaze and saw them. Flickers against the shadows. Dark creatures and blinking lights, crashing branches and hyena-like yelps. As my eyes adjusted to the dim light, I could just start to pick them out.

"Devas," Jasika breathed. "Nymphs. Pixies. Redcaps. Bogles. Knockers . . . they're all out tonight."

"They must sense something." I clutched my bag a little tighter. "I guess we're in the right place."

I took a deep breath and stepped into the dark.

The underbrush crunched and rustled around me. Needle-like branches stung my bare legs as they snapped against me, releasing the sharp, herby scent of crushed plants. A chilly breeze hissed through the woods, raising the gooseflesh on my arms. I shivered and gripped the strap of the duffel a little tighter. Why the hell had I decided not to wear a jacket tonight?

"Which way are we even going?" Dom demanded, his normally tan face ashen. The squawks and yelps from the wild fairies echoed in the distance. I almost reached out to squeeze his hand.

"We follow the chaos," I said. "Wherever the boys are, they're probably—"

High-pitched yelps and yips tore through the air. I had to jump back as a dozen dark shapes charged in front of us, their large ears laid flat like a cat's. My heart jumped into my throat. My shadelings!

"Hey, wait!" I called, chasing after them, but they dissolved into the shadows, only their sharp cries echoing in the woods behind them. Something had scared them. What was it Marsh had told me? They were afraid of the Unseelies. Mab's court would kill them on sight. And I couldn't protect them. They knew that now, didn't they?

"Stop, come back!" Dom shouted, jogging through the dark. "Wait. We won't hurt you!"

"It's no good." I scrubbed a hand over my face. "They aren't coming back. They're scared."

"But I—"

"Wait!" Jasika cried out.

I whirled around just in time to see something throw itself at her. It looked like the reverse of a satyr with the mottled, gray-skinned body of a human male and the head of a matted mountain goat. A phooka. But . . . but they weren't supposed to be violent.

"Hey!" I shouted, and since there wasn't any time to dig through the duffel bag for something helpful, I swung the whole damn thing. I heard glass shatter inside the bag as it collided with the phooka's head, sending it staggering back. But the phooka never lost its footing. It turned on me, gray hands flexed, and shrieked.

I stumbled back, fumbling with the zipper and digging

blindly through the bag. Every time my fingers brushed against a flask or a nail or an iron cross, my hand burned.

The phooka lurched forward. Fine. I dropped the bag. Just a second more. A second more . . . When the phooka came within a few feet of me, I ducked low and kicked my steel-toed boot right into its fleshy gut. It let out a horrible, throaty wheeze somewhere between a bray and a choke and fell to the ground gasping for air.

"We've gotta go," I called, instinctively running my hands up and down Jasika's body to search for any wounds. She had a few scratches, and her sleeves were done for, but otherwise she seemed safe. The phooka rose, panting, foam frothing on its lips.

"Eeeee!"

Over a dozen batlike shapes swept down from the trees, throwing themselves onto the mad creature, shrieking like a bunch of overheated teapots. The phooka screamed and threw its head from side to side, but it couldn't throw the shadelings off. Not once they dug their claws in and bared their needle teeth.

There were a lot of sincerely frightening things in this world. I'd never really thought a shadeling could be one of them.

"Don't hurt it!" Dom cried, dropping the frying pan to hold his hands up. "It's just spooked."

One of the shadelings hissed, but closed its mouth. As a unit, they grabbed the phooka's mane and jumped all at once, dragging its head to the floor. A dozen more shadelings descended from the trees, pinning the creature's limbs down. The phooka frothed and wheezed, its wide, dead eyes darting around. After a moment, it calmed down, panting as it drooled onto the leaves.

What. The. Fuck?

Dom sighed and knelt down in front of the bunch of them, hands on his knees. "Great job, guys. You really saved our asses."

The shadelings regarded him. A tubby greenish one pulled itself loose and plodded up to him.

"Maybe now you put jelly in the milk?"

Dom chuckled and nodded, holding out his hand. "Of course. Could you help keep the path clear while we look for the twins?"

The shadeling nodded and shook his finger before jumping into the nearest shadow. One by one, like a horrifying tangle of spiders, the shadelings extricated themselves and followed suit. The phooka blinked once, twice, then leapt to its feet and scrambled off into the woods.

Dom swallowed before wordlessly digging through the underbrush for the duffel bag. For all the good it would do. Everything in there was probably broken or mixed-up now. Gooding would be pissed if . . . when he woke up.

"Dom, how long have you been feeding them?" I breathed.

Dom shouldered the duffel. "Since a little after the fire. I think maybe a couple recognized me and they showed up like cats begging for food. Probably easier than getting to the church for them."

"And you just fed them?"

"You said they were friends." He glanced over his shoulder. "I'd say it paid off, wouldn't you?"

Something confusing knotted in my chest, hovering

between jealousy and relief. The shadelings were gone. They weren't mine to look after anymore, but they'd found someone new. And, clearly, he was taking care of them.

It was good. It stung like antiseptic, but it was good.

Jasika stared after the phooka's path into the underbrush. "Maybe Mab's having that effect on a lot of them," she murmured. "Think the shadelings will be able to keep anything else out of our way?"

My stomach churned, but I nodded. "We can trust them."

"Hey!" Dom shouted, pointing deep into the woods. "Is that . . ."

I turned and saw two forms a little shorter than me picking their way through the trees.

"Jake?" I called. "Ash!"

I jerked toward them, but a hand closed around my arm, holding me in place.

"It could be a trick!" Dom insisted. "We need to stick together."

The underbrush began to swallow up their forms. It could be a trap. But it could be them.

"We have to go after them," I insisted. "Jasika—"

"We need to stop and gain our bearings," Jasika said softly. "I don't trust anything we see in these woods tonight. Just give me five minutes. I know a divining spell. I can check on them."

Five minutes. In five minutes they could be lost for good. I glanced between them, tears stinging my eyes.

"Keep everyone else safe," I choked out before I wrenched my arm free. They had their people to protect. I had mine.

I tore through the woods, just barely able to keep their

costumed pinpricks in my line of sight. The boys charged through the woods, always just out of reach. I ran harder until my sides ached. My cheeks burned. My heart felt like it had been ripped out of my chest. Inhuman screeches and whoops erupted around me in a deafening cacophony, interspersed with the *bong*s and *bang*s of a frying pan connecting with something solid.

"Ash!" I cried. "Jake, stop!" They were here. Just ahead! If I could somehow make myself move a little faster, I might be able to catch them . . .

And then they were gone, swallowed by the sudden darkness. I skidded to a stop and whirled around. Dom and Jasika were nowhere to be seen. Nor were any of the wild fairies. The only sound I could hear was the steady *thrum thrum thrum* of my heart pounding in my ears.

Then it hit me. The woods smelled different, with a too-sweet undercurrent like honey. Everything was wrong. The subtle but undeniable difference between the American spruce and whatever these trees were. The light cast a haze over everything like a bluish camera lens. The way that my boots somehow made no noise on the foreign ground. This wasn't a dream.

I wasn't in Pennsylvania anymore.

Thirty-Two

I paced back and forth, trying to think of some way to get back to the others. To find the boys.

And then I saw them. Little will-o'-the-wisps bobbing above a stone path, their light warm and inviting in this wooded sea of darkness. Something deep inside me itched. This was the way to find Mab. I sure as hell wouldn't get out of here before I did just that. I took a deep breath, sent up a little prayer, and followed the bobbing, twinkling line of wisps.

"Take off your iron!" hissed a creaky voice.

I jumped back to see the haggard, gaunt figure of a woman crouching behind a tree, her large eyes glowering up at me. A gwyllion. According to the lore, all they did was creep out mountain travelers, but then phooka weren't exactly supposed to attack people, either. My hand flew to my throat, but my nail was still gone.

"Take off your iron," the woman hissed again.

When I still did nothing, the gwyllion let out a little growl of annoyance and jabbed a bony finger at my boots. Oh. Steel toes. Of course, they wouldn't want to risk it. Not after what I'd done. But then, at this point, could they really stop me?

"I'd rather keep them on."

"Then you will not pass," the gwyllion rasped, raising her chin.

"Did two boys come through here?"

"Take off your boots and you may pass. Keep them on, and you will never reach your destination."

You'd think if Mab wanted someone from my bloodline this badly, she'd bend the rules to get me. With shaking fingers, I unlaced my boots and slipped out of them, socks and all, and set my bare toes against the leafy underbrush.

"I'll be back for these," I warned, and flexed my hand and stared down the misty path. No nail. No bag. No boots. No plan. But one way or another, she wasn't getting the boys.

Morgan swam to the front of my mind. *You will have to salvage victory from loss.*

I was so screwed.

The gwyllion retracted her arm but continued to watch me with shadowed eyes, her thin lips pulled into a line. The wisps bobbed overhead in a reminder, and I took a deep breath. With only the faith that they wouldn't want me dead, I followed them up the path. It wasn't cold here, wherever *here* was, but my gooseflesh didn't go away. I rubbed my hands over my arms but schooled my expression into an emotionless mask. Whatever I saw up ahead, I wouldn't give it the pleasure of knowing how scared I really was.

The path curved up a gentle slope, and off in the distance, I saw it.

The clearing. Packed with courtiers. The massive table heavy with a harvest feast. Stringed instruments cast the same eerie melody onto the breeze as before. An uneasy feeling settled in my gut. I'd been here before. I'd done this before, only last time she'd let me believe I'd won. Was she trying to lull me into a false sense of security here?

I rubbed my sweating, bleeding palms against my dress. I knew what Mab really wanted. I could bargain with her. Jasika and Dom were still out in the woods. If I didn't find the twins here, they could still take them back to safety.

Dozens of luminous eyes fell on me, flaying me apart bit by bit. I sucked in a shaky breath. What did they see? Their foe? Their prize? Fresh meat? Or just that pest of a girl who'd been fighting for so long to keep them out of Easterton, Pennsylvania?

"I'll give you some credit. You proved to be more powerful than I expected. I think I was right to hold out hope for you."

I turned. Ice settled in my chest as Mab swept into the clearing, her dewdrop gown fluttering behind her. Somehow, she looked just as impish and lovely in real life as she had in the dreams. Her lips quirked up into a pleased little bow. "I'm glad to see you've reconsidered."

I sucked in a sharp breath and staggered back a step, but my back hit something solid.

"Ssssstay," a deep voice hissed.

I jumped back, my eyes darting up to see a horrible, bone-white face, purple blood oozing from its cracked lips. Another drone.

"I'm not afraid of you," I snapped, instinctively kicking out at it. But I'd left my boots with the gwyllion.

Clawed hands caught my bare ankle and flung me to the ground. Titters and cackles rose up from the crowd of courtiers.

"None of that," Mab sniffed. "You ought to make a good impression in my court. Come, now. If you can't make friends, then I worry you really won't fit in."

"Good. Pull out of my town and we'll go our separate ways." I scrambled to my feet, fists shaking. "I don't care who made a deal with you. You don't own me. You don't own my family."

Mab frowned. "Such defiance, Bryn. You know, you tried to kill me. I may be impressed, but that does sting."

"Good."

Mab sighed and shook her head, her mane of dark hair bouncing in the air. "I should have chosen better all those years ago. The king's sister was more trouble than I bargained for. Still, we make do with what we have. I'll not leave here empty-handed, but I will leave the choice to you. You may come willingly, or I will have them before dawn."

I swallowed. The music faded. Every courtier stood as a statue, their eyes locked on me.

Under all those inhuman eyes, I forced myself to raise my chin. "Neither. We don't belong to you."

Mab pursed her lips and plucked an apple from one of the silvery bowls. Her sharp nails dug through the skin, juice pooling like blood in her hands. "Such anger. And here I gave you a choice."

"Not much of a choice."

"You're so like your mother. It sickens me." She dropped the apple to the ground and flicked the juice away. "And that witch who promised a faithful line to me."

"She couldn't really promise that, could she?"

Mab arched a brow. "I suspect you're right. Morgan always

was a crafty one. Sometimes I think she orchestrated the hiding of all her son's little bastards from me. But no matter. I found your mother and I found you."

I sucked in a sharp breath and raised my chin. "She dealt with you because she wanted her brother's throne, right? Well, if you're after England, it's changed hands a few times now and you've come to the wrong continent."

"A human ambition. I have a throne and, thankfully, not the same foolhardy ambition as the witch," Mab tutted. "You won't have to worry about her, Bryn. She's long gone. You and your brothers are all I could track down from her legacy. I'll take you where you belong now."

My eyes darted up to hers. The horrible bitch.

"You're all just storybook characters, these days," I spat. "You've got nothing over us. Morgan's still out there, right? Why don't you take it up with her?"

"She made me a promise, Bryn. We take promises very seriously here." Mab sighed and tossed her hair over her shoulder. "But I suppose betrayal is a terribly human trait. I wonder, perhaps, if either of the twins has strayed from the other in the woods. If I told them I would only take one, which do you think would sacrifice his brother?"

Something snapped. I lunged forward, throwing her against the marvelous table, sending the suckling pig and the bread and the pumpkins crashing to the ground, their innards flying in every direction. My hands shook violently, but not so much that I couldn't press my fingers to her throat. Mab snarled up at me, knocking me back onto the table. The breath hissed out from between my teeth. I scrambled, nails scraping against wood. For just a fraction of a second, I thought I saw a red banner fluttering up among the trees under the unfamiliar stars.

"You have no idea of the honor you were born to," Mab crooned as she loomed over me. She had the audacity to actually look sad about it. "You've fitted yourself into a life too small for your potential."

I sucked in a sharp breath. My heart slammed into my ribs. I shoved myself off the table and scrambled toward the woods, but arms caught me. I flailed, kicking, scratching, biting with all the energy my ragged breath could spare. Where one hand let go, another grabbed me, pushing me down to the ground. I bucked against them, but they were stronger than I was. I was still just human enough to be no match.

"Bring her," Mab ordered coolly.

The prince stepped out, looking tall and lovely as before, save for the purple splotch still staining his cheek. I hoped it was from my blood. Clearly, it healed slowly. I hoped it hurt him.

He waved a hand behind him, and a new figure emerged from the woods. She shone like the moon in the night, but her pale hair had been strung with ribbons and flowers the color of twilight. Her billowy shift had been replaced by layers and layers of colored silk so delicate it must have been woven from spiderwebs.

Gwen's lily-pad eyes brimmed with tears as she met mine. "I told you to be careful."

"Gwen, what are you doing here?"

"She is here because she struck a bargain with me. Her service in return for the protection for her sisters. They did work, after all, to keep you from me."

Tears slipped down Gwen's cheeks, but she did not lower her head. The prince twitched his hand, and a crystal blade slid down his sleeve and into his waiting palm.

"No, wait!"

"She is mine to do with as I will, Bryn." Mab swept in front of me and folded her tiny hands in front of her.

Gwen didn't so much as flinch as the prince grasped the back of her head and pressed the tip of the blade to her throat.

"NO!" I screeched, surging forward, but there were arms on me, dozens of inhuman hands holding me back. The courtiers served their queen. Gwen didn't tremble, but she did bunch her fingers up in her silks as a single drop of aubergine blood welled up on her throat. Gwen, who never hurt anyone, who couldn't. Gwen, who'd healed my wounds and kissed my tears and welcomed me into her home day after day.

"I'm sorry, Gwen," I gasped. "Please. Don't hurt her. She didn't do anything to you."

The world went hazy at the edges, but one thing remained in sharp contrast. A small smile at the corner of Mab's lips.

And there it was. She had already won. Maybe she meant to kill Gwen. Maybe she didn't. But this wasn't just a threat. Mum, Dad, William, Gooding, now Gwen. She wasn't afraid of collateral damage. But I was. As long as I was playing her game, I would lose.

Mab's shimmering skirt rustled against the dried leaves on the ground as she strode in front of me. As she knelt down, she sighed, folding her hands over her knees.

"Bryn," she cooed. "You have lived a life that has never been your own. Caring for your family, ostracized from your peers. You fight so hard for those who have always prevented you from reaching your full potential. Imagine the freedom I offer."

My full potential.

Salvage victory from loss.

One way or another, Mab wasn't getting the boys. And she sure as hell wasn't going to hurt anyone else I cared for. I sucked in a shaking breath and forced myself to meet her gaze. This was the creature who had tricked Morgan le Fay. The horrible, otherworldly thing that had owned my mother, lost her, stolen her, then lost her again. This was the bitch who'd hurt Gwen. In her mind, the game was always going on. Even if I somehow managed to fight her off here, it wouldn't make a difference. She'd keep coming. She'd burn the world down to win.

Time to clear the board and start a new game.

"Consent," I choked out.

Mab frowned but, with a little flick of her hand, the courtiers let up their grip. I sucked in a shuddering breath and pushed myself up.

"The magic is stronger with consent," I wheezed, forcing myself to meet her eyes. "I'm the firstborn of my generation. I've been training for years. I know magic and I . . ." I swallowed against the bitter taste settling on my tongue. I wasn't a Fae. I wasn't bound by their rules. I could still lie, and Mab couldn't. "I'm not completely human anymore. Just like you wanted, right?"

Mab cocked her head, a slow smile twisting her lips into something lovely and awful. She raised her hand, and the prince removed his blade. Gwen shivered and closed her eyes.

"I'm so glad you finally came around," she mused. "I was afraid I was going to have to do something truly drastic."

I shuddered. If everything that had already happened didn't count as drastic, I hated to think what did.

My throat ached as I forced myself to meet her eyes. Somewhere in the woods, the boys were still wandering. Dom and Jasika didn't know where I was. My dad was gone, totally unaware that any of this had happened and still cursed. Still vulnerable. Father Gooding was fighting for his life in a hospital while Marshmallow looked over him, scared and alone. The water wives hid. With one deal, I could save all of them and start a game of my own, where the damage could be done in her territory, not mine. If she thought Mum had been trouble, she wasn't prepared for me.

Mab rested her hand on top of my head, gentle as a feather. "Understand. I will not lose this night. If you're holding on for your friends, your priest, your water witches, or your once-cursed father, understand that it is in my power to remove the temptation from your very heart. Once you come with me, you are mine."

I sucked in a sharp breath.

"Hold your horses," I croaked, feeling as though glass was ripping at my throat. I squeezed my eyes shut and caught my breath. This was a big moment. I couldn't let her distract me. With the Fae, the wording mattered. "I will go with you. But you must swear you will leave my family, my friends, and all of my town alone. In those exact words. No tricks."

Mab clapped her hands and let out a little giggle. "Very well. I swear I will leave your family, friends, and your little town be. If you come with me this night, no harm shall befall them so long as I hold the throne of the Unseelie. Are you satisfied?"

Not until I'd stuffed her throat with iron. But that would be a long-term plan. In the short term . . . I nodded.

"Splendid. Now, my dear, if you would?"

I forced my eyes open just in time to see *him*. My wretched, damned prince kneeling before me, holding out a bowl of pumpkin seeds, his purple welts pulling on his cheek as he sneered. Nice to know he was that breakable. He was right under Mab on my list.

Mab stood behind him, chin raised, staring down at me like the queen she was.

"Eat," she instructed.

I swallowed against the foul taste still in my mouth, staring down at the bowl. Anywhere but at the queen and the prince before me. I reached out with a shaking hand, grasping at a couple of seeds and sliding them into my mouth. It felt like eating tasteless stones. My whole head throbbed as I forced myself to crunch down on them, breaking their shells, swallowing them like chips of bark. They settled like chalk in my stomach.

"Could use a little garlic," I rasped.

The prince smirked and retreated, leaving only Mab in front of me, beaming from ear to ear like a proud mother. She held out one of her small, pale hands.

"Come, child. Time for us to return home."

I stared at her hand. If I had to spend the rest of my life fighting her, it would be worth it to keep her away from the others. But I hoped it wouldn't be long until I could return home with her head in a box.

Mab's hand tensed. "You ate our food, Bryn," she reminded me, her voice deceptively kind. "You made me a promise. You can live with me and save them all, or you can die and take them with you."

The chess game stretched before me. The prince. The drone. The fires. The book. The dreams. Every move, every strategy. But it was time to start a new game. Once I saw the new board and the new pieces, I could make up a few new rules of my own. Mab thought she'd won. All she'd done was raise me up to her level.

I let her drag me to my feet and tried not to jerk my hand away too quickly. It wouldn't do to insult her. Not immediately.

As soon as I was on my feet, the guilt began to gnaw at my belly. Penn State. Family. Duty. Friendship. Love . . . I wished I'd told Dom how much his friendship meant to me. How glad I was that he'd come here. I wished I'd had enough time to take Jasika to a proper movie or a nice dinner. That I'd had time to give in to that feeling. I wished I'd had the chance to make sure Marshmallow and Gooding were going to be okay. I wished Dad had seen me walk across the stage at graduation. I wished I could have seen Ash and Jake do the same and introduced them to the shadelings before I went to college.

I wished for so much more than this. But maybe a normal life was never an option for me.

"Gwen will be your maid, Bryn, as you will be mine. Gwen, attend her." Mab made a vague gesture with one hand before she turned heel and made her way into the deep woods. I threw one last glance over my shoulder, but Easterton, Pennsylvania, was long gone. I forced one foot forward, then another as I followed behind Mab.

Gwen fell into step beside me, looking paler than ever in the dark. I took her hand.

"Bryn, I wish you hadn't—"

"Hey." I gave her a wink, because it was better than letting on to the fluttering in my chest and the wriggling in my belly. Selfish as it was, I was glad to have someone going with me into the dark. "Remind me sometime to tell you a little bit about yellow jackets."

Gwen frowned, but she squeezed my hand and swallowed. And, together, we walked into the dark.

Epilogue

The air was different here. Tighter on my skin, like wading underwater, but too thin to suck in a lungful. My vision swam as Mab dragged me soundlessly through a dark land of night. Gwen had been taken somewhere else, but she hadn't looked frightened. I shuddered to think she was somehow already used to this place. Bright eyes followed us, shining like headlights in the dark. With every breath, a burnt honey smell clogged my nose and throat. My knees trembled, but Mab's iron grip kept me on my feet.

"This will be your room," her saccharine voice cooed. "Gwen is next door if you need to call on her. I'll fetch you when I'm ready to teach you your duties."

At last, the steel grip loosened, and I dropped back. Plush down pillows and silky furs caught my fall. Dust puffed around me, filling my lungs. I wheezed until, at last, I managed to suck in a sharp breath. Spots of darkness and color danced before my eyes until the room solidified around me.

Silvery walls undulated like crooked trees all grown together, but when I reached out to touch them, the smooth, firm texture of bone greeted me. I jerked back, wrapping my

arms around my middle as the sickening taste of Mab's pumpkin seeds flooded my mouth. This was only temporary, but I
didn't get to leave until the job was done.

I pushed myself up onto my jelly legs and staggered around
the room, my bare feet silent against the earthen floor.

I forced myself to touch the bony walls again, to feel for
anything that might function like a handle, but one twisting
column was much like another. No door. No windows. No
escape. My prison had only the pile of pillows and, in the far
corner, a shallow clay bowl decorated with pictures of berries
and ivy.

I crept forward, ready to dart away if the contents turned
out to be something sinister. But the bowl held what looked
like a liquid mirror, reflecting the intertwining bone-branches
that made up the ceiling of my prison. Mercury. It had prac-
tically been set up for scrying. Why would Mab leave something so potentially useful to me?

No. Not Mab. This was the sort of thing Gwen would do.

Bracing myself against the wall, I lowered myself to the
ground. Best to get my bearings while I was here.

A shiver stole down my spine. The mercury in the bowl
trembled, ripples dancing up to the rim. I sucked in a shuddering breath and leaned down. "Ash and Jake?" More ripples.
Tiny shadows danced across the surface. settling into a clear
picture. The boys sat on the ground next to a police cruiser,
shock blankets wrapped tightly around their shoulders. They
looked dirty and miserable, but safe. An officer next to them
had a phone pressed to their ear. Dad would know about
things by now. Maybe, now that the Unseelie had withdrawn,
things would be a bit easier for him. My heart pounded. I

wished I could have gone back and explained things to him. I wished I'd left a letter or something to let them know I was alive. All I could do was tell myself that I'd make it back to them eventually and explain myself.

"F-Father Gooding?" The ripples shifted, shadows dancing across silver. Father Gooding's chest rose and fell. Marshmallow curled up on it, her ears perked up. After a moment, Gooding's eyes fluttered open and settled on the thing sitting on his chest. The monitors next to him began to flash in alarm. Thank God. Both okay, if confused.

I swallowed. "Dom? Jasika?"

They sat on a floral couch in the Witters's living room, each holding a mug of something steaming. Their lips moved, but I couldn't make out the words. There were streaks on their cheeks. Had they been crying? Dom reached out and wrapped an arm around Jasika's shoulder, pulling her into a loose hug.

My skin crawled. I forced myself to look away. I'd broken promises to all of them. I didn't expect they'd be able to forgive me even when I did return. But they would be safe.

"All right. One more," I murmured, leaning in so close my nose almost touched the quicksilver. "Where's Mab keeping my mum?"

The quicksilver undulated in the bowl, the surface rippling. A shadow rolled across the surface until, like a golf ball had been dropped right down the center, the mercury splashed out of the bowl.

I jerked back as the little silver droplets beaded on the wall and floor. After a second or so, they firmed up and rolled back toward the bowl, mocking gravity as they settled inside. Okay.

So clearly some questions wouldn't be so easily answered. Not too unexpected. If they were, I wouldn't be here.

Very suddenly, this place weighed like sand on my back. I staggered to my feet and shuffled across the room, careful not to look too closely at the walls, and threw myself onto the fur-covered bed. Dust puffed up around me and hung in the air this time, drifting down in slow motion. I reached up. The dust pushed away from my hand, like magnets repelling each other. Maybe there was just ambient magic here. Dimly, I wondered if Gwen's room was anything like this. Or Mum's. Had she ever spent nights lying alone like this staring up at the ceiling, dreaming of the human world?

I had no doubt she'd be upset if she knew I'd done this. But maybe she'd understand. After all, she'd once been forced to serve Mab under this stupid curse. She'd escaped once. Maybe on that awful day back in Wales, she'd handed herself over to protect us the way I did. But the point was that she'd escaped in the first place. Changed her name. Found love. I could, too. But not until I found a way to break whatever contract Morgan made. Without that, there was no point to running away. Mab would just come again and again.

I let my hand drop. The dust floated down to settle around me. The bony walls seemed to squirm in the corner of my eye, and I didn't dare look right at them, just in case it wasn't a figment of my imagination.

I squeezed my eyes shut and began reciting all the weaknesses I'd learned over the years. Iron burned them. Saint John's wort, rowan, rue, yarrow, and holy water repelled them. Lies were impossible for them. They couldn't cross through running water. I'd heard, though it had never been confirmed, that maybe red could hide me from some of them. Somehow, somewhere, something had to be the key to getting one up on Mab. I just needed time to observe her. Figure out where she was weak.

There was no way, really, for me to guess how long I'd be here. But this wasn't a job to rush. Mab had raised hell for us for years.

Time to return the favor.

Acknowledgments

IRONSPARK IS A novel that was ten years in the making, but twenty years of learning, adapting, and working toward this one goal. As such, there are far too many people who have helped me on this journey to thank each and every individual. Some people know the impact they had on me. Others may never realize. But my gratitude to them remains all the same.

To the family that wouldn't let me quit when life might have distracted me, whether they understood my passion or not.

To the countless friends who listened and inspired, and who read draft after draft.

To the SCBWI Critters, who never accepted anything less than my best and, when it just wasn't working, reminded me to *Just Change Everything*.

To the authors who mentored me over the years at conventions and cafes and in their homes.

To the teachers along the way who inspired me by exclaiming and encouraging and celebrating. Who treated me as a young professional. Who reminded me that, counterintuitively, my acting classes could help me hone my writing.

To my agent, Ann, who held my hand through the excitement and terror of a debut.

And to Holly West and everyone at Macmillan for selecting *Ironspark*, and patiently working with me through this whole crazy process of preparing this novel.

Words cannot express my relief and gratitude at the support from so many incredible people.

Thank you.

Thank you, thank you.

Glossary

Banshee—A wailing Irish spirit whose mournful cries are said to foretell imminent death.

Bendith y Mamau—Also known as the Tylwyth Teg, Bendith are known to cause mischief and steal human children, leaving behind changelings. They are widely considered to be a cross between a goblin and a Fae, often using glamours to appear lovely, hiding a hideous face.

Boggart—A shape-shifting spirit generally (but not always) considered to be malicious.

Bogle—A Celtic spirit similar in many ways to a poltergeist, Bogles enjoy terrorizing humans and spoiling their food.

Brownie—Benevolent, goblin-like Fae noted for their unique tendency to inhabit and work in a human house. They will accept gifts of food from humans, but are easily offended at the notion that they are in any way employed by them. If something is offered to them to serve as payment rather than friendship, they will become offended and abandon their home.

Changeling—Also known as a crimbil, a changeling is a Fae child left in the place of a human child for any of a number of reasons. It is said that they have powerful screams, an affinity for music, and one leg longer than the other.

Gnome—Diminutive earthen Fae ranging from a few inches to a few feet tall, they are said to be generally benevolent creatures possessing a great deal of secret knowledge. It is said that gnomes have a power all their own, which they use to reward or punish people as they see fit.

Gwragedd Annwn—Also known as the water wives, these are Welsh fairies known for living in villages underwater. They are known for being incredibly gentle, such that even a playful slap on the back can cause one to retreat back into the water for years. They are considered by some to be a type of Tylwyth Teg, but are notably separate from the Bendith y Mamau.

Gwyllion—Known as the Old Woman of the Mountain, a Gwyllion is a hag known to lead lost travelers astray. It is considered to be a close cousin to the Bendith y Mamau.

Knocker—Said to be spirits, knockers are subterranean Fae who live in mines. They seldom venture to the surface, and can most often be found by the knocking sounds they make while they work. They are said to be benevolent, even protective by some. Others say they are dangerous, with pranks ranging from annoying to lethal.

Nymph—An elemental nature spirit known to inhabit a specific area of nature, such as a tree or a river.

Phooka—An Irish shape-shifter known for causing trouble and wreaking havoc. In spite of this reputation, however, they have never been known to directly attack a human.

Pixie—A tiny, mischievous fairy who delights in playing pranks. Pixies are numerous and, generally, their behaviors are benign.

Redcap—Malicious Fae who prefer to hunt those who have strayed too far from their home. It is said that a redcap's name comes from the hat it wears, dyed with the blood of its victims. The redcap must continuously seek out new victims to maintain the color of its hat.

Seelie—A court of Fae often associated with daylight and summer, the Seelie are considered to be the Fae most likely to treat a human with kindness. However, they are still instinctively mischievous, and do not take kindly to mistreatment of their territory.

Shadeling—A type of impish Fae known only to Bryn, these once-brownies can travel through shadows and demonstrate incredible loyalty. However, like most Fae, if for any reason that loyalty is lost, it can be impossible to regain.

Unseelie—A court of Fae often associated with night and winter, the Unseelie court is home to the truly malicious. Often, the Unseelie are openly hostile to others, especially to humans, and their mischief is known to give way to true harm.

Will-o'-the-Wisp—A dancing light often found in dark, marshy, or foggy places, will-o'-the-wisps are said to lead travelers through the dark. Sometimes, it may be a way home or to great treasure. Sometimes, they may only lead a traveler deeper into the dark, abandoning them when they are lost.

Check out more books chosen for publication by readers like you.

DID YOU KNOW...

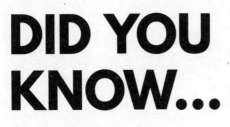

readers like you helped to get this book published?

Join our book-obsessed community and help us discover awesome new writing talent.

1

Write it.
Share your original YA manuscript.

2

Read it.
Discover bright new bookish talent.

3

Share it.
Discuss, rate, and share your faves.

4

Love it.
Help us publish the books you love.

Share your own manuscript or dive between the pages at **swoonreads.com** or by downloading the **Swoon Reads app**.